A King's Test

Merlinnus led them right up to the stone. On its white marble face was a legend lettered in gold:

WHOSO PULLETH OUTE THIS SWERD OF THIS STONE
IS RIGHTWYS KYNGE BORNE OF
ALL BRYTAYGNE

For a long time none of them spoke. Then Arthur read the thing aloud, his fingers tracing the letters in the stone. When he finished, he looked up. "But I am king of all Britain."

"Then pull the sword, sire," said Merlinnus.

Arthur put his hand to the hilt of the sword, tightened his fingers around it till his knuckles were white, and pulled.

The sword remained in the stone.

OTHER NOVELS BY JANE YOLEN

Tartan Magic
The Wizard's Map
The Pictish Child
The Bagpiper's Ghost

The Young Merlin Trilogy
Passager
Hobby
Merlin

The Wild Hunt
Wizard's Hall
The Transfigured Hart

The Pit Dragon Trilogy
Dragon's Blood
Heart's Blood
A Sending of Dragons

Armageddon Summer
(with Bruce Coville)

Boots and the Seven Leaguers:
A Rock-and-Troll Novel

Sword of the Rightful King

A NOVEL OF KING ARTHUR

JANE YOLEN

MAGIC CARPET BOOKS
HARCOURT, INC.
ORLANDO AUSTIN NEW YORK SAN DIEGO TORONTO LONDON

Requests for permission to make copies of any part of the
work should be mailed to the following address:
Permissions Department, Harcourt, Inc.,
6277 Sea Harbor Drive, Orlando, Florida 32887-6777.

www.HarcourtBooks.com

First Magic Carpet Books edition 2004

Magic Carpet Books is a trademark of Harcourt, Inc.,
registered in the United States of America and/or other jurisdictions.

The Library of Congress has cataloged
the hardcover edition as follows:
Yolen, Jane.
Sword of the rightful king: a novel of King Arthur/Jane Yolen.
p. cm.
Summary: Merlinnus the magician devises a way
for King Arthur to prove himself the rightful king
of England—pulling a sword from a stone—but trouble
arises when someone else removes the sword first.
1. Arthur, King—Juvenile fiction. [1. Arthur, King—Fiction.
2. Knights and knighthood—Fiction. 3. Middle Ages—Fiction.
4. Great Britain—History—To 1066—Fiction.] I. Title.
PZ7.Y78Sw 2003
[Fic]—dc21   2002152622
ISBN 0-15-202527-8
ISBN 0-15-202533-2 pb

Text set in Granjon
Designed by Lydia D'moch

A C E G H F D B

Printed in the United States of America

*To editor Michael Stearns, who knows how to wait,
and to my husband, David, rightful king of my heart*

Contents

There was seen in the churchyard, against the high altar, a great stone four square, like unto a marble stone; and in midst thereof was like an anvil of steel a foot on high, and therein stuck a fair sword naked by the point, and letters there were written in gold about the sword that saiden thus:—WHOSO PULLETH OUT THIS SWORD OF THIS STONE AND ANVIL, IS RIGHTWISE KING BORN OF ALL ENGLAND.

—Sir Thomas Malory, *Le Morte d'Arthur*

Sword of the Rightful King

I

Queen's Anger/ Mage's Dream

Midnight by the bell. The churchyard was deserted and in darkness. By the front door, which was but a black rectangle in a blacker mass, a large square was marked off on the ground. In the square's center stood an enormous stone, which—if the moon had been shining—would have reminded any onlooker of a sleeping bear. A dead bear, obviously. For in the bear's back was thrust a great sword, its haft pointing slantwise toward the night sky.

Summons

PRINCE GAWAINE took the stone steps two at a time, trying to guess why his mother, the queen, had sent for him. She only did that when she was angry with him, or wanted something from him, which usually came to the same thing. Either that or she was going to recite his stupid bloodlines again.

"I've half a mind," he said, puffing a bit as the steps were steep and many and he hadn't climbed them in a while, "half a mind to tell her what I've decided." He stopped on the landing and took a deep breath. "That I don't want to be king of Orkney. Not now. Not when I turn eighteen. Not ever."

He smiled faintly, having spoken aloud what he had

been thinking secretly for over a year. Though of course he hadn't said it aloud to his mother, just aloud to the stone walls.

Let Agravaine have the throne, he thought fiercely. *Or the twins.* He took a deep breath. *Or that brat Medraut.* He started up the stairs again, still taking them on the double and thinking crankily about his mother and the throne. He knew that even if they were given the throne in his place, none of his brothers would have a chance to rule, anyway. Morgause would keep the power close to her own breast, with her spiderweb intrigues, with her spiteful magicks, with her absolute conviction that he or one of his brothers should not only be king of the Orkneys but High King of all Britain. And she the ruling queen.

A blast of wind through one of the arrow slits scoured his corn-colored hair. It blew sense into him at the same time. He slowed down.

No sense running, he thought. *She might think I'm eager to see her.*

When he made the last turning, he came face-to-face with her chamber door. No matter how often he came to it, the door was always a surprise, a trick of space and time, another of her plots. Made of a single panel of oak carved into squares, the door looked like a game board and was painted black.

Gawaine smoothed down his grey linen tunic and knocked on the one blank square. The rest of the squares were warded with arcane signs, spells that only she could read. The blank square was well-worn. No one, not any of her servants or his brothers—or even his father, when he was alive—ever dared knock on any other section of the door.

There was no answer.

Grinding his teeth—something he seemed to do only when he was home, in Orkney—Gawaine knocked again.

Still no answer.

"Damn her!" he whispered.

How she loved to play these games. Her servant Hwyll had said, specifically, she wanted to see Gawaine at once. He'd emphasized the two words: *at…once*. Poor Hwyll, a nice enough man, always kind and thoughtful, but he had no backbone. She had chosen him exactly because he had none. He was a conciliator, a peacemaker, the perfect servant.

"A pus pot," Gawaine said aloud, not knowing if he meant Hwyll, his mother, or the situation he found himself in.

Once again.

He banged on the door with his fist, and cried out, *"Mother!"* His voice rose to a whine. *Hardly fitting,* he thought angrily, *for a Companion of the High King.*

———

MORGAUSE COULD hear her son's angry cry as she came down the stairs from the tower, clutching a handful of bitter vetch. She smiled.

It's good to let him stew, she thought. *A stew long boiled makes easier eating.*

She never tried to make things simple for her boys. Princes needed to be tested even more than peasants.

And my *sons most of all.*

Stopping on the stairs, she flung open one of the corbelled windows and glanced out.

The late-spring seas around the Orkneys were troubled. Ninety islands and islets, and all of them buffeted by extraordinary waves. "High wind and waves build character," she told herself. Her sons were in want of character.

Agravaine she was certain of, though he still needed a bit more tempering. And the twins—they dangled together, like rough-polished gems on a chain. Medraut was so like her, she knew his mind without working at it. But Gawaine...

Gawaine had gotten away from her. It had been three years or more since she'd understood him. It was all she could do to keep control. Of him. Of *herself* when she was with him. He made her angry when anger did not serve. He made her furious to the point of becoming speechless. Still, she needed him more than he needed her, and so she had to bring him close again. To heel. Like a hound.

Speaking a word of binding, she flung three leaves of the vetch through the window. The wind brought them back to her and she closed her hand around them, stuffing them into her leather pocket. She smiled again, willing herself to calm. Gawaine *would* be hers as he once was, the adoring and adorable towheaded first child. All of Lot's sons were susceptible to spells of binding, as had been their father. It was just a matter of patience and time. She had plenty of both.

Continuing down the stairs, she discovered Gawaine red-faced and furious, standing with his back to her door.

"I'm glad to see you, too, dear," she told him.

2

Bloodlines

GAWAINE couldn't help himself: He spluttered. All the fine speeches he'd rehearsed slipped away, and his mother just stood there smiling her damnable smile.

"Always on time," she was saying. "That's an admirable quality in a young man." Though she herself used time as a weapon.

"You..." he sputtered, "asked for me."

She was still giving him that beautiful and seductive smile that drove the men around her mad. Running a ringed finger through her silky black hair, she purred, "I always like to see my boys."

Ever a dangerous sign, he thought. When she purred, she was satisfied. Or hunting.

"Did you want something, Mother?" *There. Better to be plain about it. Not elliptical, not like her.*

"Do I always have to want something?" she asked.

But she does, he thought. *She always does.*

She held out a hand and drew him to her, and he went into her chamber, reluctantly but inexorably, as if bespelled. She went ahead of him and arranged herself, catlike, on a low wooden settle, its hard lines softened by plump feather pillows. Then she patted a place beside her with a nail-bitten hand. It was the only thing human about her, those nails, bitten down to the cuticles.

He remained standing. "Mother."

She smiled. "Son."

An uncomfortable silence seemed to stretch like silken spider's thread between them.

At last she spoke. "Do you have to go back to Arthur's court so soon? There is plenty enough to do here in your own kingdom."

So that's it! She would try to keep him here as ruler, though of course he knew which one of them would actually rule.

He shook his head. "I like Arthur's court, Mother. It's a place of knightly practices and fine company. Arthur is a prince among men."

"Put silk on a stick," she said bitterly, "and it will still look fine." Her beautiful face was suddenly fierce with anger, her eyes drawn down into slits.

"Mother," he began, but she cut him off.

"Since you refuse to be king here, under my guidance, I will let you go off south," she said, standing so that they were eye to eye. "But know this—*you* did not decide to go to Cadbury at the first. Do you remember complaining? Whining? Being afraid?"

He did, but did not want to acknowledge it.

"You had night sweats."

Startled, his eyes flew wide open. He wondered how she knew that. He had taken the sheets down to the river himself.

"But you went at last. Because *I* willed it," she said. "Because I wanted you to be my eyes and ears in that place."

"A spy!" Now he was furious and his eyes drew down into the same thin slits as hers so that for the first time he looked like her son. "I am a prince. You cannot expect me to be a spy."

"Not a *spy*, no." Her voice was suddenly smooth, a stone under fast water. She put her hand on his forearm. "Not a spy—not in the court of a man you admire. How could I ask such a thing?"

But she just did, he thought, then wondered, *or did I mistake her?*

She was smiling at him. "Not a spy," she repeated, "but still your mother's man. Of course you tell your mother all that happens at court. It is expected. As you have done for these past three years. Did you think I did not listen?"

He had in fact thought just that. She'd never reacted to anything he'd told her by so much as a blink. When he'd reported on the balls, the tourneys, the hours of practice on horse and with sword, the time Arthur had gifted him with a pair of brachet hounds, even the names of the girls he had flirted with and the one he had, briefly, loved—none of that had seemed to interest her. Now, suddenly, he understood why. But even had he known something about Arthur's policies, about his allegiances and alliances, he would not have repeated what he knew. He was not a spy. *Never* a spy. He shuddered.

If she noticed his shudder, Morgause did not remark on it. Instead she continued as if she hadn't guessed how he felt. "I want to know what Arthur says behind closed doors. I want to know which of the Companions regards him with awe, which with a certain cynicism. I want to know the Companion who is most in need of funds, which one drinks too much, and which one forgets himself with the pretty maids. Or..."—she smiled her cat smile—"the pretty boys."

"Mother, I..." He put up a hand to hold back her words, but it was like trying to stop the onrushing sea.

"You are *not* to be guiled by Arthur. I sent you there to observe, so that we may be ready when the time comes. Not to play at swords, not to speak love to unworthy maidens. You are there for us, for what we can and will be."

Her face was now fierce with her desire. It made her ugly. He hardly knew her when she was like this.

"Arthur is nothing but a petty usurper, for all you like his manners," she whispered harshly. "Some day— and soon—he will be plucked from the throne. That is the day I prepare for. The day I prepare *you* for." Her eyes glistened.

"Mother!" His voice cracked as if he were thirteen again.

"And you must beware especially of that jackdaw, that black rag of a man, that Druid priest, that..."

"Merlinnus." Gawaine put his hand on hers, but she shook him off, as if his hand were a wet, dirty thing. She had never been one for mawkish displays of affection, but she had never before shrugged him off so thoroughly. Not even when he was a muddy boy, in from a ride in the rain. So he smiled at her to hide his hurt. "His name is *Merlinnus,* Mother, and he is not really so terrible." He shook his head. "Just terribly old."

"Old? You think that is all he is? *Old?*" She shook with sudden rage, as if the bitter winds had her by the throat. In that moment she looked as old as Merlinnus. Unaccountably her hand went up to her right cheek.

Gawaine stifled his sigh. *Now she will begin the litany, the bloodlines,* he thought. *The old story that holds her in such thrall.* For a moment he looked away. *She is the only one still moved by it.* Then, fearing himself a coward, he looked back, steeling himself for the onslaught of her words.

She was not slow in getting to her point. "Together that old man and that petty *king...*" She spit the last hard word out, spraying spittle. "They have conspired to steal your birthright, Gawaine. My mother married Uther Pendragon for the High King's throne, so that her children should sit on it after he was gone. Surely she didn't marry him for love. Uther was a pig, an upstart; he wore drippings in his beard. His clothes smelled of dog. No—worse than dog. He smelled like a rutting wild boar. Did you know he once laid his filthy hands on me? *Me!* His wife's daughter, a princess in my own right. I never told you that. But he forced me, a child. Goddess—he was a terrible king and a worse man."

Her eyes had taken on the mad look Gawaine hated. No good ever came of that look. Whippings were ordered, executions announced, true loves sundered,

forced marriages perpetrated—tortures, dismember-
ments, exile. He held up his hand to stop her, though he
knew not even the gods could stem that tide. Did he believe her? He no longer tried, for she always mixed
truth and lies into her stories, like honey in poison to
sweeten it as it went down.

"My mother had no male children by Uther, so the
throne should by marriage right have come to me and
thus to you." She continued as if his weariness were not
written upon his face; her hand clutched the bodice of
her dress like a claw.

Gawaine had a sudden thought: *She* is *mad*.

Morgause went on. "But I have five sons. And all
living, all grown strong and sturdy and smart. You are
the eldest; you are to be king here of the Orkneys when
you choose to claim it, Gwalchmei."

He flinched at the use of his old name, *Gwalchmei*.
It was a wonder that she did not notice his distaste.
Only *she* still called him that. Changing it was one of
the first things he had done upon arriving at Arthur's
court three long wonderful years earlier.

"By rights, Gwalchmei, *you* should be High King as
well."

This time he could not keep from sighing. Kingship
should be about strength, not blood; about power, not
birthright. Arthur was a strong and a mighty king.
Who, then, could be better upon the high throne?

She threw her right arm up, as if summoning the old dark gods. "Gwalchmei of Orkney, High King of all Britain." She stared at him, almost fondly. "You do well to listen to me, Gwalchmei."

But he was no longer listening at all.

3

Queen's Entrance

AFTER GAWAINE LEFT, Morgause went back up the stone steps to her tower, holding up her green linen skirt so it would not tangle in her legs. She moved like a girl still, those long legs carrying her up the stone risers with ease.

That went well, she thought. *I can always persuade him. He is his father's son.*

When she reached the top of the stairs, she walked along the alure till she came to her favorite spot where she could stare out across the blue-black sea. White terns were busy bringing up sand eels while the kittiwakes and guillemots rode the waves like little satisfied housewives.

"What fools those little birds are," she said, marking them.

Above her, gannets hovered and then dove into the dark water. Great power was in their dives. They owed allegiance only to the sea and sky and took what they wanted from both. She admired them that.

Taking the gold torque from her neck and the gold circlet from her brow, she sighed. She took off the gold-and-red-enameled bracelets from her arm. Loosing the belt from her waist, with its jangle of brooches and the small jeweled dagger, she set them all on the stone. Then she let the wind work on her waist-length hair, twisting the dark loops into elf knots, as she thought how much she hated Arthur. The man who had stolen her father's crown and her sons' inheritance. Who had taken away her own right to be Britain's mother queen.

THE NEXT MORNING, in the tower room, free of her boys, Morgause plucked up a glass vial and held it up to the sun. The light picked out bits of red pulp that the pestle had not quite ground down.

She thought about the dead man in her hidden dungeon. *He* had been a spy; she was sure of it. Even though he'd not admitted any such, just wept for his mother at the last.

They always do that, she thought. *Men are but little boys when it comes to their mothers.*

He had admitted nothing, but it was what he did not say that was important. She knew deep in her breastbone that he was a spy.

A spy's heart was always worth something.

She smiled thinly and set the vial down in its iron holder.

Now, she thought, *to make the brew.*

WHILE THE BREW sat on the highest shelf, stewing, steeping, all its granularities dissolving, Morgause went downstairs to greet the messengers. She had dressed carefully for them, in a white linen overgown with eye-lets that allowed the red undergown to show through. On her black hair sat a crown of filigree gold. The torque and circlet were brilliantly shined, and she'd added four large-stoned rings to her fingers.

Her sons were off under Hwyll's stewardship to gather birds' eggs from the cliffs, something they en-joyed and that would keep them away for hours, even overnight if Hwyll could manage it.

As Morgause descended the stone stairs, she thought about the men awaiting her: messengers from all the little kings and lords and lairds and chieftains of the north. Come to her bidding.

She'd let *them* stew and steep as well, in the Great Hall. Wine and meats and cheeses had been provided, and piss pots, too, but the doors had been barred on the outside so the men couldn't leave. It was a lesson in queenship, so they'd know who was in command here.

When she arrived at the doors to the Great Hall, her guards greeted her stone-faced. Nodding at them, Morgause waited for the doors to be opened, never for a moment showing her annoyance at how long it took.

Finally the doors gaped wide and she stepped forward.

Entrance, she thought. *Or en*-trance. She meant to cast a spell upon them all.

THE MESSENGERS looked up as one from their food, except for a single man, in the far dark corner, using the pot.

The small-boned, gold-crowned woman in white seemed to glow with beauty. Her streams of black hair, her dark sea-colored eyes, all added to her mystery. She did, in fact, entrance.

"My men," she said, opening her arms as if to gather them in.

They bowed their heads.

She moved as if without effort till she was sitting on the throne at the west end of the hall. It was the warmest spot in the huge room, being close to the fire.

The great corbelled windows shone down shafts of light onto the throne, which further enhanced the sitter's stature and mystery.

"Majesty," one man cried and fell to his knees.

The others quickly followed suit.

She waited till they rose again, then waited another moment still. Then at last, when she judged all eyes were on her alone, she spoke. "Do you bring me pledges from your good masters? Will they march against the usurper Arthur under my banner? Will they set my son, the rightful heir, upon the High King's throne?"

Where a moment before there had been enchantment and single-mindedness, now there was chaos. Some of the men looked down at the floor; others studied the high beamed ceiling with fierce determination. One messenger coughed mightily and it took two men to beat upon his back to still him. Chairs scraped, dishes rattled, flagons were set down noisily upon the table. But no one answered the queen's challenge.

Morgause stood. Glaring at the men, trying to force their eyes on her by the rigidness of her posture, she cried, "Speak!"

For nearly a minute there was utter silence in the hall. Then one man cleared his throat.

Morgause turned to him. "You!" she said, and pointed. "Come here to me."

Reluctantly he moved forward till he was right in

front of her. Even more reluctantly he raised his head till his eyes met hers.

"What does your master say?" She was cold and hot at once; fury and sorrow and something else warred beneath her breast. Perhaps it was fear.

The man looked away. He spoke to the far wall. "Majesty, my master says that as long as Arthur is under the black mage's protection, as long as he is first in battle and surrounded by those who love and honor him, we cannot rise against him."

"So says my master as well!" cried someone from the crowd.

"And mine."

Their voices, like an ocean wave, broke against her small, white-clad body.

Fury won the war beneath her breast. "Fools!" she said, her voice rising slowly till the hall seemed filled with it. "Running dogs of puling, pustulant masters. Go back to them and say that I, the North Witch, Queen of the Orkneys and beyond, daughter of Duke Gorlois and Ygraine, who was afterwife of Uther Pendragon, himself the High King, will myself rid this land of the usurper Arthur. And I will do it permanently. Then I will set one of my own sons upon the throne with my own hands. After, I shall deal with all of you as you deserve." She held up two fingers, and the men seemed to cower before her, feeling the magic as dogs do whips.

She glared at them. "Arthur *will* die. And you after."

The guards threw open the doors and the messengers ran out, pushing and stumbling and fighting with one another to be first outside. Last was the man who'd been at the pot when she arrived.

Smiling thinly, Morgause held three fingers up and said something under her breath. The man dropped to all fours and, howling, galloped away, looking more and more like a whipped hound the farther he got from the hall.

Suddenly she clutched her stomach. *I should not have done that last,* she thought. *It was an indulgence. I shall pay for it tonight.*

4

Travel from Orkney

THREE DAYS LATER, in her tower room, Morgause bent over the cauldron, staring down into the roiling depths. It bubbled so quickly, she could see nothing of the dead cat, or the three tails of baby mice, or the spindly spider legs and the pulped black bodies, or the bitter herbs so carefully measured out. Just the spumy water, as treacherous looking as the seas off the isles.

Long ago she could read the future clearly in her cauldron despite the bubbling roil. It had been easier to read than her books of magic, with their long Latin incantations. She hated Latin. It was a man's tongue. There were more words in it for war and battle than for love. Yet the north magic was worse. When she could, she used the softer, sweeter, Celtic spells, though they were not to be counted on and often went awry.

Long ago magic had been so easy. But with the birth of each new son, her magic had faded. It was the price she had to pay to be a queen. At the time, she thought she had paid it gladly. Yet now, looking into the cauldron's angry bubbles, she was no longer certain. All she could make out in the roiling concoction was a water crossing.

But then, from Orkney, *everywhere* was a water crossing.

The roiling continued, but she left it, to stare out the narrow window toward the open sea. Blue sky, bluer water. A streamer of white cloud, echoed by the streaming tops of waves. The storms of spring were past, and now the sea, like a gentled horse, hardly moved at all.

And on that cold, dark blue sea was a single boat, its brown sails not yet taut with wind, carrying her sons to Arthur's court. All of them but Medraut, of course, her son born after Lot's death, who was too young and too precious to let go from her.

When the boat had left—but an hour before—she had waved to the boys from the shore. But they, so intent on the trip, had scarcely noticed. She had had their backs, not their faces.

For a moment she thought about that, how boys

always leave their mothers eagerly, hearts set on the next adventure. She was sure, however, that once the trip had settled into its steady—even boring—progress to the mainland, their thoughts would all return to her.

And their promises.

She took a small red wool cap from her belt, twisted it three times widdershins. Then she spoke the Celtic word for wind. Out on the sea, the waves began to riffle. The boat's brown sail pillowed out. The prow of the ship knifed through the water. Away from shore.

Away from the castle perched on the high headland.

Away from Morgause.

She watched until the boat was out of sight, then folded the red cap carefully, tucked it back under her belt, and went down for dinner with Medraut. He was her aptest pupil, always listening intently, his grey eyes on hers, as she talked of kingship and treachery.

GAWAINE had said good-bye to his mother without promising her anything—except to keep a careful watch on the three younger brothers she had forced him to take to court. He watched gladly, since he suspected that one of them had been charged with the spying he had refused.

At least she was keeping the youngest brat, Medraut, at home. *Just as well,* Gawaine thought, as the boat skimmed over the waves. Medraut was a snot nose, always whining, always wanting more than his share of everything: food, clothes, jewels, attention. He was spoiled, mean-tempered, sly, and even at six still clung to his mother's skirts.

As *she* clung to him, that last sad reminder of his father. Though how the old man, so sick at the end, could have sired another child was beyond thinking.

Standing at the boat's prow, his cloak tangling in the wind, Gawaine breathed deeply of the salt air. It was a smell he had known all his life. If there was one thing he missed, living at Arthur's court—which was far inland—it was the joy of riding the sea. Coming back home was always a compromise between his joy of the open waters and his need to please his unpleasable mother.

There were porpoises on either side of the ship, some of them right under the large eye painted on the prow that the superstitious sailors believed brought an easy and peril-free crossing. He shrugged. *Can't hurt,* he thought. *And it keeps the men happy.*

As he watched the porpoises leap joyously ahead, he was strangely content, as if they really were a good omen. But then he heard an odd, brutal sound. Looking around, he saw it was his brother Agravaine bent over the railing and "feeding the fishes" again, which was what the sailors called throwing up. Agravaine had no stomach for sea travel, though he had lived all his life by the sea.

"Give him some hard bread," Gawaine called to Hwyll. "And some fresh water." It was the only thing he knew that would ease the spasms.

Ever helpful, Hwyll reached into his pockets and drew out the remedy. But Agravaine waved the man away.

I have never seen Agravaine so green, Gawaine thought, but hardly cared. He had little love for his brother, who was a bully.

"Hard Hands," the servants called Agravaine, though never in his hearing. He used horses and men with equal disdain. Gawaine had heard the servants talk. Indeed, they often came to him with their complaints, even Hwyll, who was usually so competent and never tattled. Gawaine always did what he could, which was little enough—sending his own personal physician to deal with black eyes and broken bones, and his horse doctor to spirit away any animals too badly abused.

Hardly out of boyhood, his face still spotty, his hair the yellow of autumn leaves, Agravaine was already feared by his mother's household for his temper and quick fists. Yet Morgause did not attempt to control him. Her boys were always in the right, even when they were in the wrong.

Gawaine made a face. *It is not mete that a prince should act so cruelly.* He shook his head. *Such a thing would never be allowed in Arthur's court.* And then a second thought came to him. *Merlinnus will sort him out soon enough.*

He guessed that of his three brothers going to Cadbury, Agravaine was their mother's spy. It was a role he had been bred up for.

"Keep spewing, then, for all I care," Gawaine muttered in Agravaine's direction, loud enough for his brother to hear. Then he turned back to watch the porpoises.

Suddenly Gareth and Gaheris were at his elbows, speaking, as they often did, in one voice. Few of the servants could tell them apart, but Gawaine could. Even when they traded tunics and linen camisias and breeches and cloaks, disguising themselves as one another, he always knew which was which. It had to do with the way Gareth set his shoulders and Gaheris shrugged. It had to do with the fact that one listened with his head tilted to the right, the other to the left. They had never looked alike to Gawaine, even when they had been babies lying side by side in their cot.

"Do you think they're an omen? The porpoises?" they asked.

Since he had so recently thought that very thing, he nodded. "But like all omens, hard to read," he answered. "Unless you are a mage."

"A mage!" said Gaheris, shoulders rising up toward his ears.

"Like Merlinnus!" Gareth breathed.

Neither mentioned their mother's magic. Gawaine wondered if they even knew of it. It was a secret, but not an especially well-kept one. He had discovered it by accident as a ten-year-old, going into her tower room, which was usually hard-warded and locked. He had wanted to show her a doll he had made for the cook's little girl. Wanted to borrow a bit of fine cloth to wrap the thing in. The cook's girl had a harelip and no play-mates, and he felt sorry for her. He often gave her gifts.

The door to the tower room had been open, and his mother was gone—off to the high alures to shake her black hair at the sea, no doubt.

She never knew that he had entered the room with-out permission. But the memory of that cauldron squatting in the middle of the place—empty then but smelling foully, like a violated tomb—still haunted his dreams.

Worse still had been the glass bottles full of dead things suspended in heavy water, things that seemed to turn at the sound of his footsteps, and stare at him with their bulging dead eyes. Unborn creatures, most of them, though one—he was quite sure—had been a human child. He could remember the room and how it had made him feel—soiled and damned—as if it had been yesterday and not almost eight years gone by.

Gawaine folded his hands over his chest, spread his legs apart, keeping his balance without the aid of the boat's rail. "Merlinnus is a mage, yes. But he is a man first."

"Never!" said Gaheris, shoulders still crowding his ears.

"Does he eat?" asked Gareth.

"He eats."

"And does he get seasick like Agravaine?" Gaheris asked.

"I have never seen him on the sea," said Gawaine.

"Clot!" Gareth told his twin. "Mages cannot cross running water."

"That's fairies," said Gaheris. "Not mages."

"That's all magic makers."

Gaheris drew himself up so that he stood half a thumb's span taller than his twin. "Mother never crosses water. And she works magic."

Gawaine kept his mouth shut. *So they know.* He wondered how.

"Fool," Gareth said. "She came from Land's End by boat to be Father's bride."

Gawaine threw up his hands. "Whatever you two wish to believe, believe." He could tell it was going to be a long trip. And longer still once they were at the king's court. He had forgotten what incredible bumpkins his little brothers were.

GAWAINE SLEPT but fitfully on the boat's deck. It was not the wind tangling in his hair that kept him awake. Actually he quite liked the feel of it, as if it were scrubbing away all that was Orkney from his mind. But a sound on the wind, a strange moaning, niggled at him. At last he sat up, shaking off the blanket, and looked around.

The twins were close by his feet, spooned together. Hwyll was snoring lightly, well beyond them. In the half-moon's light, Gawaine could make them all out.

But Agravaine was missing.

And the moaning that had disturbed Gawaine's sleep had not been a dream, for he heard it still.

He stood, dropped the blanket, and—walking somewhat unsteadily as the boat rolled on the high waves—headed toward the sound.

It was Agravaine, of course, his head over the side of the boat, heaving dryly into the waves.

For a minute Gawaine thought to leave him there. *Good for him to feel pain once in a while instead of inflicting it.* But Gawaine could not help feeling sorry for any suffering creature. Even a pig like his brother.

He went back for a waterskin and some dry bread, then brought it to Agravaine, who was, for once, too sick to even think of going on the attack. At Gawaine's urging, he took several sips and slowly chewed on a piece of bread, then fell back against Gawaine's chest, exhausted.

Gawaine held his brother in his arms until morning brought a glassy sea. The minute the sea calmed and the sun rose, Agravaine pushed him away, saying, "If you tell anyone about last night, I shall kill you. Slowly. You will cry like a sow in labor."

Smiling wryly, Gawaine stood and walked away. It was comforting to know that some things never changed.

LORD BEDWYR had arranged horses for them at the quay, and everyone but Agravaine was glad of it. Agravaine's color had not yet returned and his mood never lightened. Someone who did not know him might have guessed that was from the sour taste in his mouth from several days of vomiting. But Gawaine knew better. Agravaine was always sour. In fact, on landing, Agravaine slapped his manservant for being slow, then after that, whipped the horse he was presented with, when it was not as soft-mouthed as he would have liked, or as handsome. Finally he swore vehemently at Hwyll.

Hwyll, being ever mindful of his station, and wary of his charge's temper, bowed and quickly got out of the way.

"You should mind your manners," Gawaine said quietly, making certain that no one else could hear this caution, "else Cadbury will be an uncomfortable place indeed. If you are so hardhanded, no one will let you in on their secrets. And how will you tattle to Mother if you have nothing to say?"

"Shut up, brother," Agravaine advised loudly, "or I will whip *you* as well." That lent a little flush to his countenance, but it was gone in seconds and he was as green as before.

"You will do no such thing," Gawaine answered, but so low only Agravaine could hear.

Still, Agravaine understood the threat in the quiet steely voice and did not speak further.

As if to emphasize his utter disdain, Gawaine turned away and chivvied the twins to their mounts like a shepherd with sheep. They bounded like lambs.

"Will he try to whip you, Gawaine?" asked Gareth and Gaheris together.

Gawaine guessed they were less curious than hopeful.

"Not if he values his whip arm," Gawaine said. *And not as sick as he is,* Gawaine thought. He got them settled and then chose his own steed, a sweet-faced gelding the color of good earth, with a white blaze down its nose.

The horses that Lord Bedwyr had sent were good, serviceable ones. Not the heavy horses for battle nor lighter ones like those the Companions rode when boar hunting in Cadbury. These were sturdy ground-eaters who would take them down south with a minimum of fuss, thirty miles a day at least, weather permitting. Fast enough to escape even the most diligent of thieves, many of whom lay in wait in the highland forests.

"Give your lord my thanks," Gawaine said to Bedwyr's man. "Tell him I will see him in Cadbury when next the Round Table meets." He handed the man a small ring with a stone worth the price of a horse.

The ostler looked up at Gawaine, his plain face wreathed with smiles. He touched his hand to his forehead. "I will do so, young master, when he returns from deer stalking." Then he had to sidestep quickly as Agravaine insinuated his horse between them.

"What did you give him? The horses are worth less than nothing. They are an insult. Small, badly conformed." Agravaine's voice was pitched to carry.

"You are not used to riding long distances, Agravaine. Orkney is a tiny place compared to Britain. These ponies are perfect for getting us south quickly." Gawaine pulled his horse's head to the right. He neglected to mention the thieves.

Hearing the unmistakable sound of the whip slashing through the air, Gawaine turned back. He raised his arm to ward off the lash, knowing his sleeve was but little protection.

The whip came nowhere near him. Instead it flicked across the ostler's back, cutting open his wool tunic and laying the flesh bare. A thin red line of blood showed that the man had been scored, but not badly. Yet.

Gawaine leaped off his own horse, ran over to his brother, and hauled him to the ground. It was so sudden a rush, Agravaine was not ready for it, and besides he was weak from two days of seasickness, so he fell heavily.

"Go, man!" Gawaine shouted out to the ostler, who hastened away into the nearby inn, slamming the door behind him.

Agravaine rose heavily from the ground, but Gawaine was on his feet, sword drawn, and waiting.

"Get back on your horse," he said, his voice a low grumble. "Do not try to attack me, brother. I am older and taller and bigger. I have not been throwing up the contents of my stomach for two days. And I have been practicing my sword strokes with the greatest master in Britain."

Shrugging, Agravaine rose. "I was just upholding the family's honor, brother. The insult should be avenged. If you—the eldest of Lot's sons—will not do so, then it is left to me."

"There was *no* insult," Gawaine said. "Get on your horse and you will see."

"My horse is useless."

"Then take mine." With little effort, Gawaine sprung up onto the saddle of Agravaine's horse, turned its head to the right, and rode south toward Cadbury and Arthur's court, knowing that Agravaine had little choice but to follow.

5

Message Delivered

THE MESSENGER had sailed two full days before the Orkney princes. He had made a hard crossing and an equally hard landing, coming ashore in such an astonishing downpour that it had all but washed the paint off his small boat.

In a fortress not far from his landing place, he reported briefly what he had found out in the Orkneys to Lord Bedwyr. Then he had been immediately sent—with a pocket packed with hard journeycake and a leather bottle filled with the raw wine of the previous year—back to the road without either a bath or a change of clothes.

"Arthur must know what she is sending," Bedwyr

had told the man. "Let no one and nothing stop you. Not thieves, not those puny lords who hate Arthur and would stop any messages reaching him. Go. Go with Our Lord's blessing." He clapped the messenger on the back with a gusto that belied the fact that he was worried about the man getting through.

The messenger's face was the color of Roman bronze from being outdoors most of his life. He had a hawk's nose with dark alert hawk eyes above it, glowering from under a leather cap covered with metal. His mustache was as taut and grey as bowstring, and his beard looked as if ash had been sprinkled in it. No one seeing that face or the ease with which he sat his saddle or pulled his long-bladed sword from its sheath would ever mistake him for easy prey.

Still, Bedwyr worried. His pudgy, homely countenance scrunched up with his dismay. He knew there were many brigands and many followers of the North Witch between his own well-guarded fortress and Arthur's Cadbury.

IN FACT, brigands did not worry the messenger on the long road. His enemies were wind and weather and the many days he had to spend in the saddle. Even a man with his natural strength wearied. A weary man is not a careful man. A careless man is a dead man. He worked extra hard to remain careful.

The messenger rode three separate horses down, the first two expiring within an hour of his unsaddling them in an ostler's stable, and the other having to be killed with a quick deep slice across the neck after it tripped and broke its right foreleg in the deep forest. That one had been an excellent horse and the messenger hated losing it, but death was the only honor he could pay it for its service. And his own carelessness.

After that he walked through the deep woods, a strong stride, but still days slower than any horse's gait.

He slept cold and hungry, for even though it was late spring, there was not much in the way of a forest larder in the northern lands. But he made it at last to a farm at the edge of the woods, where he purchased a new horse that took him speedily on to the palace. Nowhere along the way did he say where he was riding—or why. Safety lay in anonymity. This the messenger knew from long experience.

Once in Cadbury, he produced his letter from Bedwyr, with the lord's crest foiled into the wax, and was shown at once to the king.

ARTHUR WAS shifting his weight uncomfortably on the high wooden throne, his white brachet hound asleep at his feet, when the messenger was brought into the Great Hall, a boat-shaped room that served many purposes.

Bowing to the young king, the hawk-faced messenger took off his helmet and glanced briefly but longingly at the peat fire burning in the central hearth. The smoke was making its way up through the louvre, the hole in the roof.

"Have you been traveling straight through?" Arthur asked, having known such days and nights himself. The hound stirred at his voice but did not waken, for she was getting old, and once asleep, nothing much woke her.

"Aye, my lord," the man said.

"Were you assaulted anywhere along the way?"

"Nay, my lord."

"Good. Then the peace holds."

"For a careful man, sire."

Arthur smiled. "How's the back? The legs?"

"Fine, my king. Though I cannot say the same for all my horses. It took four."

"Any of them living still?" asked Arthur, suddenly grim, for he loved the large-footed beasts and hated anyone's having to use them so hard, even when he understood the necessity.

"Only the last, my lord; as for the others, I am saddened and shamed." It was plainly said and clearly from the heart. Arthur immediately took to the man.

"Give me your message quickly, then, and stand by the fire while I read it." Arthur held out his hand for the letter the messenger held.

"The message is in my head, lord," said the man. "Lord Bedwyr would not entrust it to a scribe. This letter is but my passage into your presence."

Arthur stood and walked down the throne's two steps to the man. The movement made the brachet look up blearily. Then she settled down into sleep again.

"Let us stand at the fire together and there you shall tell me what it is that has sent you on such an unrelieved journey," Arthur said. As he walked, one arm on the messenger's elbow, he nodded to his stepbrother and seneschal, Kay, who knew that he was meant to bring them both a mug of hot cider without delay.

Kay was a thin, still boyish-looking young man, who tried to appear older by sporting a flowing mustache. The mustache was red, though the lanky hair on his head was blond. It created a pied effect that only made him look foolish, like a jester without wit or wisdom for the job.

He made a face when Arthur sent him out, hating to miss any part of the message. There was nothing he liked better than being in on secrets. But he knew he could not hesitate acting upon Arthur's commands, small or large. To hesitate was to lose the king's trust, and the king's trust was the thing Kay desired most of all.

As soon as Kay had cleared the doorway, Arthur spoke quietly to the tired man. "The sooner you have delivered what it is in your head, the sooner you can sleep. Your good horse will be cared for in my own stable."

"The message is this, my lord—the North Witch is sending her four sons to your court, and they are not to be trusted. One is an assassin. So says my lord Bedwyr, who has sent many messengers riding the country on your behalf."

"Four sons; not five?" Arthur let nothing show on his face.

"The young Medraut she keeps behind her skirts at home. He is too much in her thrall to be let go. And too young to be much good here. But watch the others, my lord Bedwyr says—"

"Which one is the assassin?"

"That, alas, Lord Bedwyr was unable to discover."

"Ah." Worry lines spread across Arthur's brow. "Then let us reason this out together."

"Together?" Clearly the messenger was unused to great lords doing more than dismissing him once a message had been delivered.

Arthur smiled. "We know Gawaine well here in Cadbury. There is no meanness in him. He is a sound young man." Suddenly Arthur broke into a barking laugh, and the messenger looked startled. "I call him 'young,'" Arthur explained, "though he is but four years younger than I."

"My lord..." The messenger hesitated. Then he plunged in. "Even Gawaine must be watched. They say where I live, 'The de'il's bairns hae ay de'il's luck.'"

"And that means?"

"The devil's children have all the devil's luck, sire. He may seem sound, Prince Gawaine, and without guile, but he is still the North Witch's child, suckled at her breast on wizard's milk and gone back home at her every summoning."

The smile disappeared from Arthur's face.

At that moment Kay returned with the cups and handed one to each of them.

"And they also say," added the messenger, "'Wha sup wi' the de'il wants a lang-shaftit spune.'"

"I know that one," said Kay, a bit too eagerly. "Who sups with the devil needs a long-shafted spoon." He grinned in what he thought was a companionable way and stroked his mustache.

"Kay's last lady but one was a Scotti girl," commented Arthur to the messenger. If he thought the comment would steady the man, he was wrong, for the messenger was now in full cry against the Orkneys, as only a Highlander could be, his original message all but forgotten. And as he wound himself up with his warning, he slipped easily back into his own dialect.

"Those islands are nae Scotland," said the messenger. "And nae Britain, neither. They be Norse settled and Viking to the core. Odin be worshipped there, my lord, not the Christ. The de'il and all are alive across those waters."

"So says Lord Bedwyr?" asked Arthur quietly.

"So says mysel'," the messenger said before gratefully taking a long swallow of the hot mulled drink.

WHEN THE MAN was gone to a bed far from the Great Hall, and all the servants were dismissed, Arthur explained the message to Kay. Arthur often kept his step-brother out of state secrets. Kay had eager ears but not a closed mouth.

Kay's face turned red. He roared, "Does Bedwyr think we are stupid? Of course we know Morgause believes she has a better right to the throne than you." His voice ended on a rising note.

The brachet looked up, startled out of dreams. Then, seeing the noise was only Kay, she put her head down again.

"Morgause *has,* you know," Arthur said, "a straighter, truer line. I am nobody—fatherless, motherless, kinless—but for your father, who named me his foster child. I was put on the throne but did not inherit it."

"That is not what Merlinnus believes," Kay said. "Nor I. You are my brother in all but blood, Arthur. Besides, you were trained up to be the king."

"*We* ..." Arthur said slowly, "were trained up to it together." He said this partly because he knew it was what Kay was really thinking, and by acknowledging that fact, he salved the pain of Kay's jealousy and held Kay even closer. And partly he said it because he truly believed the two of them were equal. "We were both taught to handle hawk and hound and horse. We both practiced daily at sword and spear, axe and sling. And we learned well what a hero has to know—if not a king." Then he smiled a half smile, remembering. He had loved those lessons.

"You were the best," Kay admitted. It was hard for him to say, but it had to be said. "Though I was better at letters. Still, you must be careful, Arthur. The North Witch has a long reach, a sharp knife, and four strong sons."

"Five," Arthur answered.

"The little one does not count," Kay replied hotly. "Medraut. Not for ages and ages."

"It is the ages I worry about most," said Arthur in a calm voice. "My sword can take care of the rest." He drank down the last of the cider, now cold but nonetheless delicious. Then he set the cup on the wooden mantel that stretched the length of the hearth. The peats were barely smoldering and what heat remained was as soft as summer.

"What should we do, then?" Kay asked. "Be extra careful?"

"I am careful with everyone," Arthur said. "It is part of what High King is all about, being careful. I am careful because everyone—even you, my dear brother—would be king in my place."

Kay had the grace to look embarrassed and once again blushed red. "Not I, Arthur," he said, but they both knew it was a lie.

"*Everyone* wants the throne," Arthur repeated and walked back up the steps to the high wooden seat. He sat down on it heavily. The brachet sat up, put her head in his lap, and he absentmindedly stroked her small head. "Everyone wants it but me."

Kay did not hear the last comment as he picked up the cup and headed out of the room. Even if he had heard it, he would not have believed it. High King of all Britain was the most important position in the entire civilized world. He believed that with all his heart.

6

Castle Mage

AS THE MESSENGER was led to his room, he was so tired, his eyes began closing even as he walked. He no longer needed to remain alert, for Bedwyr's message had been well delivered. And even with the near disaster of the dead horses, he had made good time. No one was expecting the North Witch's boys for days and days yet.

Perhaps, he thought, *they will meet the black knight some call Death along the road.* He almost wished it, then crossed himself. He was a Christian now. He knew he should not make such prayers. Not when he was too tired to think out the consequences. Not without confessing it to a priest.

He started to doze on his feet, shook himself awake, saw the servant ahead of him make a quick turn to the right in the dark hallway, and hurried to catch up. As he rounded the turn, he bumped into someone, barked out an apology, then stuttered when he saw who it was. Only his Highland pride kept him from crossing himself again.

The man he had charged into was none other than the castle mage, old Merlinnus, thin and wiry, with his tangled grey beard and bleached blue eyes, the color of autumnal skies.

"My bones are too brittle for such a bruising," the old man said. The voice was soft, but the meaning was clear.

The messenger sketched a quick bow, unsure of the etiquette, but certain of the old wizard's power. Hadn't Merlinnus brought the hanging stones across the sea in a single night, setting them on the plain to tell the time at each Solstice? Couldn't he make the dead to walk, the lame to dance, and charm the old gods to worship at the Christ's cross? The messenger blanched. "I did not see you, my lord."

"I doubt you are seeing much, with eyes that red... from riding through the dust storms a heavy horse kicks up."

The messenger did not doubt Merlinnus knew his entire history without being told.

"I had a message, mage."

"For the king?"

The messenger nodded.

"Tell it to me."

"It was for the king's ears alone." The man said it quietly. One must not anger a mage.

Merlinnus made a motion with his hand, no more than a flick of annoyance. But the Highlander thought it was a magical sign and threw himself to his knees, hands above his head in a warding gesture. He trembled, and not just from fatigue.

"Stand up, man," Merlinnus said. "I mean you no harm. You are in Arthur's house."

As if drawn up again by some dark power, the messenger stood. "It was a message," he said softly in a tired, trembling voice, "about an assassin coming, sent by the North Witch."

"Morgause," whispered Merlinnus.

The name itself unmanned the Scot. He quickly recited Bedwyr's message, his own fears, and a paternoster in quick succession. He did not even notice that Merlinnus had left before his recital was done. It took the servant's hand on his shoulder and a quick shake before he let himself be led to his bed, as if the entire episode with the mage had been but a waking dream.

MERLINNUS had been on his way down to the kitchen for a bowl of stew when the messenger bumped into him. The old mage often liked to sit in the kitchen, for it was the only place that remained warm, winter and summer alike. He also enjoyed the bustle of cook and potboys around him. They ignored him when he was there, more out of fear than friendship, but it was the ordinariness of the scene that pleased him. He did not realize that, by his very presence, he changed what was ordinary into something else. The clamorous chaos in the kitchens became a quiet frenzy whenever he was in attendance. No one dared speak aloud, except to use phrases alluding to food, like *Pass the salt,* and *Grind this turnip,* and *Dust that leg joint with flour.* There were no stories full of sexual allusions, no ribald songs, no tickle-me-up tales when Merlinnus sat among them. Fear rode the mage's shoulder and turned its baleful eye on all.

But the messenger's words had changed Merlinnus' mind. The North Witch was not Arthur's only enemy—but she was the strongest. If she was really sending an assassin, she must believe herself ready to tackle even his own magicks. He had no time for soup now and instead abruptly turned and headed back up the stairs to his tower room, five stories up, where he had windows that looked out on the four major compass points. His old knees creaked and popped and groaned as he mounted each riser, but he never stopped. Pain was an old campaigner on his body's battlefield; they had walked long miles together.

Keys and a spell opened the door, and he pushed through into his cozy, messy room. Pouring fresh water into a stone bowl, he stared long and hard into it.

The water riffled as if a wind blew across it. Bending over, the old mage spoke three simple words and the water went still as glass.

At first he saw nothing. Then he saw strands of black rope tangled and blowing in the wind.

He said three more words, and the picture in the water resolved. Not rope, but hair. Long black hair. Elf knots. Then a face he knew. For a moment it stared at him as if it could see him spying. Then the face began to laugh, gentle at first and then with a hysterical edge to it. Things flew out of the mouth—dark, ugly, vile things with long tentacles dripping bane.

"Morgause," he said quietly. "Morgause." So it was true. She was still practicing dark magic, unchanged by the children she had had, hardly stopped by the aftermath of pain that always accompanied the greater spells. If he had thought to see her softened, he could no longer hold to such foolish hopes. That laughing mouth, those monsters emerging from it, told a harsher story. Her obsession with the throne of Britain was not just about bloodlines. It was about power.

Leaving off scrying, which was a difficult trick at best, he went immediately to the north-facing window. Silently he stared out, as if by staring long enough he could see beyond the mountains and the distant seas to the Orkneys and into Morgause's rooms.

Once she had been a child playing magic games at his feet. An unhealthily spiteful child, angry at her mother, angrier at her stepfather, angriest at what she considered an unjust world. He should have kicked her out of his room long before she had had a chance to learn anything from him. But he'd been flattered that a child would pay him any mind. Most children trembled and screamed in terror when he came near. But not Morgause. She dimpled and smiled and tossed her dark curls. She called him "Lord Magic" and named one of her dolls after him. He had succumbed to her seven-year-old charms.

Besides, he had needed to remain close to her mother, Ygraine, who was carrying an even more special child in her belly. A child promised to him at its inception, *the* child who would be his to nurture, train, love. A child he would put on the High King's throne.

He had never thought that nine months at his feet could have taught Morgause any real magic. She was a tot, hardly knowing more than her alphabet. She seemed to be paying him little mind, concentrating on a straw doll. Or blending flours and herbs together in a crucible he loaned her, and saying nonsense spells.

But she'd had an aptitude that her wiliness hid from him. Or he had been blinded by his own pride so that he did not see it. For learn she did. Then—and later. Only it had been a knowledge untempered by any morality, fed by anger, slyness, and hate; black magic instead of white. North magic crossed with what she had stolen from him. Magic overlarded by the unpredictable wild Celtic wood lore, which he had never trusted and so had never bothered to learn.

"Morgause," he said again into the wind. "Tell me what you are planning." As if his voice could carry the message there and back again.

He already knew what she wanted: Arthur gone, and the throne of all Britain for herself and her sons. She would have it, too, if her assassin was successful. *Even if he is not,* Merlinnus thought, *she might still win if I cannot find a way to bind the people—all the people—to Arthur. And soon.*

"Time," he said into the wind. "I need more time."

As if Morgause herself answered him, the wind spit back into his face, "No time, old man. No time."

He turned away from the north window and went to the south. Staring out, past the gates, he saw the peasants' fields freshened with spring plantings. A green and golden haze touched the trees. The old year renewing itself.

"I need to make new what is old," he told himself. "The king on the throne rethroned."

Again he turned and this time glanced out the east window. The river, like a steely snake, twisted past the walls of Cadbury. It doubled back at one point, making an oxbow in the middle of which a small rock island sat. "Arthur must be protected by steel and stone."

He sighed and turned at last to the west window. The west never signified in his thoughts, for the west looked out on the unknown. Green meadow and green lea flowed all the way to the horizon. Far off, where the green ended, he knew, was water. A tremendous ocean of it. Britain was, after all, an island, completely surrounded by water.

He shivered. He had never been good with water—only fire and air and stone and steel.

Looking over his shoulder at the hearth, he realized that once again the boy had not come to freshen the fire, and the room had grown cold. The flame in the lamp in the iron holder was out as well.

The trouble with the current boy—with *all* the boys who had served him since Arthur had grown up and become king—was that he was so afraid of Merlinnus, he could not do his chores properly. They had all found excuses to stay away from the tower room, silly excuses really. He hated that the boys feared him. And yet, he knew, their fear was a necessary component to his art.

Magic, he reminded himself, *is as much perception as reality.*

And with that reminder, he had a sudden idea. It came as all his ideas came, with a miraculous rush out of ordinary things: the view from a window, a cold fire, a memory of a spiteful child.

His idea was this: If the people believed Arthur to be their only choice—*perception*—then he would be. *Reality.* And if they believed Arthur the once-and-future king, all of Morgause's small magicks, her tantrums, her would-be assassins, would come to nothing.

Only, Merlinnus wondered, *how can I make the people believe in Arthur, now and in the future? What legerdemain will make them believe? And once that is accomplished, what further magic will make Arthur believe in himself?*

He thought once again: *I know only fire and air and stone and steel.*

And then—in a moment—he had it.

7

Dream

"I HAD A DREAM, my liege, of a sword in a stone," Merlinnus said, his voice throbbing with emotion. He pushed aside the guards at the door and, without being bidden, entered the throne room. Grand entrances were always a part of his magical success. He had become very good at them over the years. "I dreamed of such a sword and such a stone last night, my king. Stone grey as grief, with that sword stuck right in the top like a knife in butter."

Arthur had been dozing on the high-backed throne, lightly snoring. The brachet was asleep at his feet. At the wizard's voice they both startled awake. The brachet recognized the wizard and put her head back down again. But Arthur's grey eyes, unfocused and watery for a moment, went dark as steel. His hand had already reached for the sword at his belt. Then, seeing it was Merlinnus, he dropped his guard.

"It means something," the wizard continued, letting his voice fall to a whisper as he neared the throne. Another trick, but a good one. Arthur was always susceptible to that; it got his full attention. "My dreams always mean something. Do you believe in that stone and that sword, my lord?"

Arthur put his hand to his mouth, disguising a yawn as a heavy sigh, though the wizard—who had known Arthur since he was a baby—was not fooled. "Merlinnus, I have no time to believe in a sword in a stone. Or on top of a stone. Or under a stone, for that matter. I'm too tired to put what's left of my strength— and my temper—into believing your hocus-pocus today. I have found that believing you always means work." He pushed a hand through his sand-colored hair, played with the gold torque at his neck. "Besides, you *always* have dreams."

"I had this dream three times in one night." A lie, but a useful one.

"And anything that happens three times is true?" Arthur said in a teasing voice.

"Not necessarily true in every particular, my king,"

Merlinnus answered, sounding very much like the teacher he really was. In fact, unless his waking dream counted, he had not dreamed of the sword and the stone at all. But he never let details like that spoil a good lesson. Or a good story. "I have told you *that* often enough. However, this dream was very different."

"Your dreams are always *very* different," Arthur said, smiling.

Merlinnus knew that Arthur was actually quite fond of him, the way a grown man is fond of a father who has been both hard and kind. The smile was very sweet. One thing Arthur had never been lacking in was charm.

"You must listen, Arthur. It is important." Merlinnus only used the king's name when he needed to make a point. But this time his use of it was of little consequence. Arthur was vigorously shaking his head.

"More important than your dream, my friend, is the news I have just had. A messenger from..."

Merlinnus put a finger to his temple and intoned in broad Scots, "The de'il lies in the Orkneys stirring her potions wi' a lang spoon."

For a moment Arthur looked nonplussed. Then he smiled again. "You met the messenger in the hall."

Merlinnus smiled back.

"Well—you are my adviser, Merlinnus. Advise me."

"The North Queen sends assassins like spring rain," Merlinnus said. "That does not mean the crops grow any faster or truer."

Arthur leaned forward and growled. "You know I hate that kind of thing. Talk straight, old man. Do you mean you are not worried that one of her sons—whom we must accommodate, as they are highborn lords—will try to kill me while they are here?"

"No, I am not unduly worried about them." But he was. He knew he could keep an eye on one boy. Gawaine had been easy to watch. But the messenger—and Arthur—had said "sons." He could not remember how many Morgause had. She bred like a bitch—one litter after another. "Who is she sending?"

Arthur counted them on his fingers. "Gawaine will be returning. And his next-oldest brother, Agravaine. Then the twins, their names begin with a *G*. I cannot remember."

"Twins…" Merlinnus was suddenly disturbed. Twins could be a problem. In magic, anything out of the ordinary troubled deep waters. If they looked alike, spoke alike…

"The youngest, Medraut, has remained at home."

"Just as well," the old wizard replied. "Four of that brood will be plenty."

"*Should* we worry?" Arthur asked. "About Orkney

dirks on a dark night, or a sword in the belly during a mock fight or—"

"Not you," Merlinnus said. Meaning that he would do the worrying for both of them. He climbed the steps to the throne.

Arthur sighed and leaned back again. But his eyes were still steel and his mouth had thinned down to a knife's edge.

A guard opened the door and looked in. When he saw Merlinnus bending close to Arthur, he shut the door without being told.

"Now, about that sword in the stone—it is important for you to listen, Arthur," Merlinnus said.

"I have already spent most of the morning sitting here on this hard chair listening to important things," Arthur answered. "Or at least things that are important to the people who are doing the speaking. Merlinnus, you never told me that being a king was three parts ear to one part mouth."

"If I had, you would never have taken the job," muttered the old man into his tangled beard. He knew Arthur was a man for action, had been since a boy. "The Whirlwind" had been his nickname at Sir Ector's castle. The joke was that Arthur had never met a chair he liked. Or a sport he disliked.

"Most of the morning gone," Arthur continued,

"and I will have an aching head from it for the rest of the day. What kind of job is this for a king?" Arthur's right hand closed into a fist. "I want to be out hunting deer. I want to take my sword and right wrongs. But instead I sit all day on this thing." He banged his fist on the wooden arm. "This hard chair. And I listen."

Merlinnus nodded. "The ear is the seat of governance."

"There you go again!" Arthur shook his head. "I sit with my bottom, Merlinnus; I hear with my ear. And what I hear from you is too hard to parse. It reminds me of Latin. And speaking of Latin, the first thing I had to deal with this morning were two quarreling *dux bellorum*. Or is it *bellori*?"

"Belli," mumbled the mage, shaking his head. "Chiefs of war." Arthur had never been a scholar, of Latin or anything else. He could read, but did not enjoy it. *"Belli,* my lord. It matters..."

"It matters to *you,* Merlinnus. And to the church. And to some old Romans who never bothered to learn our tongue. But as for the rest..."

"It should matter to you, too, Arthur," said the mage, leaning forward and assuming his teaching expression, which consisted of lowering his eyebrows and sucking on his bottom lip. "Everything should matter to a good ruler."

Arthur gripped the carved arms of the throne to

keep from getting angry. Merlinnus knew that whenever Arthur was tired, and cranky with too much listening, he got angry.

Arthur gripped the throne so hard, his palms took the imprint of the carvings: a bear and an eagle. He turned his palms up, and Merlinnus saw the prints.

The dog saw them, too, for she was up now, and nervous because her master was angry.

"Listen, Merlinnus, I have no use for Latin or Romans this morning. *Use* matters. Not some old half-forgotten language that my people do not use. So, after the *dux bellori*—"

"*Belli,*" Merlinnus corrected automatically.

Arthur ignored him. "After them, I had to sort out five counterclaims from my head cook and his children. He should stick to his kitchens. His household is a mess. Then there were five chiefs down from the north who wanted no more than to lay eyes upon me, I warrant. Since I stood a head taller than they and shook hands with a grip they admired, they pledged themselves to the high throne. For now. Though I suspect that should I falter or lose weight or girth, or my gripping hand take the palsy, they will be on me like young lions on an old. And then I had to award grain to a lady whose miller had maliciously killed her cat."

Merlinnus shook his head.

The brachet growled, then lay down again.

"Did you know, old man, that we actually have a law about cat killing that levies a fine of the amount of grain that will cover the dead cat completely when it is held up by the tip of its tail and its nose touches the ground? Kay found it in the *Book of the Law*. Who thinks up these things?" Arthur raised his hands in a helpless gesture. "The miller owed the lady over a peck of grain." He sighed again, and again combed his hair with his fingers.

"A large cat, my lord," mumbled the mage.

"A very large cat indeed," agreed Arthur with a rueful smile. "And a very large lady. With a lot of very large and important lands. Which she mentioned in every large and important breath. Now, why in Mithras' name should I care about Latin or a sword on top of a stone when I have to deal with all that?"

"In *Christ's* name, Arthur. *Christ's* name. Remember—we are all Christians now." The wizard's tone turned sharp, and he held up a warning finger that was as gnarled as an old tree. His eyebrows began to lower again. "If you know Latin, you can know language and history. Know Latin to train your mind. As for the sword, it is *in* a stone, like a knife in butter, not on top of it. There's something of great import there. I know it. I know it. Else I would not have dreamed it." He waggled the finger at the king. "I just don't yet know what it is I know." He was convinced of that dream himself now.

"*You* can be the Christian, Merlinnus," Arthur said simply. "Not me. I still have to drink bull's blood with my men in honor of Mithras." He shivered. "Horrible stuff, bull's blood." He shook his head and smiled that sweet smile again, only some mischief lay underneath it. Merlinnus could see the boy still in the young man. "And yet I wonder how good a Christian you really are, my old friend, when you insist on talking to trees. That's a Druid's trick, not a Christian's. And once a Druid, always a Druid, as Kay says."

"Your stepbrother, Kay, is a fool. And once a fool, always a fool," muttered Merlinnus. "Even if he *can* read the *Book of the Law*."

Arthur stood and put his arm over the mage's shoulder, speaking quietly but with passion into the mage's right ear. Merlinnus blessed him silently for such compassion. His left ear was growing quite deaf.

"Kay is sometimes a fool, indeed. No one knows that better than I. But even fools have eyes and ears. And—alas—tongues that wag at both ends. Do not dismiss Kay too readily, Merlinnus. He could do us both great wrong if he feels his honor slighted. He can do us much good if he believes himself valued. With the outermost tribes already spoiling for a fight, we need to be happy in our own household at least."

"Your Latin may be awful, but you read people the way I read dreams," Merlinnus said.

"Never so well, old man. But I thank you for the compliment." Arthur straightened up and looked at the mage, considering. "Now go away, Merlinnus, and do not trouble me again with this sword and stone dream. I have more important business. *Real* business; not business of the imagination."

"Pah!" Merlinnus spit out his reply. "Imagination is the only real business of a king."

Arthur threw his head back and roared with laughter. "So you say until I show some. And then you will tell me, 'Listening is the only real business...' or 'Compassion is the only real business...' or something else you have just thought up."

Merlinnus tried to think of a withering and indignant reply but could not, for this time Arthur had caught him out. They walked down the steps from the throne together.

"Oh, and tell the guard at the door to send in the next petitioner," Arthur said. "*And* my counselors." He turned back, climbing heavily up the two stairs as if he were himself the old man, though he was scarce twenty-two years old. Sitting down on the throne, he added almost as an afterthought, "Have them send in Kay, too."

"Once I was all the counselor you needed," said Merlinnus before slipping out through the door and, as usual, having the last word.

8

May Queen

KAY PUSHED PAST the guards and into the throne room.

"That old humbug is up to something again!" he shouted. Kay was always too loud. The brachet stood up and, stiff-legged, made her way to the door, where a guard let her out.

Kay was still speaking. "Isn't he? Isn't he?" He came right up to the steps of the throne but stopped there, his respect for majesty overcoming his eagerness to learn what Merlinnus had been saying.

Arthur sighed. A real sigh this time, not a cover for a yawn. His stepbrother often affected him that way. He loved Kay and was exasperated with him in equal measure. "Merlinnus had a dream, that is all." He was careful not to mention anything about spies.

Kay mulled that over for a moment, his hand toying with the silver brooch on his tunic before asking, "A dream about the assassins? We need to think about them, Arthur. We need to plan."

Arthur shook his head. "Not the assassins."

"A new dream or an old one?" Kay asked.

"One he says he dreamed three times in a row," said Arthur.

"Then it's true. *It's true.* You know it's true. Or will become true soon enough. Anything dreamed three times in a row is..." His voice echoed loudly in the room.

"...is not necessarily true," Arthur said.

"But everyone knows—" Kay abruptly stopped talking. He knew what Arthur's response would be. The same thing that Merlinnus had tried to drum into both of their heads when they were boys.

"Not necessarily true in every particular," Arthur said. "Besides, there's no knowing if he dreamed the dream or simply *said* he dreamed it. He lies all the time, Kay, though always with purpose. And that purpose is the good of the kingdom, so I cannot call him on those lies. I can only listen and try to get at what it is he wants me to get at."

Kay ground his teeth. It was not one of his more pleasant responses.

"I worry about how well I can figure things out," Arthur continued. "I wish he would just say what he means straight."

Kay pouted. "You always listen to him and not to me, Arthur. He is the liar and I never lie. So you should listen to me. Besides, blood is supposed to be thicker than water."

"We are *step*brothers, Kay. We share no blood."

"You *know* what I mean." There was a whine in his voice now. A loud whine. It grated on Arthur's ears.

Arthur nodded. "I know, Kay. And I do value you. You are my oldest companion. My dearest friend." It was true up to a point, but Arthur knew better than to go further. Conversations with Kay always tended to go off the track and into the woods. "But, brother, it is time to get on with the day's business. The real business, not a mage's dream business. And not a silly worry about assassins who may or may not be arriving. Remember, though, I have already ruled on two *dux*..." He hesitated, recalling Merlinnus' correction. "...*belli*. Met with five tribal chiefs from the north. Considered one large lady and one impossible cook. I am not in a good mood. Luncheon would be a fine idea, and the sooner the better."

"It is not near time for eating," Kay said loudly.

"There would be a riot in the hall if I told the crowd out there that you wanted to eat instead of rendering judgment. Some of them have been waiting three days now." He pursed his lips. "But before we get to all that, I have something to make you happy."

Arthur smiled at that. Or at least he showed his teeth. He looked more like a bear—which is what his name really meant—than a man when he smiled that way. It was a smile he reserved for people who annoyed him. And for his stepbrother, Kay.

"Not like that. A *real* smile." Kay understood some things, though it always surprised Arthur when he did.

Reaching down the front of his tunic, Kay pulled out a piece of parchment. "The men did not like who was chosen for May Queen this year, and they have made a list of those qualities they think she should possess, so we will be better prepared next year." He handed the parchment to Arthur.

Arthur read aloud slowly. Reading did not come easy to him—not the way riding or swordplay did—and he pronounced each word carefully. Also, the slower he read, the fewer judgments he would have time for.

> *"Thre thingges smalle—headde, nose, breests,*
> *Thre thingges largge—waiste, hippes, calves,*
> *Thre thingges longge—haires, finggers, thies,*
> *Thre thingges short—height, toes, utterance."*

"Sounds more like an animal in a bestiary than a girl," Arthur ventured at last. "And I am not sure of your spelling."

"It is better than yours," said Kay, which was true.

Arthur leaned forward. "And what is wrong with this year's choice? A nice girl, I thought. Sweet."

"She is a pig farmer's daughter," Kay said sniffily. "And she giggles."

Arthur sucked at his teeth, something he did only when he was annoyed. "We all raise pigs, Kay. That we pay someone else to clean the sty does not make us the better. And where in this list does it say: *Giggles smalle*?"

Kay's hand went to his mustache.

"I am not fooled, you know," Arthur said.

Kay gazed at the ceiling, which Arthur recognized as his attempt to look innocent. "I do not know what you mean."

"I know the Companions are trying to find me a bride. Everyone in court from the cook's boy on up is looking out for the right girl. But I do not want one of those temporary marriages, a handfast for a year and a day."

"And...?" Kay seemed to have found something very interesting in the ceiling, because he was still staring at it.

"I am not like Queen Maeve of Connacht to change

consorts so often that I never have a mate but there is another in her shadow."

"And . . . ?" The ceiling must have been utterly fascinating. Kay could not let it go.

"And I want something more than . . . than a list of things small and large," Arthur said. "I want . . ." But he stopped because, for the life of him, he did not know what he wanted in a bride. Beauty? Wit? Intelligence? Loyalty? Honesty? A large dowry? A good family? A long patience? A gift for song? It was a puzzle for certain. Whoever became his bride would also become the queen at his side. Not a May Queen to serve for the Planting Fest until Solstice Eve, but a queen for all seasons. Someone to talk to, to confide in. To share interests. Someone who could make him laugh. He rarely had anything to laugh at, now that he was king. The list the men had drawn up did not speak to that kind of queen. He wondered if there was any list that could.

"The men are trying, Arthur," said Kay, by which he meant that *he* was trying and had gotten the men to go along with him. Kay could often bend certain kinds of men to his will.

"Very trying," Arthur replied quietly, and smiled. This time it was a real smile because he, like Merlinnus, had gotten off a real last line.

But still gazing at the ceiling, Kay did not seem to

notice Arthur's last line. Indeed, Kay had little sense of humor, especially where it touched upon himself.

"All right, then," Arthur said, and sighed. *So much for last lines.* "Send in the next petitioner."

Eager to be doing something official, Kay went back to the door and ushered in a white-bearded man wearing grey woolen breeches and a tunic tied with a leather thong at his waist. Clearly he had not dressed up for his interview with the king. He was carrying a very large bag of millet in his arms.

9

Talking to Trees

MERLINNUS HAD LEFT the throne room and gone directly outside, where he began to mull over the interview he'd just had with the king. Without thinking about where he was going, he headed toward the grove beyond the north end of the castle. His favorite oak tree grew there.

The long, cruel winter had heaved up the path, making the footing uneven and treacherous, so he walked with care. Now approaching his sixtieth year, Merlinnus did not dare fall, for fear he might break a bone. Even with his vast knowledge of herbs and potions, he could no longer count on healing easily. He had not been speaking idly when he had told the messenger his bones were brittle.

If he broke a bone, what good would he be to Arthur? Pain and fever precluded sound judgment. Sound judgment was the base on which all magic rested. And if ever Arthur needed magic, he needed it now.

How else to guarantee the throne?

Merlinnus hadn't needed a messenger to remind him of the restless tribes. He was well aware of the troubling rumors coming down from the north. It was not only the North Witch who sought the throne, though she had the best claim to it. Petty Highland kings with unpronounceable names had refused to take Arthur as their liege lord. And as for the Border lords, hiding behind the Roman Wall—well, for the most part they refused to commit themselves.

So Merlinnus trod the broken path carefully, and when he got to the roots of the oak, he gazed up at the tree fondly, addressing it rather informally, they being of a long acquaintance.

"*Salve, amice frondifer.* Greeting, friend leaf bearer. I am troubled and only your good advice will salve me."

A rustle of new leaves answered him, as a tiny wind puzzled through the grove.

"Here is the problem. The northern tribes in the Orkneys are fussing again, demanding one of Morgause's sons be named king in Arthur's stead. And the westerners, around Cornwall—curse them!—simply egg the northerners on. Those westerners are hoping for a standoff so that they might put up a king of their own. Though they would not be unsatisfied if Morgause's line ruled. After all, she's a daughter of theirs, sired by the late duke who died defending their Castle Tintagel against Uther Pendragon." He sighed. "So many claimants to the throne. So many angry people."

Another small wind ran around the tops of the trees, but only the oak seemed agitated.

Merlinnus shook his head. "What am I to do? I must make them all follow the boy, make them eager to do his bidding. History demands it. History past and history future. Royal blood runs in his veins. No one else knows, of course, but I do. He shows his lineage in his very looks, though only I seem to note it. And I do not mention it because it puts his father's reputation in disrepute." He smiled sourly. "Not that his father's reputation needs much help in that direction."

He waited for some answer from the tree and, getting none, spoke on. "Should I have expected gratitude for setting Arthur on the throne? Should I have expected imagination to accompany his heritage? And how can I dare hope he will fight to retain a crown he finds so heavy?" He drew in a deep breath. "And have I mentioned that he thinks himself unworthy?"

The oak leaves fluttered as if laughing, and around the grove, larch and beech seemed to join in.

"Well, bless me, I *did* expect it. I *did* hope for it. My brain must be rotting with age."

Again many leaves rustled in the grove.

"You ask what is good about him? Oh, *amice frondifer,* he works hard. He loves the people. He weeps for the impoverished. Cares for the needy. He longs to right wrongs. Already he is a good king. He could make a great one in time. But tell me, *e glande nate,* sprout of an acorn, do I ask too much when I hope for vision as well? *Vision!* That's what is missing in the boy. If he shows an ounce of it, they will all follow him to the ends of Britain, no matter his parentage."

This time the leaves in the grove were still. The wind had died down.

"Well, maybe you are right to be silent, tree. Blood is blood, but history has no veins. I've no other witness to his heritage, and what nobles will believe it, anyway? They will say he was gotten badly by a trick of my conniving. They will say I am both the problem and the solution. Oh, magic! That it proves to be such a hard master." Merlinnus sighed again, this time sounding much like the wind in the trees.

He looked up to the crown of the oak. "Arthur must prove his worth—to himself, to all the tribes—in some other way. Sword and stone. It will work. I am convinced of it. But how to convince the king?"

The tree, the grove, the wind, all remained still.

Merlinnus sat down at the foot of the oak and rubbed his back against its bark, easing an itch that had been there for days. "Winter itch," he called it, though he actually itched summer and winter alike. "Comes from wearing wool," he said companionably to the tree.

Tucking the skirt of his robe between his legs, he stared at his feet. He still favored the Roman summer sandals, even through the dark days of winter, because closed boots tended to make the skin crackle between his toes like old parchment. Besides, in heavy boots his feet sweated and stank, which no amount of herbal infusions seemed to sweeten. Since he felt cold now winter and summer, what did it matter that he exposed his old toes to the chill?

"Did I tickle his interest at all, do you think?" he murmured to the oak. "Or did I just irritate him. Or bore him. Young men are bored so easily. Especially by the prattling of the old." He pulled on his beard as if that helped him think. "Such a waste of time, this tickling business. I would rather just say, 'Arthur—do this and be done with it.' But I cannot, else he would learn little. He still needs to learn so very much—for the years when I am gone and can no longer teach him. So I *must* take the time now to teach him to listen and learn. But time is, alas, the one commodity I have so little of." Remembering the face with the vile things vomiting from its mouth, he rubbed a finger alongside his nose.

"I had hoped he would wonder about that sword stuck in the stone like a knife in beef. He likes beef. And swords." Merlinnus almost smiled at that. "He is still a boy, really, for all he has been king these past four years."

The grove was still silent, but the old man kept talking. "That sword in the stone, now—a nice bit of legerdemain, that. I am rather proud of it, actually. You see, it was not really a dream."

The wind picked up again and the leaves fluttered above him.

"Yes, yes, I know I *said* it was a dream. But it was not. I now know I shall have to build the thing before he will understand, though not in my tower room. I shall construct it in the catacombs under the high tor. And let some wandering shepherd find it, so I will not be connected to it. At least not directly."

Once again the leaves above him began to shake in the slight wind.

"Ah—I see I have at least caught *your* interest. Why—anyone with a bit of Latin can read the old Roman building manuals and construct a ring of stones. Or rebuild the baths under the castle. It's just that so few have the ability to read anymore. There's the pity. Or those who *can* read, won't. Like Arthur."

The fluttering leaves made a sound like women laughing.

Merlinnus smiled. "They call what I do magic, but we know better, old friend. It's knowledge and experiment, really. A little lore, a little light, and a lot of patience. Magic! It doesn't change history with a finger snap. Little by little does it. Little by little."

An acorn left over from the last season dropped down by his side.

"Well, of course I am proud of the sword in the stone. He will be, too. You are right, though. Arthur needs to do something more than just rule on quarreling dukes and silly cooks and grasping widows, more than grip the hands of small tribal chiefs. He has to fire up these silly tribes; he has to give them a reason to rally around him. He's got to be more than just another petty chieftain, more than a simple chief of chiefs. A High King does not just sit on an elevated throne. He has got to be the Rightful King of all Britain. He needs..."

A cuckoo called down from an overhead limb.

But, exhausted from his mental labors, the old man did not hear the cuckoo. Or he chose to ignore its obvious message. Instead he drifted into sleep.

This time he really did dream.

II

Mage's Dream/ King's Hope

The churchyard was deserted, but the dawn was beginning to light the sullen square. The stone in the center blushed with the rising of the sun, and the sword in the stone's middle sprang to uncertain life. The sword's shadow was a long stain along the bulge of the stone.

10

Under the Oaks

IT WAS NEARLY a week later, a week of spring skies, which in Britain meant alternating drowning rain and startling sun. The king was in a foul mood, his brother walked about as if on eggshells, and everyone in the castle had snotty colds. Cook had done a fine business in hot, spicy wines, and the infirmarer was kept busy with tisanes and compresses. Only the brachet, who seemed renewed by spring, was happy.

Merlinnus did not have a cold, but he was exhausted. His work had tired him. Day and night he had labored over his dream, hardly eating, barely sleeping. He had sent notes excusing himself from Arthur's company. He had sent Kay away with a rough word. He had even forgotten to worry about the North Queen's assassins, so caught up as he was with the sword and stone. Even a young man would have tired from such labor, and Merlinnus had not seen his own youth for ages.

But he was done. The thing was made. Morgause's sons were not yet there, so he now had time to worry. And so he went out to the oak at sunrise for a renewing sleep. He felt neither the hard ground nor the upheaved roots beneath him. That uncomfortable bed put him right to sleep.

He slept through breakfast and well into the morning without dreams.

"WAKE UP. Wake up, old man."

It was the shaking, not the soft-spoken sentence, that woke him. Merlinnus opened his eyes. A film of sleep lent a soft focus to his vision. The young person standing over him seemed haloed in mist.

"Are you all right, grandfather?"

Merlinnus sat up. He realized, belatedly, that he was getting too old to be sleeping out of doors. The ground cold had seeped into his bones. Like an old tree, his sap ran sluggishly. He could feel a sharp, stabbing pain in both his hips.

But being caught out by the youngster made him grumpy. "Why shouldn't I be all right?" he answered gruffly.

"You are thin, grandsire, and you slept so silently, I feared you dead. One should not die on sacred ground. It offends the Goddess."

That snapped Merlinnus' eyes wide open. "Are you, then, boy, a worshipper of the White One?" he asked, watching the stranger's hands as he spoke. No true worshipper of the Goddess would answer that question in a straightforward manner, of course. Instead he would signal the dark secret with an inconspicuous semaphore. The body language of the true believer. But all the youngster's fingers signed were concern for him. Forefinger, fool's finger, psychic's finger, and ear finger were silent of secrets.

Merlinnus sighed and struggled to sit upright. There were those sharp stabbing pains again, at hip and at buttocks. *No more napping outdoors till it is summer,* he told himself.

As if aware of the old man's aches, the stranger put a hand under his arm and back, gently easing him into a more comfortable position. Once sitting up, Merlinnus took a better look. The stranger was a slim boy with soft, lambent cheeks not yet coarsened by a beard. Perhaps twelve or thirteen years, by the height of him.

His eyes were the clear blue of speedwells. The eyebrows were dark swallow's wings, sweeping high and back toward luxuriant and surprisingly gold hair, cut round like a monk's and kept safe under a dark cap. He was dressed in a wool tunic over a linen camisia, both dark blue, and breeches fastened with a rawhide thong. The long cloak was blue as well, and looked as if it had known some rough traveling. The hands clasped before him were small and well formed, though Merlinnus noted that the nails on the right hand were bitten to the quick.

Sensing the mage's inspection, the boy spoke. "I have come in the hope of becoming a knight in Arthur's court."

Merlinnus nodded, but not eagerly. The boy was slight, more suited for a monastery than the rough-and-tumble of castle life. But it was difficult to tell boys this age how badly fitted they were for heroics. They never listened.

As if anticipating the old man's concerns, the boy added, "I already know how to ride and I am stronger than I look. I wish to learn the sword and lance. I know the bow. And I have never feared hard work."

Merlinnus' mouth screwed about a bit but at last settled into a passable smile. Perhaps he might find some use for this eager child. A wedge properly placed had been known to split a mighty tree. "What is your name, boy?"

"I am called ..." A hesitation, scarcely noticeable, but Merlinnus noted it. It was as if the boy feared anyone knowing who he really was and took his time to search for another name.

"I am called Gawen." The emphasis was ever so slightly on the second syllable.

Merlinnus' smile broadened. "Ah—but we have already a well-known knight by a similar name, Gawaine of the Orkneys. He is not so much older than you. Perhaps you have heard of him. He is praised as one of the king's Three Fearless Men."

"Fearless at least with the ladies," the boy answered. His voice tried to hide a bitterness, and Merlinnus wondered at that, too. "Gawaine, the Hollow Man," the boy added. Then as if to soften his condemnation, he put in quickly, "or so it is said where I come from."

So, Merlinnus thought, *there is more than a desire to learn sword and lance that brought this boy to court.* He thought briefly of spies, then dismissed the notion. This boy was not smooth enough, not studied enough, to be a spy. His condemnation of the North Witch's son was too passionate to be faked. *That I can use, too.*

Aloud Merlinnus asked simply, "And where *do* you come from?"

The boy looked down and smoothed the homespun where it lay against his thighs. Again, purchasing time to come up with the right answer. "The coast."

Refusing to comment that the coast was many miles long, that an island nation has a surfeit of coasts, Merlinnus said a bit sharply, "Do not condemn a man with another's words. And do not praise him that way, either."

"Andronicus," said the boy.

"You know his writings?"

The boy remained silent, and Merlinnus took this as assent.

Curious, the mage thought. *Not many boys can even read, much less read the classics, and certainly not boys who come to be knights.* But he did not comment upon it further. Instead he said, in a voice he usually reserved for Arthur and Kay, "Purity in tongue must precede purity in body."

The boy remained silent.

Annoyed by that silence, Merlinnus lifted a finger and added, "That is my first lesson to you."

"I am too old for such lessons." The tone was sulky.

"None of us is too old for lessons," said Merlinnus, wondering why he felt compelled to continue. "Even I learned something this week."

"And that is . . . ?" Sulkiness gone, the speedwell eyes opened wide with interest.

"It has to do with the Matter of Britain," the mage said, "and is therefore beyond you."

Young Gawen cocked his head to one side. "Why should the Matter of Britain be beyond me, Magister, or beyond any who live here in this land?"

Merlinnus smiled to himself. *That was quick! And well said.* He was beginning to like the boy.

"Give me your hand." He held his own out, crabbed with age.

Gawen put a small hand forward, and the mage ran a finger across the palm, slicing the lifeline where it forked early.

"I see you are no stranger to work. The calluses tell me that. What work it is I do not know. Or how long you have done it. A month's calluses might be as hard as a year's. Whatever work, it is *not* the Matter of Britain. That is the stuff for kings and mages."

Gawen withdrew his hand without a word.

Merlinnus wondered what other secret that hand might have told him could he have read palms as easily as a village herb wife. Then, shaking his head, he stood.

"Come, boy, before I bring you to court, let us go and wash ourselves in the river."

The boy's eyes brightened again. "You? You can bring me into the court at Cadbury?"

Clearly, Merlinnus thought, *the boy is from far away if he does not recognize me. There was no hint of falsity in that eager question.* The old man smiled. "Of course, my son. After all, I am the High King's mage."

"Merlinnus." The boy whispered the word without fear in his voice, only a sort of respectful pleasure.

Merlinnus was so delighted at that, he let the boy have the last word.

11

Visitor to Cadbury

THEY WALKED companionably to the river, which ran noisily between stones. Willows on the spongy bank wept leaves into the swift current.

Using the willow trunks for support, Merlinnus sat gingerly on the bank and eased his feet—sandals and all—into the cold water. It was too far and too slippery for him to walk in.

"Bring me water to bathe with," he said, thinking in this way to further test the boy's quick-wittedness.

Gawen stripped off his cap, knelt down, and held the cap in the river. Then he pulled it out and wrung the water over the old man's outstretched hands.

Merlinnus liked that. The job had been done, and quickly, with a minimum of fuss. Another boy might have plunged into the river, splashing like an untrained animal. Or begged to be told what to do. Gawen had solved the thing on his own.

As he wrung out the water, Gawen muttered, *"De matri a patre."*

Startled, Merlinnus looked up into the clear, untroubled blue eyes. "You know Latin?"

The eyes were suddenly hidden, the light in them shielded by long lashes, as if a hand were held before a candle to hide its flame. "Did I say it wrong?" The question came out in a breathy whisper.

"'From the mother to the father,' you said. In Latin."

"That is what I meant to say." Gawen's young face was suddenly transformed by a wide, relaxed smile. "The brothers taught it to me. Some sort of prayer, I think."

Merlinnus knew only two monasteries along the coast, and they were both very far away. The sisters of Quintern Abbey were much closer, of course, but they never took in boys. *So this child,* he thought, *has come a very long way indeed.* That explained not only the reading and the Latin but the callused hands. The monks did not shy away from hard work, nor did their boys.

He did not say any of this to the boy, of course. Let

the child think he had fooled an old man. All he said aloud was, "They taught you well."

Gawen bent down, dipping the cap once again in the river. This time he used the water to wash his own face and hands. Once the trail markings had been erased, Merlinnus could see he was exceedingly handsome. Almost *too* handsome to be a knight. More the stuff of wandering players or minstrels. Girls would go foolish around him.

Wringing out the cap thoroughly, Gawen stared piercingly at Merlinnus. Cap in hand, he asked, "Now will you bring me to the High King?"

"You will do," said Merlinnus, by way of an answer. "By the tree, you will do."

As THEY NEARED Cadbury, walking slowly up past a mass of bluebells toward the turf-and-timbered fortress, the enormous gates yawned open. Set atop a hill and surrounded by a shell wall of stone, with a single high guard tower at the southwest corner, was Cadbury Castle. A dry ditch encircled the whole.

They walked past the outer bailey, and Gawen gasped at the hurly of people racing around in the courtyards and forecourts. He stared through the haze of cook fires that made the place seem magical even in the middle of the day. Here were the quarters of the guards, the stables, the storehouses, the forge, the well.

"Come, boy," said Merlinnus, and they continued into the inner bailey where the double keep tower stood. "This is where the king himself stays."

If Gawen had gaped at the confusion of the outer bailey and its residents, the inner was even more complex.

"Great Hall, kitchens, private chambers, king's stables, king's well, workshops," Merlinnus said, counting them off on his fingers. "And..."—he was extremely proud of this—"the chapel."

Gawen nodded.

The Great Hall was enormous, over sixty feet long and half as wide, made of wattle and daub. Topped by a straw thatched roof, it was an impressive sight. To its side and attached were the king's quarters, with a high tower.

"The safest part to be," Merlinnus told him, pointing to the hall, "should an enemy try to take Cadbury..."

"The king has enemies?" Gawen asked.

"All kings have enemies," said Merlinnus. "It is in the nature of kingship."

"I understand."

"But should an enemy want to take *this* castle," Merlinnus repeated, gesturing freely with his right hand, "they would have to breach barbicans, moats, ditches, high walls with archers perched atop them, drawbridges, more walls, portcullises, more walls. An unbreachable fortress has stood on this very spot for hundreds of years."

"Very safe," the boy said dryly.

Was there a hint of laughter behind that soft voice? A spy's laughter? Merlinnus strained to find it, then gave up. He would take young Gawen at his word, at the face of his word. For now.

Behind the castle, beyond the far gates, loomed the tor, a high, slumping hill sparsely covered with grass that was well grazed down by sheep. The hill was rumored to be hallowed, a place of fairies, of witches, of devils. Though others feared to go near it, Merlinnus had explored the place thoroughly, inside and out—for the place was hollow and mazed with caves. All he had found there were rats, bats, and an occasional goat that had wandered away from a flock. It had been the perfect place to build a secret workshop, with a passage to it from the Cadbury dungeons. The workmen who had dug the place for him had done it at night and were all gone—dead of natural causes or sent over the seas to the Continent. He had bespelled them so that they could never tell what they knew. Only he had knowledge of the place now—and Arthur.

Merlinnus did not mind encouraging popular fancies about the tor. In his work, superstition was an aid to getting things done. For a moment he wondered if he should mention the place to the boy, but Gawen was still agape at Cadbury itself.

No need, then, to bring it up, Merlinnus thought. *Yet.* He smiled to himself. For a child from the coast, who had been educated by monks, such walls and moats and barbicans must seem miraculous enough. But for the competent builder who planned for eternity, architecture was the true miracle. Merlinnus had long studied the writings of the Romans, whose prose styles were as tedious as their knowledge was large. He had learned from them how to instruct men in the slotting of the great timbers; how to build a system of water troughs and baths.

Well, all he had really needed to build such a castle, such a kingdom, was the ability to read—and time. *Yet time,* he thought again bitterly, *for construction as well as for anything else is running out on me.* He was getting old too soon, and the kingdom was not yet solidly under Arthur's capable feet.

This boy—this boy is the key to everything. Merlinnus did not know how he knew this, but he knew. All his life he had been touched by such knowledge and did not set it aside lightly. The boy had arrived for a reason and, once Merlinnus discovered what it was, he would use it for Britain's sake.

"Come," he said to Gawen, "stand tall, knock hard, and enter."

Gawen squared his shoulders and then, following Merlinnus' instructions, hammered on the wooden doors.

As soon as the guard had checked them out through the spy hole, they were let in.

"Ave, Magister," said one guard, with an execrable accent. It was obvious he knew that much Latin and no more. But at least he had tried. Merlinnus rewarded him with a rare smile.

The other guard was silent.

Gawen was silent as well, but his small silence was filled with a growing wonder. Glancing sideways, Merlinnus saw the boy taking in the stoneworks, the Roman mosaic panel on the entry wall, all the fine details the mage had insisted on.

"An awed emissary," he said to the boy, as he had said to all the boys he had trained, "is already half won over."

Gawen nodded.

That pleased Merlinnus. The boy obviously understood what he meant. Not like the other apprentices, boys whose minds had remained closed to his teachings.

A boy who listens well, he thought, *will be well trained.* He put a hand on Gawen's shoulder, feeling the fine bones beneath the jerkin. "Turn here."

As they walked, Gawen's head was constantly a-swivel: left, right, up, down. Wherever he had come from had obviously left him unprepared for such splendor.

The last hall opened into an inner courtyard where pigs, poultry, and wagons vied for space. As a lone grey mastiff hound walked toward them, Gawen breathed out again in a noisy sigh.

"It is like home," he whispered.

"Eh?" Merlinnus let out a whistle of air, like a skin bag deflating.

"Only much finer, of course." The quick addition was almost satisfying, but not quite. It created an unsatisfactory disjunction; a join not well matched.

A boy traveling on his own from a monastery would not know so fine a place. Would not need to justify his response.

Merlinnus wondered suddenly if he were using the boy, or the boy using him.

That was an uncomfortable thought. He put it aside to worry over later, like a bit of the skin that lies aside a torn fingernail.

It was a puzzle.

Merlinnus did not like unsolved puzzles. They were dangerous.

12

Fledgling

 "To the right," Merlinnus said once they were inside the castle itself. He shoved his finger hard into the boy's back. "Right."

Gawen turned quickly, wordlessly, as graceful as a dancer, but did not outpace the old man.

It is a performance, Merlinnus thought, *quite masterful in its own way.* Now he was seeing the boy in a different light, more shadow than sun.

Recognizing the mage, the guards at the door to the Great Hall opened it without a moment's hesitation.

Merlinnus stepped in front of the boy. "Come," he said gruffly.

As they entered the room, with its high wooden ceilings, Arthur looked up from the paper he was laboriously reading, his finger marking his place.

Merlinnus noted with regret that Arthur was once again reading well behind his finger, like a boy in his first year of tutelage. *But at least he reads,* Merlinnus thought, *unlike his father. Or any of the kings before him.*

"My liege," Merlinnus said, though he did no more than sketch a bow.

The boy, he noted, did a proper bow, one leg forward, and a fully sketched hand. It did not sit with his being a monastery boy. Or at least not one who had spent years there. That bow came from a court and castle, not a monks' hall.

"Ah, Merlinnus, I am glad you are here," Arthur said, ignoring the boy. "We've been worried about you this past week. No one has seen you."

Merlinnus knew that Arthur was not meaning the royal "we," but that he and Kay had been worried. They would have spoken together more than once about his whereabouts. Old as they were, they were still his boys.

"Are you all right?" Arthur asked.

Merlinnus nodded. Surprisingly, he suddenly felt more than just all right. He felt completed. The sword in the stone *was* the key!

"There is a dinner tonight with an emissary from Gaul," Arthur was saying, "and you know I cannot speak their language."

"Eh?" For a moment, happy in that completeness, Merlinnus had lost the thread of the conversation.

"The language of Gaul, old man. It simply glides across my ears. I need a translator. If you are indeed well, will you be there to help?"

Merlinnus nodded again.

"And there is a contest I need your advice on. Here." He drew a list from behind him. He had obviously been sitting on it for some time, for the parchment was creased. "The men want to choose a May Queen to serve next year. They do not like this year's choice." He made a face.

"And why not, my lord?"

"Kay says she giggles."

"Giggles?" Merlinnus sucked on his lower lip. "Of course she giggles. All girls giggle. I do not understand."

"How can you, you old celibate? But it is not this year's girl they are concerned with. I think they are hoping to thrust someone on me as my queen. They have drawn up a list of those qualities they think she should possess, this paragon, this perfect woman. Kay wrote it down."

Kay, Merlinnus thought disagreeably, *is the only one of that crew who can write.* He took the list and scanned it. "Head...waist...hips, calves." He shook his head in disgust. "It sounds more like a shepherd's list. Or a butcher's."

By his side Gawen stifled a giggle.

"They are trying—" Arthur began.

"They certainly are." Merlinnus handed the list back.

"They are trying to be helpful," Arthur said curtly. He finally looked at the boy, studying him for a full minute as if trying to fathom who the child was. "And who is this fey bit of work?"

The boy bowed again, though none such was called for. "I am called Gawen, sire. I have come to Cadbury to learn to be a knight. I know how to ride and I am stronger than I—"

Arthur rolled his eyes and turned to the old mage, interrupting the boy's speech. "Is he to be yours? He is too small for knighthood. And too...slight to even apprentice to a smith or an ostler." Then he looked back at Gawen thoughtfully.

Merlinnus knew what Arthur meant. That whatsoever it was the boy had come for, he was certainly not built to be a fighter. *Better to claim him now before he breaks his heart on helm, aventail, byrnie, gauntlet, greaves. Before he is bullied and broken by the master of swords.*

"Sire, I am not afraid. I will for certain grow." The boy was almost in tears. "I *must* learn to be a knight. I *must* become one of your Companions."

Arthur leaned toward him and spoke quietly but with complete authority. "To be a squire takes patience. You must spend years cleaning the leather, polishing the steel. And years more working with lance and sword. Then, and only then, you may become worthy of being someone's household knight. But even though you make knight, you will perhaps never be a Companion. For the most part they are lords of the realm."

Merlinnus was silent throughout this recital, eyes on the boy and his reaction. Gawen stood absolutely still, as attentive as a fox following a hare.

Arthur continued, "There are but a few places at the table reserved for others, who by heroic effort and not by blood deserve to sit there. Is it not enough, boy, to have come to Cadbury to serve?" By the end of this speech—a long one for Arthur—his voice had softened as if he felt some kind of pity for the boy. Then he turned his steely eyes back to the mage.

Merlinnus thought, *Better to keep the boy close, whoever he is—minstrel, runaway, or fledgling spy.* "He is mine, sire."

Gawen looked sharply at the old man. "But, Magister, I would learn the sword. Really, I am stronger than I—"

Merlinnus allowed himself a small smile. "For whatever work you wish to do here, know this: The mind is sharper than any blade. And like a blade, it has edges and a point. Be content with me, child. You shall use your strength in my service and it will serve us both well."

Gawen got that sulky look again, like a spoiled child who has been denied a sweet.

"How old are you, boy?" Arthur asked suddenly. And before Gawen could answer, Arthur began battering the boy with questions, as if proving his own mind sharp as a sword. "Are you a Christer, a Grailer? Or do you worship Mithras or the Mother? Are you well-bred?" He turned back to Merlinnus. "Is he?"

"Well-bred, certainly," the mage replied, remembering the Latin and the elegant speech, even without the slip about how much the castle looked like home.

"I am thirteen," the boy said.

Merlinnus had in their walk from the woods already revised his estimate of the boy's age several times over. He guessed from the boy's manners, his quickness and ease with strangers, that it was two or three years further than thirteen, but said nothing.

"My own mother follows the Goddess but my father the Grail, so I know both," Gawen said.

So... Merlinnus thought, *not an orphan sent to a monastery, then.*

"And worship neither?" Arthur leaned forward on

the throne. It looked as though he were interested in the boy's answer, but Merlinnus suspected he was just shifting position on the hard chair.

"Pardon me, sire, but that is between me and my god." The boy's cheeks flamed red, but otherwise he did not seem discommoded. Just stubborn.

"I will pardon you, boy, but know this—if you serve me, you serve my god," the king said.

So, Merlinnus thought, *Arthur is listening. Something about this boy quickens him. That is interesting indeed,* and he tucked this item away in his mind's cupboard with the rest.

"I thought I made it clear the boy serves *me,*" Merlinnus put in. And then to soften the rebuke added quickly, "And you, Majesty, have yet to make clear which of the many gods in Britain you will stick with yourself!"

Arthur leaned back against the chair and laughed. It was a buoyant and boyish laugh.

Merlinnus began to laugh, too.

The burly guards at the door smiled at one another, not really having heard the conversation, but just because they loved their king and were pleased when he found something to laugh about.

Only the boy remained solemn. Merlinnus suspected it was not because he had no sense of humor. Rather he did not yet dare to laugh out loud at the king. Or with him.

After a moment, Arthur arched his back and put a hand behind him. "Damned throne's too hard. I actually prefer a soldier's pallet. Or a horse." He stood and stretched like some sort of large sandy-colored cat, scattering several scrolls. "That is enough for one day, I think," he said, gesturing to the scrolls. "I will look at the rest tomorrow." He came down the two steps and whispered in Merlinnus' right ear. "When you gave me this kingdom, old man, you forgot to mention how hard a chair the high throne is."

"And would you have made a different choice, sire?"

Arthur once again roared out that boyish laugh. "No. Probably not. But I would have requested a different throne."

Merlinnus pretended shock. "But that is the High King's throne. All the kings of Britain have sat upon it. Without that throne, you would not be recognized as the High King."

Arthur nodded. He turned slightly and looked straight at Gawen then and said, "Of such things is a kingdom made. Hard to credit it."

Gawen suddenly spoke up. "Would not a cushion on the seat do, Majesty?"

Arthur laughed again. "Out of the mouths of children. Would it not do, Merlinnus? A cushion?"

The mage's mouth twisted about the word *cushion*. But he could think of no objection. It was the quiet

hominess of the solution that he found somehow offen-
sive. *Certainly it would work. But would it make the king
less...manly? Less powerful? Less...*

"It will work," he said at last. "Only do not let there
be any embroidery on it."

Arthur laughed again.

"And now, my lord," the mage said, "I have more
important things to discuss than cushions." He thought
he would have liked a cushion himself at that moment
and sat down, rather hurriedly, on the risers that led to
the throne.

Arthur sat down next to him. "The assassins?"

The mage shook his head. "The sword and the
stone, Arthur."

"Very well. Let us talk."

"In my workroom," Merlinnus said. "I would not
have ears hear that should not. If you will accompany
me there." He tried to stand and found he could not.
Unaccountably both his knees were too weak to hold
him. *Old,* he thought. *I have suddenly grown old.*

"I will not only accompany you," the king said, "it
looks as if I will have to carry you." He stood and pulled
the old man to his feet, but gently. "Give me a hand with
him, boy, and we will see how strong you really are."

Gawen was quick to offer the mage his hand.

"I can walk," Merlinnus said testily. He certainly

had not meant the king or the boy—and especially not the guards—to see his weakness. "I can walk myself."

"Then lead the way," Arthur said and, winking at Gawen, added, "and we will catch you should you fall."

When there was no quick answer, Arthur smiled. Finally he had had the last word.

13

Dungeon

THEY WOUND through the castle halls, down three flights of stairs. Often they paused on the steps to let the mage catch his breath. The walls were softened with large tapestries, and the millefleurs on them were made of many-colored threads that seemed to glow against the grey stone. Gawen nodded at the tapestries and several times ran a finger across the stitching as if counting what lay on the cloth.

When they reached the dungeon, dark shadows danced upon the walls. The entrance to the dungeon was guarded by a large bronze head, its deep eye sockets filled with blue enamel. It was Arthur's wish that the dungeon stayed empty. Arthur preferred to make friends of his enemies. But the threat was always there.

At the far end was the darkest cell. They went into it. Merlinnus touched three stones, left, right, center, and then again, then backwards. The stone wall sprang open. Behind it was a wooden door.

Merlinnus pulled up the keys that were hooked by a golden chain to his belt. It took three keys and a spell spoken in a strange tongue before the door opened.

"Not Celtic," Gawen whispered. "Nor Gallic. Nor Latin."

"Greek," Merlinnus told him.

Gawen shook his head. "I do not know Greek."

"I will teach you." It was a promise, spoken like a threat.

The king seemed little impressed. "Why so much security, Merlinnus? No one who values his soul would dare come here." He laughed quietly. "Except me, of course."

"Of course," Merlinnus grumbled.

"You used to let me wander into your rooms whenever I wanted to, back at Sir Ector's," Arthur added.

Merlinnus turned. "Back at Sir Ector's I was a simple apothecary and you were the foster son. No one cared what we did there."

The door creaked open.

"And now?"

Gawen answered for him, piping in brightly. "Now you are the High King and he is the High King's mage. A spy would be well paid to gain entrance to this place."

Arthur reached over and grabbed Gawen up by the collar. "And are you such a spy?"

"If he were, would he have warned you?" Merlinnus said.

GAWEN GAZED around the room. It was a hodgepodge of tables both large and small on which stood pottery amphorae, glass bottles, and metal burners encrusted with foul matter. Hanging from the beams were bunches of dried herbs, still fragrant from the last spring: moly and mint, yarrow and lambsfoot, tansy and thyme.

A small pallet lay in the corner. Gawen guessed it was a daybed for naps. *Who would sleep here, surrounded by so much dampness and dark?* Gawen knew the answer. The mage slept here when he was deep into his work.

Merlinnus beckoned with one crabbed finger and Arthur picked up a torch. Then he and Gawen followed the old man down a long hall that seemed carved out of stone, more cave than castle. Gawen put out a steadying hand to one of the walls. It was damp.

They came at last to a huge vaulted room with stone pillars hanging from the ceiling. A stream ran along one side of the place. Gawen shivered. The room was cold and unwelcoming and strange. In the middle of the place stood a block of white marble with veins of red and green running through.

"I wrapped the thing with cloth," Merlinnus said, nodding at the stone. "It took seven men to get it down the castle stairs and into the dungeon. They knew not what they were carrying, of course. They transferred it to a small open wagon with wheels. I hauled it the rest of the way into this cavern myself."

This made Gawen wonder even more. The mage **did** not look strong enough for pulling any such thing.

"They were eager enough for the payment of gold coins," Merlinnus said, "and even more eager to leave the dungeon behind." He chuckled and Arthur laughed with him.

Gawen did not see the humor.

Sticking out of the top of the stone was the hilt of a sword that was covered with wonderful runes. *In silver,* or so Gawen thought.

Merlinnus led them right up to the stone. On its white marble face was a legend lettered in gold:

WHOSO PULLETH OUTE THIS SWERD OF THIS STONE

IS RIGHTWYS KYNGE BORNE OF

ALL BRYTAYGNE

———

FOR A LONG TIME none of them spoke. Then Arthur read the thing aloud, his fingers tracing the letters in the stone. When he finished, he looked up. "But I am king of all Britain."

"Then pull the sword, sire," said Merlinnus.

Arthur smiled and shrugged. He knew he was a strong man. Except for Lancelot, possibly the strongest man in the kingdom. It was one of the reasons Merlinnus had chosen him to be king. He handed the torch to Gawen, who held on to it with both hands.

Then Arthur put his hand to the hilt of the sword, tightened his fingers around it till his knuckles were white, and pulled.

The sword remained in the stone.

"Merlinnus," he growled, furious at the old wizard, "what goes into stone must come out of it." He bit his lower lip. "This is witchery and I will not have it."

"And with witchery you, Arthur, will pull the sword from the stone when all others have failed. You—and no one else." Merlinnus smiled benignly.

Arthur let go of the sword. "But why do we need this...this legerdemain? I am *already* High King of all Britain."

Merlinnus looked at him sorrowfully. "Because I hear grumblings in the kingdom. Oh, do not look slantwise at me, Arthur. There is no magic that I cannot counter." He shook a finger in the king's direction. "I have spies, and they tell me who is unhappy with the High King and who is not. There are those who refuse to follow you, who refuse to be bound to you and so are not bound to this kingdom, because they doubt the legitimacy of your claim."

The king snorted. "And they are right, old man. I am king because the arch-mage wills it. *Per crucem et quercum.*"

Gawen seemed startled at Arthur's use of the Latin.

Merlinnus was startled, too. "How did you know that?"

"Oh, old friend, you are not the only one with reliable spies." He laughed, but little mirth was in it this time. "And some of them even know Latin."

Merlinnus stared into Arthur's eyes. "Yes, you are king because I willed it. But also because you earned it. This bit of legerdemain, as you call it—"

"This witchery!" interrupted the king.

Merlinnus persisted, "This legerdemain will have them all believing in you, as I already do."

"And I," whispered Gawen.

"*All* of them," Merlinnus said, ignoring the boy's obvious adoration. "To bind Britain you will need *all* the tribes."

Arthur looked away to stare at the stream, which was making a soft *shu-shush*ing sound as it wound by the side of the wall. He looked at it for a very long time. At last he smoothed down his tunic, as if wiping his hands, and turned back to stare at the mage.

"Do those few tribes matter?" he asked Merlinnus. "The ones who paint themselves blue and squat around small fires. The ones who wrap themselves in filthy woolen blankets and blow noisily into animal bladders, calling it song. The ones who dig out shellfish with their toes and eat the fish raw. The ones who hang their enemies in wooden baskets from trees and let them starve. Do we really want to bring *all* of them into our kingdom?"

Merlinnus turned to Gawen. "Can you answer him, boy?"

Gawen drew in a deep breath, as though he knew this was a test he dared not fail. For a moment he seemed to be framing his answer in his mind, testing it for clarity, then said, "They are already part of your kingdom, Majesty. They just do not know it yet."

Merlinnus smiled. "The kingdom of which you are the king now and for the future," he added. "It is not you who has to be convinced, it is the people."

Arthur said softly, "I thought the people loved me."

For a moment it looked as if Gawen was going to reach out and touch the king on his arm but then, as if thinking better of it, pulled his hand back, saying simply, "The ones who know you do."

Arthur smiled at that, then shifted his eyes back to the stream. "Are you positive I will be able to draw the sword at the proper time?" He looked back at Merlinnus and the boy. "I will *not* be made a mockery to satisfy some hidden purpose of yours."

"Put your hand on the sword once more, Arthur."

Arthur turned slowly, as if the words had a power to command him. He went back to the marble stone, which now seemed to be glowing with power. He reached out, but before his hand actually touched the hilt of the sword, he stopped, which took an incredible act of will.

"I am a good soldier, Merlinnus," he said over his shoulder. "And I love this land."

"I know," the old man told him.

With a resonant slap, the king's hand grasped the sword.

Merlinnus muttered something unintelligible in a voice soft as a cradlesong.

Arthur gave a tug and the sword slid noiselessly from the stone.

Holding the sword high above his head, Arthur turned and looked steadily at the mage. "If I were a wicked man, I would bring this down on your head."

"I know."

Gawen drew a breath and held it.

Slowly the sword descended. When it was level

with his eyes, the king put his left hand to the hilt as well. He hefted the sword several times and made soft, comfortable noises deep in his chest. Then carefully, like a woman threading a needle, he slid the sword back into its slot.

"I will have my men take this and place it in the chapel courtyard so that all might see it," he said. "All my people shall have a chance to try pulling the sword."

"All?" Merlinnus asked.

"Even the ones who paint themselves blue or blow into bladders?" added Gawen.

"Even the ones who do other more disgusting and uncivilized things," Arthur said, laughing. "I even have in mind to let the kingdom's mages try."

Merlinnus smiled back. "Is that wise?"

"I am the one with the strong arm, Merlinnus. You are the one who provides the wisdom."

Merlinnus nodded. "Then let the mages try, too. Even the North Witch. For all the good it will do them."

Arthur put his hand back on the sword's hilt.

"But one thing more," Merlinnus said.

Arthur looked over his shoulder. "It is always one thing more with you, old man."

Merlinnus smiled. "We will leave the sword and stone here and let them be discovered by a shepherd."

"Why?" asked Gawen. "Does that not make things more difficult?"

Arthur smiled, too. But his smile suddenly had much sadness in it, as if knowledge and kingship lay heavy on his shoulders. "He wishes to be removed from the sword and stone. He wants no one to know that he had a hand in it. In that way it will not be magic that names me king—but fate."

"But you are *already* the king," Gawen said. "And a great one."

"No, boy, I am a good king. But I *would* be a great one."

"With my help," Merlinnus said.

"And mine," added Gawen, passion in his voice.

Once again Arthur's fingers curled around the hilt. "It is a fine sword, Merlinnus. It shall honor its wielder. Whoever he may be." He pulled at the sword.

This time it did not move.

14

Hard Work

ARTHUR TURNED and left and they followed.

As they walked back through the dungeon, Merlinnus said, "I shall find a shepherd and make his sheep lead him here, through the tor."

Arthur turned and glared at him. "Do it," he said to the old man. "Only do not tell me when or how." He left them, taking the steps two at a time.

Merlinnus, with Gawen following, made his way back to the inner room.

"I do not understand," Gawen said.

"Admitting one does not understand is the beginning of wisdom," Merlinnus said. He smiled paternally at the boy. "What is it that puzzles you particularly?"

"How King Arthur could not pull the sword at all, and then a second time and it slid out easily," Gawen said.

Merlinnus gave a short, sharp bark of a laugh. "Magic."

But Gawen was not so easily satisfied. "I *know* it is magic. But what kind? Surely if I am to be yours..." He stopped and a shadow passed across his face. Then he resumed speaking, "Yours, and not pledged to the master of swords, I should know this."

The mage's face turned dark and a series of deep lines suddenly etched across his brow. "That I will not tell you," he said. "I was once guiled by a child to reveal more than I should. And now she squats like a toad on that knowledge."

"The North Witch?" breathed the boy.

Merlinnus nodded. "So I will not be beguiled again. I like you, boy. You are quick and subtle and know when to be quiet and when to make noise. That last, by the way, is an admirable quality not usually found in a boy your age. But—"

"But you do not yet know me well enough to trust me." Gawen's voice was soft.

"I trust few," the wizard said softly. "And even those few I trust I tell little."

The boy's face grew thoughtful. At last he said, "I, too, Magister."

Merlinnus knew better than to pursue that gift. But he tucked the information away to think about it later. "Come, we must clean this place of its secrets so that when the shepherd finds this miracle"—his hand gestured broadly at the stone wall, which was now grey in the fading light—"there will be no other secret for him to steal."

"He would not dare..." Gawen said.

"Would he not?" Merlinnus' voice was suddenly hard. "Then you do not understand the real world, boy, shut up as you were in a monastery."

"A monastery?" The boy's voice broke on the words, and then his eyes shuttered. "Yes," he said quickly, "we had little knowledge of spying in a monk's cell."

But it was too late. Merlinnus knew then for certain what he had already guessed. This boy, whoever he was, had not been trained by monks. Which meant he was some sort of noble runaway come to Cadbury to make his name. Living rough in the woods for a while would explain the callused hands. He was possibly a second or third son. Which, of course, meant more politics. Merlinnus sighed.

"Anyone *would* dare," he told Gawen, "but they would not know what it is they see. Still, if they sold their knowledge to a mage..."

"Like the Witch of the North..." Gawen added.

"...my secrets *could* be discovered." Merlinnus did

not add what they both knew, that if young Gawen was a spy, the secrets were already compromised. But he did not for a moment believe that behind such an innocent face stood a wicked master, no matter what else lay hidden in the boy's past. And if he were wrong about the boy—well, boys disappear all the time and no one finds them again. He shuddered. It compromised his magic to think that kind of thought.

THE BOY and mage worked well into the evening, hauling bottles upstairs to the tower room, settling them into the oak livery cupboards. Then they took down hanging herbs to be wrapped in soft cloth and stuck in the cupboards as well. All the scrolls that had been littering tabletops were rolled tight, tied with ribands, and stacked in a large wooden chest that was carved with runes of power. A covering of wool and silk topped the scrolls. It was heavy for just the two of them, but they managed.

"Why was this not all put away when the stone was first brought down here?" the boy asked.

Good question, Merlinnus thought. *I like a boy who asks good questions. Such a boy will listen to answers.*

Aloud he said, "It was only a simple stone when it was carried here, and well disguised. It could be dropped with no more than a broken toe to result. Besides, I had much still to do before the stone was ready to receive the sword. And after—well, I had no boy to help me clean up."

"But now you have a boy to do the work?" Gawen's smile eased the sting of what he was saying.

"Your coming is clearly a godsend. I do not have much time." He did not say how little. Sometimes saying such out loud proved it true.

Gawen nodded, clearly at ease with this explanation. He glanced around the room as if studying it. *Not like a spy,* Merlinnus thought, *but like a contented house-wife checking her work.*

"A bit more, my boy, till we are done."

When all was put away to his satisfaction, Merlinnus had the boy sweep the floor of the tower room and carry the detritus upstairs in a basket. There they emptied it over the wall, scattering the pieces to the winds.

"Now go to the kitchen and fetch me some dinner."

As Gawen went out the door, he added, "And something for yourself as well."

THE KITCHENS had the wonderful yeasty smell of bread. There were several dozen loaves of good-quality white cooling on a long table near the ovens. About the same number of black were just now being taken out of the ovens with the long bread paddles. On another table sat the trencher breads made for the servants. Gawen was unsure which Merlinnus would want.

Ale had been recently brewed, too. The heavy malt smell attested to that. Gawen had also passed barrels of wine, marked WHITE or RED or MALMSEYN.

Fresh game hung in a separate room: rabbit and pheasant and geese and woodcock, and large hams and mutton and joints of beef as well. Soon it would be time for the early lambs to be slaughtered. In a smaller pantry were rounds of cheese and vats of milk ready to be skimmed, as well as amphorae full of olive oil. A castle had many mouths and, Gawen knew, all of them were hungry.

Coming into the main kitchen, Gawen spotted the cook, a broad man with a spectacular wen on the side of his nose. The cook sat on a chair that reminded Gawen of King Arthur's throne, and he was directing his minions rather than doing the actual cooking himself. His face dripped with sweat, even though he was stripped down to his camisia and leather breeches.

"Cook," Gawen shouted over the noise of the kitchen, for there was no other way to be heard in the place, "Magister Merlinnus would like his evening meal."

Cook nodded. "Hungry from all that plottin' and plannin' is he?"

Gawen nodded back.

"I'll gie ye summat fer he, but ye will have to carry it oop yersel'."

Gawen nodded again.

"And best ye tak summat fer yersel'. That old wizard'll ferget to feed ye."

"He already said I could..." Gawen started.

However, it was clear Gawen's audience with Cook was over. Two of the kitchen boys gave Gawen a hand choosing what to put on a tray.

"Here, ye try that mutton," said one, shoving a large slab toward Gawen's face, while the other popped several boiled potatoes onto a trencher for him.

Only then was Gawen ready to go back up the many stairs to the tower, with a tray overflowing with a chine of mutton, a quart of beer, a quart of wine, a dish of buttered eggs, and a half loaf of the black.

"He likes the black, do our mage," said one of the boys. None of them volunteered to help carry the heavy tray.

Gawen managed to get the tray to the tower without spillage, but it was a close thing. By that time Merlinnus was fast asleep on the bed, snoring, his mouth wide open and showing a full set of yellowed and broken teeth.

Setting the tray down on a nearby table, Gawen drew a coverlet over the old man and left. But not before snatching another potato from the mage's tray. It had been a long day.

III

King's Hope/
Prince's Danger

The stones of the churchyard and the stone of the church walls and the stone with the sword were all one color: the grey of sin, of celibacy, of mourning. The sword in the stone was grey as well, but it had a life to it, the blade the grey of lake water and the hilt the grey of vapor rising over the lake.

15

Riding South

FIVE DAYS OUT found Morgause's sons camped near a river. It was the first time they had found such a good spot. Gawaine wondered if it were *too* good and set three men to stand watch, including Hwyll, who was handy with a dagger if not a sword. He could always count on Hwyll's even temper not to get them into a brangle unless he was certain of danger. Unlike Agravaine, who always found danger even when there was none.

Agravaine complained, of course. He had been complaining every step of the way, since he had been expecting to stay in castles with some great lords, or at least in comfortable inns each night. He felt insulted and ill used and was not choosy about whom he whined to. Gawaine suspected that he was still feeling sick from the crossing.

However, the twins enjoyed the freedom of camping from the start.

"Mother would never have allowed..." they began together, then smiled at each other. That Mother would not have allowed seemed to be the biggest compliment of all.

Gawaine had nodded. "But Mother is not here now. She is busy at home ruling other folks' lives." (*And ruining them,* he thought bitterly.) "We want to get to Cadbury on the fastest road possible. Besides, as long as we are still in the Highlands, what few inns there are, are scarcely safer than the road. Often they are run by cutthroats and thieves. And the great lords hereabouts are not all friendly to Arthur."

The twins had listened, but whether they heard him or not, he could not tell. Still, they at least seemed happy enough with the arrangements.

THIS NIGHT the twins were exhausted and, wrapping themselves in their woolen cloaks, fell asleep quickly.

Gawaine sat up by the fire, trying to think about what he should tell the king about his mother, about his brothers. Or wondering if he should say anything at all. Loyalty to family had been drummed into him from birth. But loyalty to the king was something he had learned on his own.

Hearing a noise, he turned. When he saw it was only Agravaine, he looked back to the fire.

"Tell me about Arthur," his brother said, making no attempt to dress up his interest. He sat down heavily by Gawaine's side.

For a moment Gawaine thought to ask if Agravaine wanted to know for himself, or for their mother. But then he decided it did not really matter if Agravaine were the spy. He would speak the truth, but only such truth as his brother needed to hear. Agravaine would know what he wanted to know soon enough, anyway. Cadbury kept few secrets.

"The king is my size, but bigger all around," Gawaine began.

"Fat?"

"Muscle."

"And..."

"He is four years older than I am, but already the veteran of many battles."

Agravaine smiled. "A good man to have at one's back, then?"

Sighing, Gawaine nodded and added, "He is honest, caring, and totally without vanity."

Agravaine chuckled. "No man is without vanity."

"So speaks a vain little boy," Gawaine said.

"I am no boy."

"You are fifteen."

"I have a dog, a horse, a house, and a woman at home. What more makes a man?" Agravaine asked.

"Mother gave you the dog and the horse. Your house is a cottage by the river, where you played as a child. And the woman..."

"Be careful what you say, brother." Agravaine was still looking at the fire, but Gawaine knew he was also watching every movement from the corner of his eye.

"The woman was given you by Mother, too. To make a man of you." Gawaine said it carefully but not without intent to hurt.

Agravaine threw a stick at the fire. "And it worked."

"No," Gawaine said, "it did *not* work. A man is more than the sum of such things."

"I bet you never had a woman."

"If I have or not, it is nothing I would boast to you about," Gawaine said, more angrily than he meant.

Agravaine stood. "I have a sword, too." His voice was sullen, like a child's.

"You can have sword and whip and a hard hand. That still does not make you a man." Gawaine sighed. "Go to bed, Agravaine."

"Are you telling me man to child?" The voice was still sullen, and slightly dangerous, too. He was drunk on anger and years of being the second son.

"I am telling you brother to brother. Go to bed. We have another, longer ride tomorrow." Gawaine stood as well, turned on his heel, and went over to the cloak that Hwyll had set out for him. Picking it up, he wrapped it around his body and lay down, sword at his side. He was rigid with anger, mostly at himself for getting into such a spat, like two farmwives over a fence.

Agravaine made some rude noises, but at last he, too, found a sleeping cloak.

Gawaine waited until he was certain his brothers were all snoring before he allowed himself to drift off, certain that Hwyll and the others would keep them from harm.

BY THE TIME they came within a day's ride of Cadbury, none of the boys was on speaking terms.

Gawaine was at wits' end. He had spoken hurriedly to Hwyll as they kitted up the horses that last morning.

"It is not just Agravaine, though he is the worst," he said. Anger had made a pronounced line between his eyebrows, and his handsome face was almost ugly with it.

"Agravaine is a second son and feels the weight of it every day," Hwyll said. "I know. I was a second son as well, though with much less riding on any inheritance."

"That he is second to me is not my fault." Gawaine gentled the sweet-faced brown gelding he'd given to

Agravaine, as if by soothing the horse, he could soothe himself.

"Not your fault, no. But it is your *duty* to overrule him," Hwyll said. "With a harder hand than his if necessary."

"You do not understand..." The horse nuzzled at Gawaine's neck and he pushed it away gently.

"I do not need to understand," said Hwyll softly. "I need to speak for your mother. And she would tell you this: Agravaine only follows one rule."

Gawaine waited, though he knew what Hwyll was going to say.

"Power."

Gawaine nodded. He did not doubt that he could master Agravaine, but he did not want to. He just wanted to get to Cadbury and be shed of them all. The twins, too. For they had turned out to be whiners and complainers once the trip had gotten too long and rain in the valleys had broken into their sleep night after night.

Why, he thought, *why am I cursed with such brothers?* And then added to himself, *And such a mother?* But he did not say any of this aloud. To say it aloud would be dishonorable. If he prided himself on anything, it was his honor.

Turning to Hwyll, he said, "Arthur will sort him out."

"Agravaine will hardly listen to someone he considers a usurper." Hwyll finished saddling the last horse, his back to Gawaine, but his shoulders were tense with their conversation.

Oh, by the gods! Gawaine thought. *That old mother curse again. Hwyll is hers, not mine, if he thinks of Arthur in that way. I shall have to bend him to me.* "Then why has Agravaine come?"

Hwyll turned and held up his hands, palms to the sky. His plain face, with its bicolored eyes, smiled at him. "Your mother sent him, my lord. How could he refuse?"

16

Hard Hands

THE ROAD SOUTH was rutted and ruined by recent spring rains. Only the Roman bridges still stood, strong testimony to the late masters of Britain. Every arch proclaimed that mastery.

The horses alternated trotting and walking, making swift time even on the awful roads. They moved best when given their heads, not reined in or pulled roughly about. Only Agravaine failed to understand that—or refused to listen—and so his poor horse was the slowest of all, and suffered many a kick because of it.

Finally Gawaine could stand no more of his

brother's harsh treatment of the gelding. He stopped them all on the top of a small hillock, which was one deep valley from Cadbury.

"Time for a break," he said. Then he got off his little mare and marched over to Agravaine. Before his brother could dismount on his own, Gawaine hauled him off his horse.

Agravaine fell onto his side with a loud thud that broke no bones but bruised his pride. He stood up slowly, grinding his teeth. His face was a map of feral fury.

"If you cannot ride without injuring your mount, you will walk," Gawaine said.

"I will *not*," Agravaine countered, and without warning, threw a hard punch that landed glancingly on Gawaine's cheekbone, beneath the right eye.

The pain was excruciating, radiating up to the top of Gawaine's head, and pulsating in his ear as well. He could not remember ever feeling such pain, and the embarrassment of the blow was as much of a shock as the blow itself.

Shaking his head to try to clear it of the pain, Gawaine barely kept from falling, and at the same time, he hit back, a strong right fueled by both anger and shame. As he had already warned Agravaine, he was bigger and stronger and had trained well under Arthur's master of arms. But the pain in his face caused him to miss his target, which was his brother's nose.

Instead he hit Agravaine in the throat.

It was an awful blow and Agravaine staggered back, gasping and reeling, and finally falling down in a faint.

No one was more surprised than Gawaine. Or horrified. He knelt by his brother, shouting, "Breathe, you knave, breathe." He was crying as he shouted, the tears coursing down his face, which would have embarrassed him even more had he realized it. "Breathe, Agravaine."

At first, the twins had cheered the fight, calling out for Gawaine and Agravaine indiscriminately. But when they saw that Agravaine was really in trouble, they jumped from their horses and ran over to help, whereupon they simply got in the way.

It was Hwyll who sat Agravaine up, stuck his finger in the boy's mouth, and hauled his tongue forward.

Agravaine took one small, then two very large breaths, and began to shake.

"Get me a cloak," Hwyll shouted to the other servants.

Someone brought a sleeping cloak, someone else a wineskin. They wrapped Agravaine up well, gave him plenty to drink, then after a bit, stuck him back on his horse, where he slumped over like an old man, unable to keep his balance.

With Hwyll on one side of the horse and Gawaine on the other to hold Agravaine in place, they walked slowly across the last valley toward Cadbury.

BY THE TIME they spied the twin keeps and the blazing torches illuminating the high curtain walls, it was well into the night. Agravaine was snoring brokenly and Gawaine was sporting a shiny black eye.

The guards recognized Gawaine and opened the gate. The king's own physician was sent for. Food was brought into the Great Hall for those who could or would eat.

But Gawaine refused the food and the comfort. Instead he accompanied Agravaine to the infirmary—a series of dark cells off a long hall—and lay all night by his brother's side.

As he lay listening to Agravaine's stentorious snores, Gawaine tried to pray. He even got up once or twice and fell to his knees, speaking to the gods in Norse and English, in case any were within hearing. Speaking to his mother, too, for with her magic, she might also have taken notice of what had happened.

"I will not lose my temper again," he promised aloud. "I will only seek the right. I will be kind to my brothers. I will treat all men *as* my brothers. And my brothers as good men. I will..." But at that point, exhausted and emotionally spent, he lost the thread of his prayer and only felt stupid, insignificant, and weak. "I promise I will follow Arthur's will," he ended.

Then he climbed back onto the pallet, turned over on his side so that he was back-to-back with Agravaine, and fell into a stupor that was less like sleep and more like a little death.

HOWEVER, the twins were not exhausted at all. In fact, they actually seemed strengthened by the results of the fight. Finding the Great Hall, they sat at one of the long tables and talked to anyone who would listen about the fight. And plenty were willing, for fresh gossip was always in demand. Cadbury was really a small town.

"Gawaine hauled him off his horse," Gaheris began.

Gareth interrupted, "The earth shook."

"There were horns, I think," Gaheris said.

"Hunting horns," Gareth added.

"No, dragon horns."

The men laughed.

"It was magic!" they breathed together.

By the time dried fruit, cheese, and black bread had been brought to the table—and several large flagons of wine had been consumed—that fight had grown to epic proportions. Suddenly it included a green knight, several evil swordsmen, a dragon, a chimera, a wizard, and a fair lady to be saved.

In the morning, too embarrassed to set things aright,

Gawaine said nothing. Surely the twins' version was preferable to the truth—that he had beaten his brother who now lay sick unto death in the infirmary.

MORGAUSE WAS SITTING at one of her long, narrow apothecary tables reading in the *Book of Ancient & Diverse Magicks*, when she felt pinpricks between her shoulder blades. She looked up.

It had to be one of her boys.

Standing, she went to the stone basin that sat atop a stone plinth. Carefully she poured water into it—water from a running stream, not something that had been sitting and stewing in its own weak juices.

Then she waited until the water settled, sprinkled a handful of spy-all into it, letting the ground leaves settle to the bottom. She popped a pinch of the same herb into her nose and breathed it in, careful not to sneeze. Scrying was a ticklish business.

Finally she leaned over the water and spoke a small spell.

> *With heaven's eye, let me spy.*
> *With heaven's eye, let me fly.*
> *Show all, and I will witness!*

Slowly a picture shaped itself in the water, as if it were in a glass. Not a clear picture, of course. And it always had to be of one with whom the scryer had some sort of intimate connection: blood, lust, hate were good connectors, though a picture was only one-half of a truth. Scryers could see but could not eavesdrop. A real spy was needed for that.

In the picture she saw two of her boys—Gawaine and Agravaine—lying together in a bed.

"Humph," she snorted, thinking that Arthur was so impoverished in his splendid Cadbury, he could not afford separate beds for each of them but had to sleep them together like merchants in a second-rate inn. It made her smile.

Still—why had she been called? There had been no mistaking the prickles on her back.

Agravaine had his back to her, but Gawaine was turned toward her. She leaned closer and saw his blackened eye.

"Well," she said aloud, satisfied. "If they are being beaten, they will turn to their mother for comfort." She thought of ways to comfort them. It was a short list.

17

Brothers

ARTHUR CAME to the infirmary for a visit at sunrise, and Gawaine stood, shifting from one leg to the other, trying to explain what had happened. It seemed to Arthur that the boy was trying hard not to actually darken his brother's reputation, as if family honor was suddenly more important than truth.

Arthur liked that about Gawaine. About the attempt. He really was not a very good liar.

"It was my temper, more than his. Really," Gawaine said. "I did not mean to hurt him."

Only the more he talked, the worse things sounded, and Arthur knew he had to intervene. "I broke Kay's nose once, and though he has long forgiven me, I have never forgiven myself."

"Really?" Gawaine's face suddenly smoothed out.

"Really," Arthur said, though the circumstances had been quite different, because he had been younger and smaller than Kay and had fought him over a sword they had both wanted. Kay won the battle simply by falling heavily on top of Arthur, blood spurting from his nose till Arthur had agreed to end the battle so Kay's nose could be seen to.

"Thank you, my lord," Gawaine said, falling to one knee and bowing his head. He reached over and took his sleeping brother's hand. Then he held that hand and his own up till Arthur took them both.

"I pledge my brother and myself to you, my liege."

Arthur patted Gawaine's head almost absentmindedly. "There, there," he said. "The king pardons you."

Gawaine sprang to his feet.

"And you know, do you not, that I cannot accept your brother's pledge till he gives it himself. Awake." Arthur stared long into Gawaine's eyes.

At last Gawaine looked down. "I know, sire," he whispered. "But—"

"No buts. Now, how is your mother?" Subtlety was never one of Arthur's virtues.

By the darkening of Gawaine's face, Arthur guessed

that all was not right at home, and for some reason that made him utterly happy. He liked Gawaine. It was impossible not to. He liked him and would have been terribly disappointed if Gawaine had been his mother's assassin.

"She is ... well, sire," Gawaine said.

"Good. *Good.*" Arthur looked down at Agravaine and smiled. "No more charging dragons and green knights, then. I wouldn't want your mother mad at me."

"Oh, she never could be that," said Gawaine, and blushed as if he knew that Arthur knew it was a lie.

BACK ONE DAY *and I have lied to my liege lord,* Gawaine thought bitterly. *Mother would be so proud.* He went down to the kitchens to see if he could find some breakfast.

Desiring no company, he filled his plate with some slabs of bacon and fresh brown bread just out of the oven. Then he nodded at the cook, who called out to him, "Dost want more, laddie?"

Gawaine shook his head. Cook had always had a soft spot for him, ever since he arrived as a homesick boy named Gwalchmei and had hung about the kitchen for warmth and comfort. "No more just now," he called back.

Cook nodded as if he understood.

I wish I *understood,* Gawaine thought. Not since that first homesick week had he been so uncomfortable at

Cadbury. *Is it my brothers only?* he wondered. *Am I afraid I will be judged by their actions?*

He took his plate up the stairs to a walkway and set it high up on a crenellation. The wind was soft here, not like the constant wuthering of the sea winds at home. He enjoyed the lambent air. Like the kitchen, it was warm and comforting.

Standing and eating, he looked over at the high tor, a quarter mile from the castle. He shuddered as he gazed at the place, that frightening, eerie site of magic, mystery, faerie that was slumped like a mage's hat. It made him think of his mother.

It put him off his food.

No, he thought bitterly, *my brothers are not what worries me, not what gripes at my bowels.* As if in response, his stomach growled mightily. *It is Mother. And her spy.*

He spit over the side of the wall as if to get rid of the bad taste in his mouth, when another, even more awful, thought hit him.

What if she has bewitched me and I am her spy? Only I do not know it. He had no doubt she had the power to do such a thing, and he wondered if he should tell the king.

Or, scarier still, the king's mage.

AGRAVAINE SLEPT through the morning but woke soon after Gawaine returned. He seemed to have forgotten the fight entirely and instead looked about the room as though he were wondering where he was and how he had gotten there. Then he licked his lips, as if he had a terrible thirst, and croaked something. Gawaine thought it was "Water."

Gawaine pointed to a tray on which sat three cups of wine, indicating the middle one. "Try the mulled wine," he said. "The infirmarer assured me that would soothe your throat the best."

"An infirmarer?" Agravaine croaked. "Why should you be speaking to him? Who is ill?" The roughness of his own voice should have told him.

"You are," said Gawaine, still smarting from guilt.

"Nonsense!" Agravaine retorted, swinging his legs over the side of the bed and standing in his bare feet. Made for someone smaller, the nightshirt barely reached his thighs. Gawaine was surprised to see how hairy his brother's legs were.

Why, he is *a man,* Gawaine thought, *and not a boy any longer.*

Agravaine swayed a bit as if he had not yet gotten his land legs back, though they were more than two weeks from the sea. Gawaine put out a hand to him and Agravaine shoved it away roughly.

"Have I had the flux? Was it the sea voyage? I *hate* the sea!" Agravaine's voice was hoarse and whiney.

A hairy boy, Gawaine corrected himself. "Do you remember nothing?"

Agravaine put a hand to his head. "Not the sea. No. We were camping. I remember now. For days. No soft beds. No soft—" He got a hard look on his face, a mixture of anger and surprise. "You *hit* me."

Remembering what Hwyll had said about Agravaine and power, Gawaine answered in a soft but stern voice, "And will do it again unless you climb back into that bed."

Agravaine glared at him but sat down again on the bed, and Gawaine pulled the coverlet over him. "I will see that you are moved to a fine apartment with the twins and me shortly."

"How shortly?"

"When you hold down your food and drink a full day, *and* the infirmarer gives you leave to go." Gawaine turned and walked to the door. "I will get you something now."

"Wait!" Agravaine cried out.

Gawaine turned back.

"When I am better..." Agravaine said.

"When you are better..."

"I will beat you, brother. Be minded that I will."

Gawaine laughed. And here he thought he had tamed Agravaine. "I doubt it," he said, all guilt forgiven. "I am still older and bigger than you." He walked out the door, carrying one of the cups of mulled wine.

———

THE TWINS were waiting in the hall.

"Is he well?" asked Gareth, setting his shoulders and trying to look taller than he was.

Gaheris shrugged. "Is he calm?"

Smiling at his brothers, Gawaine said, "He is well. But he is *never* calm."

They laughed, their voices eerily the same.

"Do you want to see him?" Gawaine asked.

They nodded.

"Then go in. But do not rile him."

They looked at Gawaine as if begging him to go with them.

"I have seen enough of Agravaine for a while," Gawaine said, shooing them inside like geese.

They laughed again and pushed through the door, into the infirmary.

Gawaine left them to it. He did not worry at all how they would do with Hard Hands. Agravaine was never mean to the two of them, for they posed no threat to him and, besides, they were under their mother's protection.

HWYLL WAS in their apartments, folding some of the linen.

"I am glad you are here," Gawaine told him. "Nice to talk to a grown man who knows the family and—"

"How is he?"

"Like a wild boar," Gawaine admitted. "Now that he remembers what happened, he is furious. And ready for more."

"You are harder on yourself than on him," Hwyll said, kneeling down and putting the linens in the bottom of the cupboard. "He needs rough handling, that one. He worships power and only power can control him."

"And *you* can do that?" Gawaine said.

"I am a servant," Hwyll said, composedly. He stood, turned, and winked at Gawaine. "And I never argue where I can wheedle."

If Gawaine was surprised at Hwyll's statement, he contrived not to show it. "Then wheedle away," he said. "I do not want to go back and butt heads with him again."

"Ah—two stags in a grove," Hwyll said. Then he picked up a fresh tunic of Agravaine's and started out the door.

GAWAINE STOPPED at the kitchen to leave his dirty cup. He had to step aside because Kay came charging by him.

"Cook!" Kay shouted, waving a hand in the cook's general direction. "The king needs some of that honey wine. And a good helping of your brown bread slathered in jam. Strawberry, not blueberry. Now!"

The kitchen, which had been cozy and quiet, came to bustling life.

Kay, Gawaine thought, *has a way of bringing chaos to anywhere, though always in the service of the king.* "Hello, Sir Kay," he said.

For a moment Kay stopped. When he saw who it was, he broke into a big grin. "Heard you were here! Heard about the dragon and the green knight and..." Then unexpectedly his face went dark and cautious.

Gawaine shook his head. "All nonsense," he said.

Kay waited.

"A fight between my brother and me," Gawaine said, his cheeks suddenly burnished as if with fire.

"Did you get the better of him?" Kay asked.

"Yes, but..."

Kay smiled, his face almost handsome with memory. "I got the better of Arthur once. A long fight but a fair one. Just to show him who was boss. I am the older, you see. Got that out between us, and never a moment's trouble since." He nodded as he told the tale. "I broke his nose and when it was put to right, told him we would never fight again." He grinned broadly. "And so we haven't."

Remembering Arthur's side of the same story, Gawaine said simply, "That was very brave of you, seeing how big Arthur is and all."

Kay's grin went away and his face got a bit grey.

"Well, it was a long time ago and we were both boys. And he the younger. And he wasn't the bigger then, though he is very strong now. *Very!*"

"Still..." Gawaine said.

"Still!" Kay echoed Gawaine. Then he turned and called to Cook, "Where is that wine? Where is that bread?"

I wonder if this is the sort of thing Mother wants to hear, Gawaine thought suddenly. *About how memory serves the heart and not the mind.* He shook his head, knowing he would tell her nothing, no matter how many spells she had put on him.

"When I am done with the king's needs," Kay said, breaking through Gawaine's maunderings, "I will check on your brother Agravaine. I know a salve or two myself that even the infirmarer does not. And perhaps Agravaine would like someone not in his family to talk to."

"Perhaps," Gawaine said. Then he quickly added, "Thank you, Sir Kay," and meant it.

18

Prince's Choler

WHEN KAY ARRIVED at the infirmary, Agravaine was sitting up and arguing with the infirmarer, an old man with a large wattle on his grainy neck.

"Do not touch me," Agravaine was saying. His voice grated, like a chicken scratching through pebbles.

The infirmarer—a man called Brother Josephus, though he was neither a monk nor a priest—was used to settling recalcitrant princes. He was often called to Arthur's side, or Kay's, or any of the Companions', to treat their ailments. "Now, now, my son," he said, his hand on Agravaine's shoulder.

Angrily but ineffectually, Agravaine batted the hand away.

"So much choler for one so young," Brother Josephus said as Kay watched from the doorway. "Perhaps a good leeching—"

Agravaine roared, "No bloodletting!" and tried to get out of bed.

With a practiced move, Brother Josephus held him down as if Agravaine were no more powerful than a mayfly.

That made Kay chuckle. He remembered Brother Josephus doing the same to Arthur when the king had a high fever. It was a matter of the placement of the hands and, in particular, the thumb. He had often wondered if the infirmarer had some notion of magic, for he was so much stronger than he looked.

Agravaine let out a frustrated gurgle and settled back down on the bed, but he was a lion crouched, waiting for his chance. When the old infirmarer turned away to reach for the wooden casket in which he kept his medicines, Agravaine jumped up and grabbed him around the throat from the back.

"I said not to touch me, you old fraud, you sorry infirmity, you excuse for leechery!" he screamed.

"Guards!" Kay shouted, leaping onto the boy's back. "Guards!" Agravaine bucked like a horse; Kay's legs whipped about and hit the chamber pot, which crashed to the floor.

The guards tumbled into the small room, separated the three, bound Agravaine's hands behind him, then looked to Kay for guidance. Before Kay could think what to do, Agravaine spit at him.

The boy's eyes were wild, steely grey and dark blue as the winter seas around Orkney. Spittle drooled in a string from his mouth. "Write to my mother," he screamed. "Send for her if you dare. She will straighten you out. You and your precious king."

"You can be sure," Kay said in his precise way, "that I shall write to her. She should know how you act in company. It will not please her to have such knowledge, but have it she shall." And thinking he had the last word, he turned and left.

But behind him, Agravaine called out, "She will have your guts, silly man. And grind them into powder."

GAWAINE HAD put all notions of spying aside and settled into the kitchen's rhythms. Often before, he had given thought to what life would be like if he had been born a cook's boy instead of a prince. It had never seemed too bad. Always a warm place to sit, a list of things needing to be done. Dough in, bread out. The simplicity of it all was appealing.

And then he remembered how much he loved hunting and riding and dancing with pretty ladies.

There is a simplicity in that as well, he thought.

He had just started on his third slice of jammy bread when a commotion outside of the kitchen brought him to his feet. Someone was running, calling his name.

Gareth barreled in, almost toppling one of the cook's boys who was carrying a tray of fresh-baked breads. "Gawaine, Gawaine, come quick. Hwyll said you might be here. Or in our room. Gaheris went to look there. This place is a maze. I have gotten lost a dozen times and..."

"And what?"

Gareth tilted his head to one side. "Agravaine. He is in trouble."

Taking a deep breath, Gawaine said, "What kind of trouble?"

Gareth shrugged. "Hard Hands trouble."

Oh, dear Lord, Gawaine thought. "Who has he hurt?"

"The infirmarer."

"How?"

"Tried to throttle him. Sir Kay came in and had to break it up. He broke a chamber pot over Agravaine's head."

"Oh, dear." Gawaine rolled his eyes. "Where is he now?"

"With Hwyll."

Gawaine took another deep breath. *Then everything will be all right. Hwyll will make everything all right. He always makes things right at home.* "And where are they now?"

"In the dungeon."

"Oh, Lord!" This time Gawaine said it out loud.

GAWAINE RAN AHEAD of Gareth because he knew very well how to get to the dungeon. The Companions sometimes had ceremonies there to worship Mithras, where the priest could not find them.

Taking the steps three at a time, he thought, *I will not break my neck for Agravaine,* but he did not slow his pace. The farther down inside the bowels of the fortress, the colder and damper things became. He had never noticed that before.

Rounding the last turning, he saw the bronze head with its blue-enameled eyes, then noted that the iron gate was ajar. For a moment he looked over his shoulder. Gareth was well behind him. He heard voices— one loud and one soft—beyond the gate. He raced toward them.

At the fifth cell—one with old straw on the floor and bars instead of an iron door—Hwyll was speaking quietly to a raging Agravaine, who was pacing the cell still in his thigh-length nightshirt.

"We will get you out soon, my prince. Do not worry yourself," Hwyll was saying.

"I am not worried. But *he* should be. I will kill him."

"Who?" Hwyll's soft voice asked.

"The infirmarer. Sir Kay. The guards. Everybody. Can you get word to Mother?" Now Agravaine was bellowing. "There is nowhere to sit in this piss hole. My head hurts. My throat. Are they laughing at me? I will kill them. I need to lie down." He threw his head back and howled like an animal.

"My prince, my prince," Hwyll cautioned, "do not let them see you this way."

Gawaine's approach was not noticed during this tirade. *Indeed, an army,* he thought, *would not have been heard.* When he touched Hwyll on the hand, the man startled like a poacher's deer.

"My lord," Hwyll said.

"Is the man dead?"

"The infirmarer? No. But—"

"No *but*s needed. If the man is not dead, why is my brother in here?"

"Sir Kay thought it best—"

Agravaine came over to them and, holding on to the bars, screamed, "I will kill him!"

Gawaine shook his head. "Shut up, Agravaine. And

no more talk of killing anyone or we will never get you out of here."

Agravaine shut up, but his eyes were still wild.

Just then Gareth skidded to a stop by them. "Someone is coming."

Gawaine looked up, nodded. "Not just 'someone.'"

"The king," Hwyll said, making a deep bow.

Agravaine stepped back from the bars.

Walking close to the cell, Arthur stood for a moment, feet apart, and cupped his chin in his left hand. He was dressed in black, and there were ink stains on his fingers. His right hand was never far from his sword. "Kay tells me we have a problem."

"I will kill him!" Agravaine cried but nowhere near as loud as before.

"I think not," said the king calmly. "He is necessary to the smooth running of this kingdom. You could always try a duel, of course, but Sir Kay has even beaten *me* on occasion. And you know that *I* can beat anyone. As king I have to."

Gawaine knew the occasion, of course. Arthur had just spoken of it hours before. He did not explain this to his brother.

Agravaine's face had taken on a sly, sulky look. "I *will* fight him." His voice was still rough, and he came close to the bars of his cell. As he opened his mouth to say more, Arthur's left hand shot out and caught him by the neck of his nightshirt.

"You may fight anyone you choose," Arthur said, "so long as they are of your own rank and size."

Agravaine's face was suddenly a bright strawberry red, though with shame or embarrassment or anger or constriction, Gawaine could not really tell.

"But you will never...never...*never* harm a lesser soul," Arthur said. "Not a boy or girl or old man. Not a woman or serf or beggar. If my kingdom is about anything, it is that. We who are strong are to be the caretakers of the weak. Do you take my meaning, sir?"

It was the *sir* that did it. Agravaine nodded. "Yes, my king," he whispered back.

"And," Arthur continued, "if any knight of mine misuses his power, I have sworn to strip him of title and lands. If I will do this to a knight, who outranks you in name and birth rank, do you think I would hesitate to do it to you?"

Agravaine shook his head.

"Then give me your word on this and we will speak no more of it," Arthur said.

Agravaine's voice was suddenly full of awe. "I promise I will be as you would have me, sire."

Arthur grinned and let go of Agravaine's collar. "I am sure of it."

Gawaine allowed himself to breathe.

Meanwhile, Arthur had picked a key from his belt, put it into the lock, and turned until there was a loud clicking sound. Then he opened the door, holding out his hand to Agravaine.

Taking the king's hand, Agravaine went down on one bare knee.

Gawaine marveled at his brother's capitulation. Only moments before he had been a madman, and now this ... this groveling. Then he remembered that Hwyll had said that the one thing that could control Agravaine was a show of power. *I wonder how Arthur knew that?* he thought. *How he knew about Agravaine's need to be treated man to man.*

But then he smiled. Arthur knew everything.

THEY WENT OUT of the dungeon, Arthur in the lead. Hwyll lent a shoulder to Agravaine, who was quite exhausted and red-faced from his morning's labors, like a two-year-old after a tantrum. He smelled like one, too. Gawaine refused to touch him.

"Now, my good Orkney prince, I want you well," Arthur said, his voice floating back to all of them. "It is important." He halted and turned. "I will be calling the Companions together shortly. We meet in six days around the Round Table. I expect you, Gawaine, and all of your brothers, to be there."

"I will," Agravaine answered, as if Arthur had spoken only to him.

I will be there, too, Gawaine thought grumpily, *in my regular place.*

If Arthur noticed the sulkiness of Gawaine's face, he did not respond to it. Instead he said suddenly, "And Gawaine, I am going deer hunting this afternoon. Will you attend me?"

Gawaine's jaw dropped. An invitation was the last thing he had expected.

"Well?" Arthur stood with his hands on his hips.

Gawaine shut his jaw forcefully.

Arthur waited, none too patiently.

At last Gawaine spoke. "I . . . I will, sire." And then with real enthusiasm added, "Oh, I will."

LATER, IN THE throne room, the king was besieged by those he loved best.

"Are you mad?" Merlinnus asked, and Kay agreed with him.

Arthur gave a short, sharp bark of a laugh. "No. I think not."

Kay leaned over the throne and said hoarsely, "But we know his mother has sent an assassin. To go off alone with him, out of the castle, is the very definition of madness."

More quietly, Gawen spoke, and the king had to

lean close to hear. "I know Gawaine, sire. From . . . another time. And place."

Arthur's eyes became steely. "Yes?"

"And he is not to be trusted."

Sitting back against the throne, Arthur said, "Well, I know him from *this* time and place. And I trust him. I rather think if any of the boys is the problem, it is Agravaine."

"But you are not certain," Kay cautioned.

Arthur nodded. "I am not certain."

"But sire—" Gawen tried again.

Arthur cut him off with a movement of his hand. "I said I was not certain. And I am no fool. Gawaine does not know that I know about his mother's plans. I will be on the alert." He ran his hands through his hair.

"You *must* be mad," Kay said, trembling.

"Very," Merlinnus agreed.

"Damn it!" Arthur said, slamming his fist down on the arm of the throne. "Do you three think so little of my skills? I am twice the fighter Gawaine is. He is a boy and I a man. I will be on my guard and he will not. What better way to find out his mind than by taking him far from all that might influence him here? Just the two of us in the woods and on the lea. Two companions hunting."

"Let me at least bespell—" Merlinnus began.

Arthur stood. "No spells. No soldiers. And most of all"—he walked down the steps of the throne and away from them, turning his head at the last to call back to them—"no more discussion." Then he strode out of the hall, the white brachet at his heels.

Merlinnus and Kay stood for a long while in silence, but Gawen could not keep still.

"Magister, we must do something. Truly." Merlinnus would not look at Gawen. "Sir Kay?"

Finally the mage said, "Soldiers, definitely, but far enough away so that he is not aware of them."

"I agree," Kay said, his fingers toying with his mustache.

"I count on you, Kay," Merlinnus said.

Kay pursed his lips solemnly. "I will not fail you, Magister."

"You never do," Merlinnus said, patting Kay on the shoulder, though he'd said the exact opposite of what he was thinking.

Gawen breathed a deep sigh of relief.

19

Off on the Hunt

GAWAINE MET the king at the portcullis. Both were in their leather hunting costumes and, except for Arthur's great ruby ring, the signet of power, neither wore any jewelry.

Arthur sat upon a white horse named Boudicca and Gawaine on a grey called Hag. Each had a short sword at his side, the flat pommels covered with horn, and a five-foot Saxon yew bow slung across his back. A quiver of arrows hung on each man's belt. Capering around Boudicca's legs, as spirited as a pup, the white brachet hound had taken on new life.

Before they could leave, Kay raced across the forecourt, calling out and breathing hard as he ran. "Arthur!"

he cried. When he caught up to them, he put a hand on Arthur's knee.

Arthur looked down and shook his head. "I *am* going, you know."

"Then take care," Kay said quietly, so Gawaine should not hear.

"You are like an old man, startling at shadows," Arthur whispered back. "Now let me go."

"Keep an eye on the boy," Kay said. "If he makes so much as a move toward—"

"Do not teach me how to protect myself," Arthur said. He pushed Kay's hand from his knee and turned to Gawaine. "Are we ready?"

Gawaine grinned, unaware of Kay's worries. "Ready, my lord."

Arthur kicked the horse with his heels and pulled back so hard on the reins, Boudicca rose up on her hind legs. The movement sent Kay scuttling away.

The brachet raced ahead of them as first Gawaine, and then Arthur, rode out under the portcullis, across the road, and up the small rise that led to the forest.

As soon as they were out of hearing, Kay called, "Guards!" Suddenly there were six guards on horse-back, all well armed and armored, by his side. "Do not let them get too far, but do not let them see you, either."

The men nodded.

Kay said again, "They *must* not see you. The king would be angry to know he is being spied upon."

The leader of the small contingent looked down at Kay. "*Are* we spying on him, my lord?"

"You are keeping him safe," Kay said.

"Safe from what?" the leader spoke softly. "If I may ask such?"

"From assassins," Kay said grimly. "Sent by the North Witch."

"Lord Gawaine?"

Kay put a finger to his nose and nodded, but did not speak Gawaine's name aloud.

The guards waited until Arthur and Gawaine were over the hump of the hill, and then Kay sent them on, thinking, *I have done what Merlinnus asked. But is it enough?*

The question so worried him, he went back inside the tower. There he belted on his own sword, grabbed up a bow and quiver of newly fletched arrows—though he was never that good a shot—then came out again, saddled his brown mare, and went after the men.

THE AFTERNOON was one of those glorious spring-tides, with a blue slate of sky, and birds singing on almost every branch. Both Arthur and Gawaine found themselves grinning much of the time they rode, like boys let off from lessons.

When they entered the forest, not far from where Merlinnus had his favorite oak, Arthur pulled Boudicca to a halt.

"We may be followed," he said to Gawaine.

"Followed, my lord?" There were light worry lines on Gawaine's forehead as he frowned.

"Kay has an overweening sense of protection."

"What is he protecting you from, my lord?"

Arthur laughed. "From life!"

The boy laughed as well.

"So here is what I plan to do," Arthur said, leaning forward and whispering low enough that Gawaine had to lean in to hear him. "We shall go through this small forest…" He used his forefinger to draw a map in the air. "Then plunge into the river, ride downstream about a hundred yards, come back out, and race away about a hundred more yards, where there is a second stream. There, we go into that one and then immediately back the horses all the way to the river again, where we will go on another hundred yards, coming out the other side."

"Covering our own tracks, my lord?" Now Gawaine's face was bright with enthusiasm.

"Exactly. It should fuddle them for a bit while we get away."

"'Them'?"

"My bodyguards." Arthur grinned again. "Are you game?"

In answer Gawaine gave two sharp kicks to his grey, and sped off toward the river.

Arthur was taken by surprise. "Hoy!" he cried out, then clapping his heels to Boudicca's side, he quickly followed after. The little brachet, tongue lolling, went, too.

THEY RODE EXACTLY as Arthur had outlined and within an hour had left their keepers far behind. Cresting a hill, they found themselves at the edge of a high, grassy meadow rimmed with patches of *guildes,* that corn yellow flower also called gillyflower.

There on the far edge was a doe and her fawn.

They reined in the horses and dismounted, and Arthur patted his leg so that the brachet came to him.

"Guard!" he said sternly, and the dog stood at attention, keeping an eye on the grey and white mares.

"How shall we take them?" Gawaine asked.

"Never take a doe with her fawn," Arthur said sternly. "Is that what passes for hunting in the Orkneys?"

"Well . . ." Gawaine's face took on a sulky, hurt look.

"There will be a stag nearby. I am sure of it." Arthur wet his finger and held it up to the air to test the direction of the wind, then made a contented sound. He pointed. Closer to them, head up and already alarmed, was a large buck with a wonderful set of antlers. By his side was a second doe, as wary as her mate.

Arthur dropped at once to his belly, and Gawaine

followed suit. Then they began to crawl under the shelter of new bracken and leafy trees, till they were close enough for an arrow to have a chance.

When they stood, both does and the fawn were gone, but the buck was still staring out, to where the horses were grazing unconcernedly.

Nocking their arrows swiftly, Arthur and Gawaine pulled back the bowstrings and let fly at the same time. Both hit the stag, one high on the shoulder, one in the neck, and he fell heavily to his knees.

"Well done!" Gawaine cried even as Arthur was sending another arrow toward the staggered buck. It hit him in the eye, and the creature fell over onto his side, silently, like a mountain crumbling.

With a whoop, Arthur raced across the meadow to the deer, bent down, and slit the dying buck's throat to save it further pain. When he looked up, Gawaine was racing toward him, his bow missing, but his sword held high.

"What . . . ?" Arthur hurriedly stood, furious that he should have so misjudged the boy, his mother, the times. He put his now bloody hand to his own sword and was just bringing it up when Gawaine swept by him and, with a yell, swung his blade at a masked man dressed all in black who—with five others—had come out of the trees, attempting to encircle the king.

The ferocity of Gawaine's attack surprised the lead

man, and he was already down on his knees with Gawaine's blade in his bowels.

Arthur wiped his sword hand quickly on his tunic so that it was not slippery with stag's blood. Then he gripped the hilt of the sword with both hands and plowed into the muddle of masked men, with a battle cry loud enough that the brachet left off guarding the horses and ran to her master's side.

With his first blow, Arthur struck off one of his attackers' arms and hacked halfway through the knee of another.

That left three men standing against two.

"To me!" Arthur cried, and Gawaine turned.

"Yes, my lord!" He ran to Arthur.

They placed themselves back-to-back and, with the brachet harrying the three men who were left, Arthur and Gawaine made swift work of them for, though they were outnumbered, the king and prince were well trained at this sort of bloody work.

But one assassin, as he died, gutted the little hound with his blade. She collapsed to the ground with an awful howl that went on and on and on.

Arthur knelt beside the brachet and picked her up tenderly. Her intestines, hot and bloody and tangled, spilled out across his arms.

"Na, na!" the king crooned, weeping, holding the dog as if she were a baby, rocking her to his chest. The dog shuddered and whimpered. "Na, na. Go gentle, my angel, my lovely, my pet."

The brachet looked up at him, eyes glazing over. Arthur took out his knife, still red with stag's blood, and drew the blade quickly across her throat.

When he looked up again, Gawaine was standing above him, holding something out to him. It took him a moment to realize that the thing was a man's head, caught up by its hair.

"This is the one that killed your brachet, sire. Do you want the rest?" Gawaine was painted in blood, his blond hair matted with it. He gestured to the side. All six bodies lay separated from their heads. The ground was soaked with their blood.

Standing, Arthur said none too gently, "I am more Roman than Celt, Gwalchmei. We do not take heads here."

Gawaine dropped the terrible thing on the ground and squatted down beside it. Then he turned his face aside and vomited into the grass.

Still holding the dead dog, Arthur came over and put a hand on the boy's shoulder. "First kill?" he asked gently.

Gawaine nodded.

"It never gets easier," said Arthur. "But it never gets harder, either."

Just then there was a sound of horses' hooves.

Arthur set the dog down carefully and stood again, his sword at the ready.

Wiping his mouth on his sleeve, Gawaine stood up as well and stared at the force barreling toward them. He shuddered and whispered, "Too late."

Arthur nodded. "We shouldn't have done such a good job losing them." He waved to his guards, who came galloping across the meadow to his side.

"Sire," the captain said, saluting him. "We caught these two with your horses."

There were two men, tied with the binding of the three narrows—wrists, ankles, knees—slung over Gawaine's grey mare. One was an older man with touches of grey in his close-cropped hair, the other hardly out of childhood.

"Good work," Arthur said, suddenly aware that he and Gawaine were both covered in blood. "If someone will gut that deer, and bring it back to the castle, you and your men will have venison with me tonight." He picked up his dog, wrapped her gently in his cloak, and mounted Boudicca. Gawaine got on behind the captain. Then, leaving four men to bring in the deer and the corpses, they rode swiftly and directly for home.

20

Aftermath

"I WARNED YOU..." Kay began as he and Arthur rode.

"You warned me about Gawaine," Arthur said. "And it was he who saved my life."

"It would not have needed saving," Kay went on doggedly, "if you had stayed at home."

"A king cannot be casked up in his castle," Arthur said, just as doggedly, because he knew that Kay was in the right, and he didn't want to admit it. "Not all day and all night because he fears the bogies and boggles."

"Because he rightly fears assassins," said Kay, "a king takes precautions. And does not find ways to fool his guards."

"I did a good job," said Arthur, though the bundle in his arms told him otherwise.

Kay would not be cozened. "You *could* have been killed. We were warned—"

"These were not men sent by the North Queen." Arthur was positive of that.

"And you know that how?"

"They were poachers, thieves. They were after the deer, my horse, my sword, my ring. And they were not well trained in fighting. It was more like a slaughter than a battle." He held up his right hand, where the ruby glittered, redder now because it was flecked with blood. "The North Queen does not send a group of masked men to find me out-of-doors. She favors nights and poison, or a viper in the bed."

"She favors anything that gets the dark deed done," Kay told him.

"You sound like a poet."

"I sound like a prophet."

Arthur shut his mouth before he said something he would later regret, and they rode the rest of the way in silence. But the little dead brachet was like a stone in his arms, and her death was like a stone in his heart.

WHEN THEY GOT back to the castle, the guards set up a great cheer—for Gawaine and for the king. The corpses of the dead men were laid out upon the ground, their heads set back on the stumps of necks. No one could name them and no one would claim them, not even the two who'd been captured alive.

"We just saw the horses, my lord," the boy told Arthur. "Such horses could buy us a year's worth of food. Maybe more. We had no knowledge of the others."

"I do not believe that," muttered Kay, stroking his mustache.

Arthur shook his head. "Sometimes," he cautioned, "coincidences of that sort *do* happen."

"Only in ballads, sire," said Captain Cassius.

"Put them in the dungeon," Kay counseled. "I can find out more about this sort of coincidence there."

"The dungeon?" For a moment the king looked nonplussed.

"No," Merlinnus said. He had just arrived, having heard the commotion. Young Gawen was at his side, close as a shadow, and trembling. The mage's voice seemed strong as ever, but his hands gave him away, for they were shaking. Clearly the sight of Arthur covered in blood had unnerved them both. "Not the dungeon. Arthur—we do not want them there. Too..." He hesitated. "Too cold, too damp, too—"

Arthur nodded. Until the sword and stone were discovered, best to keep people away from the dungeon. It was why he had gotten Agravaine out of there so quickly. "Too far for easy access," he agreed. Turning to the captain, he ordered, "Take them to the guardhouse, where I can speak with them later. At my leisure. Now I just want to clean up. And Gawaine, I suggest you do likewise. Blood under the fingernails is especially hard to dislodge."

But first Arthur went around to the garden where, by himself, he dug a grave and laid the loyal little brachet down, under an apple tree that was white with blossoms.

MORGAUSE HAD WATCHED the aftermath of the fight in her scrying glass, when Gawaine had held out the severed head and Arthur had refused it.

"Pah!" she said, spitting to one side, and thinking how weak a king he was to disdain the blood gift. Did the man not know that keeping the head meant keeping the corpse's ghost subservient? In Eire, where many of her best fighters came from, the heads of the slain were hung up by their hair in sacred groves. If she thought her own people would revel in it, she would do the same. But they were more Northmen than Celts.

She was sorry, though, that the masked men had not killed Arthur, even though they were none of hers. Better the king died at someone else's hands so as not to taint the throne for her sons. But Gawaine had done the right thing. His own life had been threatened. He had to fight the men. And now he was Arthur's brother in blood. Completely trustworthy. *Perhaps*—and here she smiled slowly—*even his heir.*

Briefly she gave thought again to poison or a viper in the bed, but dismissed any such.

They would know then, she thought, *and the killing would be laid at my feet.* She had sent her assassin forth with a much better plan.

ARTHUR WENT to the guardhouse to question the men. He was not pleased to see that they had been badly treated by the soldiers. The boy, who gave his name only as Will, had two black eyes. The other, a sullen-mouthed man in his mid-forties, was breathing through what seemed to be a broken nose.

"I apologize for the roughness of my soldiers," Arthur said to them. "I give you my word, it will not happen again."

The boy nodded his head, deep enough to be a bow, but the older man grabbed him by the arm. "None o' that, Will. There's no royal blood there."

"None I know of," Arthur cheerfully admitted. "But blood does not make a good king, any more than it makes a bad thief."

"An empty belly makes a thief," muttered the older man. "Well I know it."

"Why are your bellies empty, then?" asked Arthur. He was not just making conversation, or trying to trick them. He really wanted to know. "Last year was a good harvest."

"Aye, for the tax collectors," the man replied.

"And my da died," Will put in, "and my mam sold herself to a new husband to pay for our farm. And Uncle James, here—"

"Shut thy mouth, boy."

It was the command of a familiar.

"Did you not know the other men, then?" Arthur asked suddenly.

"No," Will said, "though one of them, the dark one, came through our village once to—"

Uncle James shoved his elbow into the boy's side, but not fast enough.

Arthur believed the boy. He did not trust Uncle James, but young Will seemed steeped in innocence. "Tell you what I am to do with the two of you."

"Hang us, I warrant," James said gruffly, and unbidden tears began to shine in Will's eyes.

"Ah, I expect not," Arthur said quickly. "Perhaps it is because I do not have king's blood in me but am of the people. Rather than hang you, I am going to let you go, and give you each a copper coin. In a year, you shall return to me to show me how that coin has prospered you." Arthur was satisfied to see that the older man's jaw gaped open at this strange sentence. "He who has done the most with what he has been given, shall be given more. He who has done the least shall be put in my dungeon."

"Why should either of us return, then?" the older man asked.

It was a sensible question.

"Honor," Arthur replied, as if that answer said it all.

21

The Price of Honor

"YOU CANNOT THINK to let them go like that," Kay said, when he heard. "It is like something out of a minstrel's story. A year to prosper in. What were you thinking?" He and Arthur were standing by the fire, warming their hands. The day—like many spring days—had suddenly turned cold, as if remembering its closeness to winter. "To let them go?"

"They are already gone," Arthur said.

Kay looked up at the ceiling as if the two thieves were there. Then, not finding them, he returned to staring miserably into the fire. "They will say you are soft, Arthur."

"Maybe *they* will say I am honorable."

"Those two were stealing the king's horses."

Arthur turned and put his hands on Kay's shoulders. "Those two did not know the horses belonged to me."

"They knew the horses did not belong to them," Kay said sensibly.

Arthur took his hands from Kay's shoulders and walked closer to the fire. He felt a sudden chill through his body. *Perhaps I was too hasty,* he thought. *Perhaps only a rich man can indulge in honor. Perhaps I shall never see the two of them again.*

"And now," Kay was going on, "you have taught the people a fine lesson—that not only is it safe to steal from the king, but that a thief will be rewarded for his thievery."

"Only an unsuccessful thief," Arthur said, trying to make light of the situation.

"Arthur..."

"I did not mean any such lesson, and you know it," Arthur added angrily. But deep inside, he feared Kay might be right.

EACH CLUTCHING the king's copper, the two thieves headed north as fast as they could. By evening, alternately walking and trotting, they were thirteen miles along the road.

At a crossroads Will gave up his copper to his uncle, but not without a hot word, which only served to get him a bruised cheek in addition to the black eyes. The two were standing toe-to-toe in the middle of the road, arguing, which was why they didn't hear the man on horseback coming.

By the time they were aware of him, it was too late. He had ridden them down, leaped from his black horse, and—holding his sword at the ready—dared them to stand and deliver.

"We have naught to give you, my lord," said James, holding out his empty hands to the fair-haired stranger, for both coins had already been secreted in his shoe.

"I know you have copper coins," the man said. "Indeed the entire village of Cadbury knows."

"How do they know, my lord?" asked Will, but his uncle laughed bitterly.

"Rumor goes on wings; the truth limps after," James said.

The fair-haired stranger almost smiled at that. Then he came to the point. "I will trade you those copper coins for silver—and a dagger."

"That is no trade," young Will said, "but an angel's gift."

"What murder would you have us do?" James asked, bluntly, for in his experience nothing paid so well in this world.

"'Murder,' Uncle?" Will was appalled.

This time the stranger threw his head back and

laughed. "Fair question," he said. "And if I spoke murder, would you quail at it?"

"Depends," James said, wiping his hands on his coarse tunic.

"On what?" asked the stranger.

"On the person to be killed," James said.

"I will none of this," the boy said. "Thievery is one thing, but my mam would kill me if I turned to murder." He headed off down the road.

The stranger looked after him with calculating eyes, but the boy did not see this, or he would have returned at once.

Meanwhile, James had bent down and gotten the two copper coins out of his shoe. He held them to the stranger, who was once more looking at him. "My honor, lord."

The stranger put a hand to his leather pocket and extracted two gold coins. "And mine."

"So to this bloody business, then?"

"No blood at all. I have a dagger given me from the Far East, a magnificent thing that only a king should own. But I do not want Arthur knowing it comes from me until later. And there is none," the fair man said, "in Cadbury who can keep a secret."

"And I?" James asked.

"You have lately been with the king. He will know to trust you if your story be well told."

James smiled. "A gold coin will guarantee I be the greatest teller Cadbury has ever known."

The fair-haired man smiled, though his eyes did not. "I am sure of it." He reached into his pocket and drew out a silk-wrapped packet containing the dagger.

"Can I see it?" James asked.

"Not till you unwrap it for the king," said the fair-hair stranger.

"And what guarantee do you have that I do not just run off and sell the bloody thing?"

"What guarantee do you have that I not kill you on the spot?" There was no animosity in the threat, just a bare promise. "As I have found you here, I can find you anywhere, should you betray this trust. And unlike the king"—the man smiled broadly this time—"I do not care who likes me."

Gulping, James took the silk packet. "The king shall have the dagger by the morrow."

THE NEXT DAY, Arthur was once more sitting at his desk, struggling with a piece of parchment and words that did not fit as easily on the page as in his mouth. He slammed his pen down. "Get me some ale. By the rood, this is thirsty work."

Sitting by his side, Gawen smiled. "You make it harder, sire, than it ever need be. Just form the words in your head and let your hand take care of itself."

"You sound like my old master of the sword," growled Arthur, remembering the grizzled man with affection.

"It is the same principle," Gawen said, and went out for the ale.

While the boy was gone, Arthur tried to think of the pen as a sword, making it work on its own while he merely thought the words. Then the pen broke, splattering the few words already on the page with splotches of ink.

Arthur got up, picked up another pen, and went to stand by the fire. As he used to do with his wooden sword, long before the master of swords let him hold the real thing, he held the pen lightly and concentrated on *not* concentrating. The pen made words in the air. Good words. Solid words.

Suddenly he remembered that it had taken many long months of wooden swordplay before he had been ready for the steel.

"But damn it, I *wanted* the real sword and I do *not* want the pen," he told the fire. "Besides, I have scribes who can do my writing for me." He longed to call one in. He knew what Gawen would say: He had soldiers who could do his fighting for him as well. He did not understand why, but he wanted the boy to think well of him.

"Where is that ale!" he shouted, looking longingly at the door of the throne room and willing it to open.

And open it did.

A guard poked his head in. "Sire, that thief is back. The old one. The one you gave the copper to."

Arthur was stunned. How many in Cadbury knew about that copper? And then he shook his head. Hadn't he *wanted* it known? Wanted his people to think him a good king, a magnanimous king? "Why is he here?"

"He says he does not need to wait a year; he has to show you something." The guard hesitated. "It is a dagger, Majesty. I do not advise seeing him."

"Take the dagger; send him in," Arthur said, thinking, *I might be magnanimous, but I am not stupid.*

James came in and went on one knee. "My king."

"Back so soon?" Arthur asked. "Or do royal years run somewhat longer than yours?"

"I have already made a profit on your copper, sire, and thought you should know," the man said, though his voice seemed somewhat sinister, or at least not inspiring much confidence.

"Stand up, man. I hate talking to the tops of people's heads," Arthur said.

James stood. "Can I show you?"

Arthur shook his head. "Any man can make a one-time profit. My task to you was to make the profit last the year."

"But this concerns... my *honor,* sire," wheedled James.

Arthur realized that the man, like so many of those who sought his aid, would not go away easily. Better to find out what this amazing profit was, then send him off. He expected within the year that James would be in the dungeon or swinging from a tree somewhere, but that young Will would have bought his mother a farm. He would stake his *own* honor on that. "Then show me."

"It was the dagger, sire. The one I was not allowed to bring in."

The man was tiresome. He brought to mind that fat lady of means, the one with the dead cat. Arthur went back to his desk and sat down heavily. "Very well, call the guard in."

James went, got the guard, and on the king's instruction was given the silken-wrapped dagger.

"Bring it here and let me see," said Arthur.

GAWEN WAS just coming up the stairs from the kitchen with the mug of ale for the king, when Gawaine and his brothers came galloping down. Agravaine bumped heavily into Gawen, causing the ale to spill.

"Here there!" Gawen cried. "That's for the king."

"Let me brush it where it's spilled," Gawaine said, in way of apology, starting to run his hand over Gawen's tunic.

All of Gawen's long-held hatred of the prince roiled

to the fore. "No need. No need." Gawen turned away violently, and at that very moment, there was shouting beyond the king's door.

The guard hastily flung the door open, and Gawen and the guard and the four sons of the North Witch could see the king being set upon by a man with a large jeweled dagger in his hand. It was the man, not the king, who was shouting. Oddly, what he was saying was, "Stop it! Bloody hell! Stop it!" as he struck at the king over and over.

"Sire!"

Gawaine and Agravaine dashed in, edging the guard aside. Gawen was right behind them. The twins remained at the door, juggling to see what was happening.

None of the boys had a weapon, and the guard's lance was for show only, not battle, but Arthur was already keeping the assassin away with—of all things—the sharp edge of his pen.

The man kept striking at him, over and over, clumsily, as if the dagger were doing the ill work and not the hand. Still, those strikes kept getting closer and closer.

At the last, Arthur aimed his pen like an arrow and flung it as hard as he could right into the assassin's face. It hit him in the left eye, and he toppled, just as the deer had done two days before, screaming in agony on the floor. Still his hand and the dagger tried to strike out at a now-unseen enemy.

Gawen ran to the king, who was red-faced and breathing hard, beads of sweat running down his face.

"Sit, Arthur," Gawen said. The use of the king's name lent the command some force, and Arthur sat.

Gawaine kicked the dagger from the man's hand, and it spun around three times widdershins, resting near the fire. At the same time, Agravaine, his face a fury, swung his foot up and crunched down on the old thief's face, sending the pen straight through into his brain.

"Stop!" Gawen cried. "The mage will want to speak to him."

But it was too late. The thief was dead.

And later, when they went to retrieve the dagger, it had vanished.

All that was left was a gold coin in James's hand, minted somewhere on the Continent.

"THE DAGGER was enchanted, of course," said Merlinnus afterward. "It used the man and not the other way around."

Arthur nodded. He was lying on his bed, though he did not feel a bit sleepy. The infirmarer had insisted on his resting. He had made Arthur drink a posset, which tasted like the sort of thing Sir Ector's wife had brewed up when he was a child and could not sleep.

"Who but the North Queen could have made such a spell?" Kay asked.

"Any of a half-dozen mages from the Far East, I suspect," Merlinnus said. "Though I agree it was probably she."

"Could *you*?" Kay was in the mood to challenge everyone and everything. The face of the dead man, with the pen through the eye, would not leave him.

"Why should I?"

"Arrrr!" Kay turned his back to Merlinnus and spoke to Arthur. "It was all your own fault, you know."

Arthur shrugged. "Of course it was. All of it. From start to finish. That I admit. But nothing happened. I am fine. No harm done. Except to poor old James there. And now we must think about what this all means. How this man could have been corrupted by Morgause. How he found that dagger—or was given it. And if given it, then by whom?"

Kay added quickly, "And why the North Queen's boys came in when they did. And why Agravaine killed the man before we could talk to him. And—"

Merlinnus quickly intruded. "All good questions. Some of which I will try to answer myself. But now, Kay, I think Arthur needs his sleep. Though you might stand guard yourself this night."

"That I will!" Kay said. He turned and went to the door, looking over his shoulder. "That I will!" Then he went out.

Arthur tried to sit up. "A good move, that. It will make him feel useful."

"I know, I know," Merlinnus said, pushing him back down on the bed. "And, Arthur—I was not fooling about sleep. The infirmarer has given you enough syrup of aloe in that posset to put a horse down. So let it take effect, or you will be regretting it in the morning."

Arthur yawned. "I am already regretting it." But he lay back on the bed like a small, bidden child, the smell of violets around him. The infirmarer had sprinkled his pillow with dried flowers known to bring uninterrupted sleep. In minutes the king was snoring.

BUT MERLINNUS did not sleep that night. Long he looked into his books of magic, his scrying mirror, and the various parchments on which he had made notes about spells. He hummed through his nose as he read, and he coughed and hawked up sputum, wiping his nose and mouth again and again on his voluminous sleeves.

Soon the floor was littered with things the mage had read and discarded. Gawen kept trying to pick them up and place them carefully away.

"Go to bed, boy," Merlinnus said at last. "You are

making too much of a fuss for my liking. Magic needs silence and contemplation."

Gawen knew better than to point out that Merlinnus himself was a roomful of noise. Instead, shutting the door, Gawen went down the stairs, not to sleep but to relieve Kay at the king's door.

Merlinnus did not even hear Gawen go. He was too deep in thought.

"I know Morgause is behind the attack," he muttered. "I am certain of it." But he could not figure out how she did it. *A dagger that wields the man instead of the other way around? Quite a piece of wizardry, that.* He had to admire the skill behind it, even as he hated the maker.

But his own skill was greater, as she would soon find out.

And, as Arthur himself had said, no harm done. The assassin died, the king slept, and a larger magic was about to be unfolded.

When the sun rose, the old mage went to bed. No wiser, but wise enough.

IV

Prince's Danger/ King's Hand

Now the sun on the churchyard floor made the slate look like water. The stone with its hard prow and metal rudder seemed some alien boat afloat on a grey sea. Where the boat was headed, though, no one seemed to know. Or care.

22

The Marvel

THE NEXT DAY a marvel was discovered.

A shepherd named Tom, going after three of his missing sheep, stumbled into the high tor. He went at first daylight; he would never have ventured in otherwise. The small wonder was that he returned, with the sheep *and* all his wits. Especially because he'd so few of them before, or so ran the gossip. He returned as well with a tale of a greater wonder inside the vaulted chamber.

"A stone," he said, "with a sword sticking out of it, like a knife in butter. A sword. Fit for a king. And words."

The people in the town laughed at that description and they puzzled about the words, but like Tom, they could not read, so how were they to know what was meant?

Tom was not the sharpest man in the crowd, but he was smart enough to tell his wife and she went directly to the priest about the discovery. The priest, in turn, was quick enough to tell a guard, who was interested enough to mention it to the captain, who was intrigued enough to tell Sir Kay, who, as always, told everything to the king. Along the way Tom, his wife, the priest, the guard, and the captain let bits of the marvel loose into the ears of the people of Cadbury until all the castle and the village was abuzz with it.

WHEN KAY REPORTED what had been told him by the captain, Arthur turned his grey gaze toward the ceiling as if all the answers to life were written there. He had slept well, almost—so he thought—like the dead. Then he crossed himself quickly, in case such thoughts brought bad luck. He doubted Kay had slept at all. "Let us go and see this great wonder."

"It might be a trick," Kay said.

"Of course it is a trick," Arthur answered. "But I still want to see it. We will go in force. A guard of fifteen, I think, plus Cassius."

"Do I send for the mage?" asked Kay. "We could use his protection."

Arthur shook his head. "The last person I want on this little trip is the wizard. But his boy can come."

Kay waited for him to explain further. When he did not, Kay bowed and went to form the party. He did not always agree with Arthur, but he knew when *not* to push.

So he found the captain of the castle guard, Cassius of the White Hand, so known because he had been wounded badly in a battle as a young soldier and his hand had almost bled out to white before it was tended to. Kay instructed Cassius on the particulars of the mission.

The captain nodded and was quick to gather fifteen of his best men.

Next Kay went to the kitchen, where he suspected he might find Gawen.

"Ye've just missed he," said Cook. "Carrying and fetching for the old man."

"A big tray of stuff," added one of the boys, a snuffling truant with a missing front tooth. "He will be slow a-stairs."

Kay turned on his heel and left at a run. He caught up with Gawen on the last set of steps, the ones up to the mage's tower.

"There's to be an expedition," he said stiffly. "You're to come."

Gawen turned those blue eyes on him. "An expedition?"

"Into the tor."

"At whose behest?"

Kay opened his mouth, closed it, then opened it again, like a trout out of water. He was not used to being questioned by boys. "The king's."

Nodding, Gawen said, "I'll tell Merlinnus."

Kay leaned forward. "The king says not to bother him."

"But—"

"King's orders," Kay said, laying a finger to the side of his nose and winking. It was his way of pulling Gawen into his small conspiracy.

"I *have* to tell him." There was steel in the boy's voice, which surprised Kay.

"Best not," Kay returned.

"He will know, anyway. He always does." Gawen's usually open face seemed to shut down. "You do not want to anger a wizard."

"*You* do not want to anger the king," said Kay.

They stood toe-to-toe, glaring peevishly at each other, when the tower door suddenly flew open. Merlinnus peered out. "Is that my breakfast?" he asked in a wavering voice.

"Merlinnus." Gawen turned. "There is an expedition—"

"I am not well today," the old man said, waving a hand at them. "Go in my place, child. Tell the king."

Gawen went up the last of the stairs, handed the mage the tray, closed the door quietly, then turned to gaze down at Kay.

Kay stared back.

They both had triumphant looks on their faces, but neither one spoke a word more as they hurried down the stairs to meet with the king.

THE SOLDIERS CAME behind the king and Kay and Gawen, marching in the old Roman style: two straight lines, counting off as they went. Captain Cassius marched with them. The counting was to show they were fearless, or so they would have their enemies believe.

The first four were bowmen; the rest carried spears and swords. Over their outer tunics, they wore their fighting leather tunics, and over that each wore a coat of mail with a leather belt at the waist.

If the captain had had his way, there would have been double that number of men, but Arthur had refused.

"We are not at war," Arthur said.

"We are *always* at war," said Cassius, but Arthur chose not to hear him.

Behind the soldiers came a ragtag company of towns-folk, all willing enough to venture a ways up the tor, but not into it. They knew all about the tor and its magic. A man might fall into the place, but to go there a-purpose took more courage than any of them was willing to own.

The tor was slumped on one side, and covered sparsely with grass and sheep droppings. Every few yards was another slide of rocky scree. A single huge oak stood at the top, gnarled and bent with age and the constant wuthering of the wind. Halfway up the tor was the entrance to a cave, for this was a hollow hill, a lonely place, reeking with dark power.

"Fairy Gate," whispered Kay, who actually would never have dared go in on his own. It was not that he was afraid of magic or the unknown; he had a positive fear of tight, enclosed spaces. Even the twice-yearly celebrations to Mithras in the dungeon made him queasy.

Several of the guards were as nervous as Kay, but for different reasons. Yet they did not have the freedom to say so. One man, a hero of three battles, turned the color of whey as they entered the mouth of the cave. But he did not complain. To do so would have meant daring his captain's scorn, or his fellows'.

The soldiers, the king, Sir Kay, and young Gawen went in.

The townspeople stayed outside.

Clouds covered the sun and all the signs were for rain, but rain did not come.

23

Sword in the Stone

INSIDE THE TOR Arthur led the way as if he knew where to go. No one remarked upon it, but Arthur knew what they must be thinking: that his kingship gave him the ability to find his way through the maze of tunnels. That, or God's favor.

Only he knew the truth. He was not king because he had the heart and the mind to be so. He was not king because he had taken the throne by stealth or might. He was king because of magic. Because Merlinnus willed it.

And he knew the way through the cave because Merlinnus had drawn him a map, which he had studied long night after night.

Arthur kept going forward—directly, swiftly, surely—into the cavern, where the sword in the stone waited, that bit of legerdemain that would confirm for all time his right to the throne.

Everyone would believe it.

Everyone but Arthur himself.

He ground his teeth and went on.

CAVES DID NOT trouble Gawen. On the trip down the coast to Cadbury, caves had been the safest places to stay in. Besides, Gawen—along with Arthur—understood the real reason for the expedition into the tor.

The soldiers knew only of the wonder. And the worry about keeping the king safe. Gawen knew the whole story and was there, surely, to be Merlinnus' eyes and ears.

Besides, Gawen had already been in the cavern with the king and Merlinnus and knew there was nothing to fear. Gawen also understood why Merlinnus had acted as if he were too sick to go along. The less people associated the old wizard with the sword-stone thing, the more they would believe the legend on its side. Oh, they would know it for magic, but not the maker. *Better so,* Gawen thought. *Much better so.*

As they walked through a darkness that was lit only by the flickering of torches, Gawen thought of the words to be used later to describe the place to Merlinnus: words like *cold, damp, dank, gloomy, murky.*

Should I mention that the shadows of the marching soldiers seem lumpy and dwarfish, capering along the sloping walls?

Should I say the cave smells of rot and doom, a heavy, musky stink? Gawen shrugged. Probably some of that was really the reek of sheep droppings. And the sweat of fear.

I can describe the sounds, too, Gawen thought. *Merlinnus will like that. I can say that though the men have given up on their marching count, there is a constant shuffle of feet. Now and again someone coughs, or clears a throat. It all echoes in a muffled sort of way.*

Smiling, Gawen realized, *I could make a story of it. Or a song.* But Gawen had little talent for either.

THEY CAME to the center cavern, and there, as the shepherd had promised, was the wonder itself.

Arthur smiled tightly. Certainly coming upon it through the winding tunnels without Merlinnus by his side lent the stone a certain majesty.

A collective sigh ran around the vaulted room as the men surrounded the object. For a long moment no one moved toward it. Even Captain Cassius was cautious.

It was Kay who finally walked up to the stone and put his left hand on it, carefully, as if fearing the stone might be searing hot with magic. His right hand—the one that held the torch aloft—did not waver.

Arthur had never been so proud of him. He knew that Kay hated caves, had always refused to explore them when they were boys. Kay was probably sweating profusely and glad that it was too dark for the men to notice. But his right hand and the torch were rock steady.

When nothing seemed to happen to Kay or his hand, he bent over and held the torch close to the legend, speaking the words out loud to the men, most of whom could not read.

"'Whoso pulleth out this sword of this stone is rightwise king born of all Britain.'" Kay straightened up and cocked his head at Arthur. "But you already are..."

"...king of all Britain," Arthur finished for him. "I know."

The men grumbled their agreement.

"But clearly this is meant to be one last test," Arthur said, pointing at the stone.

"Never heard of such a—" Kay began.

"A test is never to be shirked," Arthur said, his voice strong, regal, forbidding argument.

"Then, sire, put your hand to the sword," Cassius urged.

"Not here, my good captain. Not now," Kay shook his head vigorously.

Arthur agreed at once. "Not here," he said, "where none but us can see it. Not now, without proper preparation."

When it was clear no one knew what Arthur meant, Kay added, in a voice made louder by the echoing cave, "The king needs to go to church and to confession and...and then in full public gaze, so that all men might see, he will take this final test and pull the sword." He touched the sword with his right forefinger, letting it travel languidly partway down the hilt. "He will."

"Not here and not now," Arthur interrupted, running a hand through his hair, "for I need to think about this." Though he had done all his thinking already.

GAWEN WENT OVER to the king and smiled up at him, saying softly so that only the two of them could hear, "The stone does have majesty, Majesty."

The king smiled crookedly.

"But the cavern feels somewhat like a set for traveling players," Gawen added.

"I expect only you and I feel that way," Arthur replied, leaning over. "Look around. What do you see?"

Gawen looked at the soldiers and at Kay. "People beguiled."

The king nodded.

"But then, they have given themselves to the idea of majesty already, sire, which is itself a kind of ensorcellment," Gawen said. "I mean no disrespect."

"How old is that head on your young shoulders?" asked Arthur.

Older than you know, Gawen thought, *different than you can ever guess,* but did not say it aloud, adding, "I expect all kingship is wizardry."

Arthur turned and stared at Gawen. "What do you mean by that?" His voice was not sharp, but still probing.

"I mean that people need to believe in their leaders and their laws for the things to work," Gawen said. "And that is certainly a kind of magic."

"Ah." Arthur breathed, then put a hand to his chin and stared at the stone. "I think that is what Merlinnus has been trying to tell me. I wish he would speak plain."

Gawen laughed. "Then he would not be a wizard!"

Arthur laughed as well and Kay, unable to bear being left out of the conversation, came over to hear the joke. When neither of them could explain it to him, he got a huffy look on his face.

Immediately Arthur put his arm around his stepbrother's shoulders. "Kay, I never saw a braver thing than when you stepped up and clapped your hand on that stone."

"Really? Never?" Kay's face lost its huffy look.

Gawen stepped back into the shadows. There were times and places that could not and should not be intruded upon.

24

Courtyard

THEY SENT BACK to the castle for a cart, which took well over three hours. Since neither of the two big dray horses could be persuaded into the high tor, the guards themselves had to drag the wagon in, set the heavy stone onto the cart, and then haul it out again.

By the time the horses were rehitched to the cart, stomping their enormous feet, it was nearing supper.

And by the time the creaking cart with its heavy burden was at the castle, it was past time for eating.

"Put the stone in the throne room," Kay advised. "It reeks of majesty."

"No," Arthur said, "it will go in the churchyard so everyone can see it. That stone belongs to all the people."

SO BY MOONRISE it was set down right where the king wanted it.

A crowd soon gathered and the few who could read told the legend to the others. Some cried it a wonder, others a miracle. A few said that it was a dark artifact and should be buried at the crossroads, but they were quickly hushed. Several people raised their voices to declare their allegiance to the king as he was, without further testing.

But not—Arthur noted critically as he stood at one of the windows and listened—*not all of them.* He sighed loudly. *Not even most of them.* That hurt, though in their place, he guessed, he would have said the same.

He noted Gawaine down there with his younger brothers jostling for a sight of the stone, as well as Bors and Bedwyr and several other Companions. Every soldier in the castle seemed to have come for a look.

"What happens now?" Kay whispered to Arthur.

"What God wills," said Arthur, though he was thinking that by *God,* he probably meant Merlinnus. "We will discuss it in three days with the Companions at the table."

"But, Arthur," Kay said, his hand hovering near

Arthur's shoulder though not—here in the open, where anyone might see—actually touching the king, "Arthur, should we wait till then?"

"You may do what you will, but I plan to have supper now, bed soon, and then ready the castle for the Round Table with my men." He waved at the crowd, and then turned and was gone before Kay could properly frame a reply.

SOMETHING MADE Morgause rise from her bed and go to the scrying basin again. To do such strong magicks twice in three days was hard. Every muscle in her neck and back ached from the work of the day before. She was half blind from gazing so intently in the water. Her nose had bled for hours after the spy-all had scraped it raw. Magic was a hard master and a worse mistress.

But this new prickle between the shoulder blades made her get up. First she gulped down two raw pigeon eggs, following with a glass of red wine. The eggs for her muscles, the wine for her blood. Then she wrapped her silken robe about her and began the rites for the scrying.

This time she did not understand at all what she saw: a glimpse of Gawaine's face, then the twins, and reflected in their eyes some great lump, like a stone boat, with a rudder sticking out.

It made no sense, yet from the look of awe on their faces, she could see it was important. They did not go closer to the thing, or otherwise explore it. How could she know unless they showed her?

"Damn!" she cried aloud, and hit the water with the flat of her hand, destroying the image and causing a feedback of magic up through her arm that ran like a jolt of lightning to her heart. Her eyes opened wide and she had to take a deep breath. "Hecate be damned. Odin be damned. I have no idea what it is I see."

She would have to send doves to her assassin, and he, in turn, would have to send one back with news. All that would take time. But not right now. Right now she had to sleep. If she was to make any sense in the next days, if she was to do things right, she would have to sleep.

She barely made it back to her bed before sleep, like a bad habit, grabbed her by the throat and would not let her go.

GAWEN WAITED until most of the people were gone, especially Gawaine and the twins, who trailed behind him. The one thing Gawen did not want to do was come upon Prince Gawaine again here, in front of the church, with time to contemplate each other. Not that Gawaine would offer any sign of recognition. He had not done so before. And even a small mirror—like the one in the mage's tower—showed Gawen how big that difference was now. Besides, Gawaine was never one to look too deeply at a boy.

Only at women, Gawen thought bitterly. *Still, best take no chances.*

Clinging to the shadows, Gawen waited until night had almost completely set in before moving up close to the stone.

The king had been right to set the stone so, Gawen thought. It looked more majestic, more solid, and less magical in the courtyard. It was infinitely more believable in front of the church.

Placed right by the front door, on a blue-grey paving stone, the darker grey of the boulder was like a leviathan rising up in a grey sea. The sword gleamed silver in the half-moon light, and the blade seemed to be made now of water, now of steel. Gawen held out a hand toward it, pretended to grasp it, but did not touch the hilt.

I should tell Merlinnus, Gawen thought. *I should go to him now and tell him all.* But then, strolling unhurriedly toward the keep, a second thought came, this one out loud. "Let him wait. I shall tell him the truth when I get around to it."

25

Helping a Mage

IN THE MORNING the castle was a-bustle with the wonder in the churchyard.

As Gawen went from the tower room down to the kitchen, and back again with a tray of food, the story of the stone was being embellished and enlarged like an old tapestry in the hands of new sewers, till it was nothing like the tale Merlinnus had heard that morning.

"Do not entertain me," Merlinnus had warned.

So Gawen had kept the recitation unadorned and straightforward.

But what came now from the mouths of cooks and serving maids, from ostlers and soldiers, from men and women and children alike, were tales of the stone all out of keeping with what Gawen knew. They said it had flown to the tor from Eire, from Jerusalem, from the banks of Queen Mab's faerie kingdom. They said it was big as a horse and shod with iron, as small as a hedgehog and bristly all over. They said the sword was silver, gold, encrusted with jewels. It sang in six voices. It was silent as a tomb. Who pulled it would rule England, Britain, the Continent. Who pulled it would sit at Jesu's right hand and Odin's left. Who pulled it would be king forever, the savior returned to earth, the earth redeemed for good this time. Who pulled it would doom the kingdom, the island, the world.

Gawen knew the thing was none of these, that it was but a sword in a stone, and a trick.

In fact, Gawen was well tired of it. What *Gawen* wanted to talk about was the Round Table, but no one seemed interested in that.

Gawen had not seen the table room yet, as it was kept locked when not in use. The table itself, though—who in Britain did not know of it? It had been made in France, created a-purpose so that no knight might boast of sitting higher than his peers. That was Arthur's idea, of course. Or perhaps the idea had first been Merlinnus'. Of what Gawen knew of the two of them, that coin had two heads.

After asking around for a day, Gawen finally found

one of the pages, a boy named Geoffrey, willing to tell more. Of course, first they had to talk of the sword and the stone, and Gawen simply nodded at every wild rumor Geoffrey spun out as truth. Geoffrey was a dark-haired, dour boy, a southerner, and at last he got to the stuff Gawen was waiting for.

In a slow drawling voice, he said that inside the table room there were banners on the walls with the devices of the individual knights.

"A dragon for the king, of course," he said in a way that made even that information sour.

"Of course," Gawen agreed, though secretly wondered if a bear might not have been more appropriate. There was something very bearlike about Arthur, shaggy and strong.

"And a heart for Lancelot, the king's true man, and a lion rampant for Tristan, and..." Geoffrey drawled on and on.

Gawen stopped listening to Geoffrey's litany, despite only moments before being desperate to know everything about the table and the room it was in. Now Gawen suddenly wondered, *Can I get in on my own? Can I see for myself?* Merlinnus had been right to demand that Gawen tell of going into the tor with Arthur and the soldiers in its barest form, unadorned and un-ornamented. No one ever told things straight.

Gawen began making a dozen plans, plans of how

to get in to see the table, to touch it, to sit in one of the Companions' chairs. All of the plans were much too complicated and dangerous.

"Is that what you wanted to know?" Geoffrey asked suddenly, a hand to his mouth, yawning.

Gawen was brought back from all that scheming with a mental thud, and nodded. "Yes, thank you." But it was *not* what Gawen wanted to know at all.

Who could tell the truth? Only one person.

Gawen escaped from Geoffrey and climbed up to the tower room, taking the steps as Arthur did, two at a time, on legs too short to make such going comfortable for more than one flight of stairs.

At last at the top, Gawen knocked on the door. Three times, then once, then three times again so that Merlinnus would know who was there.

"COME," MERLINNUS whispered, frustrated to be interrupted at his work. Setting down the beaker he had been holding, he carefully washed his hands in the stone basin. He recognized the knock as Gawen's, and while he liked the boy, had not expected him for hours.

The liquid in the beaker made a fizzing sound. Luckily he had not yet started to heat the infusion.

"Come," he said a second time, louder.

Gawen pushed into the chamber and, without

adornment, asked, "Can you get me into the Round Table room, Magister?"

"In time," the old man said. "In time."

"But how *much* time?"

Merlinnus laughed. "Thus speaks a boy." But when he saw Gawen's face close down and get a strange, secretive look, he guessed there might be mischief afoot unless he gave a real answer. He did not want to lose this helper, for in these past few days the boy had become miraculously indispensable, not only following instructions to the letter, but even anticipating some of them. The boy was not a magic worker; clearly his skills lay elsewhere. He was attentive, smart, careful, observant, and able to speak to the mighty and the small. He was also, it seemed, becoming a favorite of the king's, for he made Arthur smile. "You will be under my protection and therefore one of the pages to serve during the next meeting of the Companions."

"But that is *two days from now*!"

At first Merlinnus thought the answer was a complaint and was ready to caution the boy again. But then he saw how Gawen's eyes had cleared, how his face seemed lit from within as if a candle had been set there. Then the mage understood that the boy was thrilled that it was such a short time till he got into the table room. He smiled. "Arthur has called the Companions together earlier than the Solstice. He means to tell them about the sword and the stone and what it all portends."

"The legend on the side is not enough?" Gawen asked.

"A legend is never enough," Merlinnus answered. "There must be explanations and exegesis; there will be arguments and counterarguments; there must be anger and sadness and friendship." Merlinnus' mouth pursed. "In short, it will be like every other Round Table session."

Gawen sighed. He looked ecstatic. "And I will be there."

THE TWO DAYS seemed to fly by, though Gawen worked so hard, there was scarce time to contemplate what was to come.

First duty, of course, was helping Merlinnus—which meant bringing him food as well as getting his robes cleaned. Gawen came up with the idea of sorting out the mage's books and scrolls, which were higgledy-piggledy all over the tower room: on tables and under them, behind the bed and under the covers, on windowsills and even in the slops closet. The order Gawen settled on was putting the books on the shelves of an empty wardrobe in alphabetic order, starting with *An Advisory to the Getting of Wisdom*.

Secondarily, Gawen helped out in the kitchen.

"Ye have a talent for baking, a light hand," Cook said, taking full advantage of the fact.

And thirdly, Gawen helped scribe three Actes for Arthur: one about the stone, one about a pilgrimage to the Holy Well of Saint Madron's, and one about taxes. Kay was too busy getting things ready in the table room to do it.

"Besides," Kay had explained to Gawen, "you have a better hand for scribing than I." He said it honestly, but there seemed quite a bit of regret in his voice. "Must be all that time with the monks."

So Gawen headed to the throne room, where Arthur seemed to be in a foul mood, glaring down at his desk.

"The people," Arthur said gloomily, ripping yet another precious sheet of vellum in two, "the people hate taxes."

"The people hate starvation even more," Gawen said. "Perhaps you could explain that their taxes go to things like granaries to be held against the time of need."

"What a good idea," Arthur said. "I thought their taxes went to armories to help defend them in times of war. But granaries is a wonderful idea. How did you think of it?"

"It is done in my...where I come from," Gawen said.

Arthur stared at Gawen for a moment, his eyes narrowing. "Which is where exactly?"

"Far, far from here," Gawen said truthfully.

"North?" Arthur asked.

When Gawen did not answer at once, Arthur's eyes got even narrower, but he held out the scribblings on the two torn sheets.

"You draft it, then," Arthur said.

"You trust me to do so?" Gawen's breath seemed caught somewhere between throat and mouth.

Arthur nodded and abruptly turned back to the other sheets on his table.

"FROM HOW FAR north does Gawen come?" Arthur asked about three hours later when Merlinnus came into the throne room. Gawen had gone back to the kitchen at Cook's behest, having scripted one and a half of the Actes and promising the king he would return quickly.

"Along the coast," the mage replied. "Why?"

"I was thinking about the North Queen's assassin," Arthur said.

"He is dead."

"I think not." Arthur's face was closed down, as if shutters had been drawn across it.

"Ah . . ." Merlinnus waited.

"That old thief had not the subtlety to be the queen's tool. And he seemed as surprised by the dagger as I. Perhaps even more so."

Merlinnus nodded. "I never thought him her prime man, but I am glad to hear you think not, as well. Do you suspect the assassin to be her son?"

"Gawaine?"

"The other one."

Arthur shook his head. "Agravaine is not smart enough. Besides, I have made him mine."

That news startled the mage. "How did you do such a thing?"

"Ah, Merlinnus," Arthur said. "You know magic and I know men."

"The twins?"

"The twins are too young."

"No one is too young for the North Witch to corrupt," said Merlinnus with a bitterness he did not even try to disguise. "But I thought we agreed the assassin was inconsequential."

Arthur stood and stretched. "I still want to know."

"Well, young Gawen is not the one," said the mage. He suspected many things about the boy, but being an assassin was not among them.

"Are you certain?" Arthur walked over to the hearth and held his hands out to the embers. "It is important to me."

The mage knew it was warmer outside than in, that the stone walls of Cadbury held in the cold. He joined Arthur at the hearth. Then, making a sudden decision, he said, "There are things about Gawen that puzzle me, Arthur, and you know I do not like puzzles."

"Hah!" Arthur replied.

Merlinnus ignored the king's outburst, and kept on. "Gawen knows too much for a youngling. His skills are odd ones, versatility without much depth. And there is some raw wound he has not yet staunched that bears upon the North Queen's eldest son."

Arthur grew quiet and listened.

"But I am certain he is not an assassin. Nor do I believe he would harm you or yours. His loyalty to you, Arthur, is without question."

For a moment Arthur was still. Then he threw his arm around the mage and gave him a hug. "Thank you, old man. Thank you!"

The display disquieted Merlinnus since he did not know what to make of it. But he did not ask. Asking direct questions of the king might get him an answer he did not want to hear.

26

Round Table

True to his word, Merlinnus chose Gawen as one of the pages to serve at the Round Table, and so Gawen was let in with the twelve other boys who were to be personal messengers for the knights. They were dressed alike, in blue tunics colored with woad, soft camisias underneath, and leather breeches. They were each given a gold brooch shaped like a bear to wear at the neck.

"Thirteen be a wicked number," said Cook when he was told. Gawen had burbled about the appointment to everyone that morning while helping with the baking.

"Not in this case," Gawen replied, refusing to be cast down from the heights of delight.

"Mark my words," Cook answered back, lifting his long wooden stirring spoon like a stick of judgment, "summat bad will cum of it." Then he dipped the spoon into the soup he was making for supper and gave Gawen a taste.

"Needs thyme," said Gawen.

"So do ye, boy," said Cook, laughing. "So do ye."

WHEN THE GUARDS opened the doors to the Round Table room, the boys galloped in like colts let out to pasture. A bit shy, Gawen held back and thus was one of the very last to enter.

Though Gawen knew what to expect—having questioned all the boys and halved their answers—that first glimpse of the round hall and its great table was awesome. Gawen went in with the others to wait instructions from Kay. The boys were made mute by the place, their usual high spirits well contained. Hardly anyone spoke, and the few words they exchanged were in whispers.

What struck Gawen most about the place was the light that slanted through the high corbelled windows and coursed like blazons across the Round Table.

The table itself was painted with a pattern of lines radiating out of a central circle. Around the table's circumference were inscribed the names of the twenty-four knights, with Arthur's name at the place opposite the entrance to the room. On his left one place stood empty.

"The Siege Perilous," said Geoffrey, whispered in his gloomiest voice. "The Seat of Great Peril."

"No one," explained another boy, named Ciril, who had a wandering left eye, "no one can sit there who is not pure of heart." The eye notwithstanding, Ciril was a handsome boy, with the often astonishing golden beauty of the northern tribes.

"Have you sat in it?" Gawen asked them, both shyly and slyly, for certainly if any were pure of heart, these two boys were. They were both less than thirteen and though they had spent their years at Cadbury, they seemed to know very little.

"Do not even jest about that!" warned Ciril in a harsh whisper.

"Knights only," Geoffrey added. "In fact, only he who will be the Grail Knight dares sit there."

Gawen held up a hand and, in a quiet voice, stated, "I have no intention of going near the thing. I was just wondering."

At that moment Kay came in, dressed in striking red.

"There went a year's supply of madder root," whispered Geoffrey, and Kay glared at him.

The boys were silenced anew.

Stroking his mustache before beginning to speak,

Kay gave them each a long, slow look, then handed out their chores.

"Ciril—check with the master of swords to see that all are ready."

Ciril took off like a thrown spear.

"Mark, you must speak with Mistress Elaine to ensure that the bedchambers are prepared." Kay nodded at the boy, who was out of the room as quickly as Ciril.

One by one the others were sent away, and Gawen, the last of them, was told to remind Cook that the flagons of wine had not yet been sent up to the hall.

"White, red, Malmseyn, and the new Rumneye are all to be included," Kay said.

"Yes, my lord," Gawen said, making a quick bob toward the seneschal, winning a big grin.

BY THE TIME Gawen returned from the kitchen, where Cook had grumped about the reminder, the Companions were already seated around the table. None of them was as brilliantly dressed as Kay in his reds, favoring instead the plainer woad blues or the green from dyer's weed.

Gawen was disappointed, hoping to see some sort of parade, with drums and banners and shields and the hammer of spear butts pounding on the floor, the way it was done elsewhere when knights of a kingdom got together. This seemed no more than a meeting of fighting men, with bread and cheeses in wooden trenchers on the table before them and, soon after, the forgotten wine to keep their spirits up and their tempers down. Still, the glorious hall and the table itself lent a kind of majesty to them all.

Behind the Companions, on wooden benches set against the wall, were their personal servants and close relatives. Gawen knew very few of them yet, except for Gawaine, with his blandly handsome face, and his three brothers behind him. Their noses and cheekbones were the same, and they all had the knotted look on their faces of sailors or folk who lived by the sea. Another man, with bicolored eyes, sat with the boys. *A servant,* Gawen thought, *or a stepfather or perhaps an uncle.* He seemed to be keeping them still.

Then Gawen caught the eye of the man seated at Arthur's right, whose blazon was a large red heart. The man had a face of a fallen angel, both ugly and beautiful at the same time, with a sweep of dark hair that began with a long white streak at the widow's peak and went straight back, like an arrow.

For a moment Gawen and the man stared at each other.

As though he recognizes me, Gawen thought uneasily. *Knows me for who I am. But how can that be? We have never met.* Gawen glanced down to break the look between them, unable to bear the implied connection.

Just then Merlinnus swept into the room. The boys all leaped to their feet, as did the servants, though the Companions did not.

For the first time since Gawen had come to Cadbury, Merlinnus was in full wizard's garb. The black robe that Gawen had so carefully cleaned was now somehow spangled with strange stars, the sleeves lined with silver cloth. The mage wore a soft dark cap that covered his ears, and from the back of the cap a strand of golden orbs dangled.

"Magister," Arthur said and nodded.

"Majesty," the mage returned, bowing his head slowly.

The rest of the Companions nodded to him, too, but the mage seemed to ignore them. Sweeping around the table, he was silent until he was by Arthur's left hand, standing behind the Siege Perilous. Then for the first time he spoke to the knights. Gawen watched the whole as if it were a dumb show, thinking how Merlinnus was masterful in the way he played the part of mage.

"My lords," Merlinnus said, finally acknowledging them all by a single long look that was at once familiar and commanding.

The Companions stared back in silence.

Like a long, unwinding skein of yarn, the silence stretched on and on. It was Arthur who finally spoke, cutting the skein, knitting it up with easy familiarity. "Our mage has an interesting offer, my lords. Listen carefully. The fate of all Britain—for now and in the future—lies in this puzzle."

The knights, and the men and boys behind them, began a buzz of inquiry, which Merlinnus stopped by raising his hand. "I wager it is no surprise to any of you that there are some kingdoms and some lesser kings who do not count Arthur as their liege lord."

A number of the men turned to stare at Gawaine and his brothers behind him.

Merlinnus acted as if he noticed none of the accusatory looks, saying, "Some have indicated they want proof that Arthur is fit to sit on the throne of Uther Pendragon."

"Who says he is unfit?" An older, somewhat heavyset and homely knight stood, his eyes hooded.

"Lord Bedwyr," whispered Geoffrey on Gawen's left. "He has always been the king's true man."

The man with the fallen angel's face stood and drew his sword. This he carefully placed before him on the Round Table. Speaking in a low voice with the soft vowels of the Continent, he said, "I challenge any who would so say."

"Sir Lancelot du Lac," Geoffrey added helpfully.

Gawen thanked him with a nod.

The mage smiled and looked with steely eyes, first at Bedwyr, then at Lancelot, and both men sat down.

But before Lancelot sat, his eyes sought Gawen's again. This time it was the knight who looked away first.

Merlinnus began speaking again. "Do not draw swords against one another, my lords. Not in the chamber where you are brothers. Nor against the very tribes we would woo. Instead, Arthur will offer each and every man in each and every tribe in the kingdom the same chance to be High King."

"Who ... ?"

"How ... ?"

"What ... ?"

The room blazed with sudden consternation.

"What *nonsense* is this?" Bedwyr was back on his feet. "I have no wish to be king. I follow Arthur and am satisfied." His round face was flushed.

"And I!" Lancelot was standing again.

"And I!"

"And I!"

All around the table, men rose. Some quickly, like Gawaine, some more slowly. But in the end they were all standing, shouting their loyalties into the close air.

Arthur alone remained seated. But he put his hand up and drew their silence to him. "For the sake of Jesu," he said, "listen to the whole before you rush in to save my honor." Then he did a very strange thing. He winked at Merlinnus.

Merlinnus smiled.

"Sit down, my friends, my Companions. Sit." Arthur's voice pulled the knights back into their seats, though it was another minute before the room was settled enough for Merlinnus to begin again.

"My lords," the mage said, "as many of you already know, there has come to us, through some mysterious work of magic, a sword known as Caliburnus that is set in a stone."

This startled Gawen. *When had the sword acquired a name?* Then, smiling at the subtle genius of it, Gawen listened further.

Merlinnus continued, "It is as if the blade has pierced the very heart of Britain." A murmur crept around the room, like the shadow of speech, only no words could be discerned. Ignoring the murmur, Merlinnus went on. "Only one man in all of our island can be the surgeon to remove that blade without splitting the stone in twain. I am convinced that man is Arthur. However"—and here he raised the point finger on his right hand dramatically—"however, if there is some other man or boy who can do the deed, I swear that I will follow him instead. And to him I will pledge all my magicks."

"And I will follow him as well," said Arthur. "With all my heart."

"What if the Witch of the North draws the sword?" cried Bedwyr. "She may be a woman, but she has the heart of a man. What if she can somehow change this sword and this stone so that one of her own brood can draw it out?"

Agravaine was on his feet before Hwyll or Gawaine could caution him. In a voice still harsh from the blow his brother had given him, he cried, "Beware how you speak of my mother, old man."

But Arthur, too, had risen. "If *any* of King Lot's sons can draw the sword, I will pledge them my kingdom and my life. They have as much right to try as any."

"Maybe more," Agravaine cried harshly, but at Hwyll's urging, he settled back down on the bench, unaware of the blaze across his older brother's cheeks that bespoke deep shame and embarrassment.

Arthur turned and spoke directly to Agravaine. "Maybe more, indeed," he told the boy. "I have never denied it, sir."

Agravaine looked stunned at the public admission, his mouth agape. His eyes, Gawen thought, seemed to offer some sort of pledge to the king, though his mouth did not.

"How do we know this is not a trick sent by an enemy, to divide us one from the other, to separate us from our true king, Arthur?" Sir Lancelot asked, and Arthur turned to face him.

"I have asked the same, my dearest Companion," Arthur said. "And Merlinnus has assured me this is true magic, a test, for the good of Britain." He turned and nodded at the mage, who stared back at him without moving, then the king sat.

As soon as Arthur was in his seat again, Merlinnus pushed the Siege Perilous to one side and bellied up to the table. He rolled up his right sleeve so that the silver cloth showed. Then he made a fist of his right hand and the veins popped up like old meandering rivers down his wrist, disappearing into the folds of cloth.

"Who rules Britain must have strength of arm more than the blood of kings." Merlinnus banged his fist on the Round Table and Gawen jumped at the sound. "What do the Highlander Scotti care if our king's blood is Uther's? Or Vortigern's? Or Lot's? Think of the dark little Picts—who is Uther to them? What Saxon will bend the knee to Lot's kin? Yet they will *all* follow power."

The men at the table mumbled to one another, and the word *power* was heard often. Merlinnus waited until they ran out of breath.

"So the king offers this trial to *all* the men of Britain," Merlinnus said. "Whosoever...*whosoever* shall pull the sword Caliburnus from the stone by the summer Solstice, that time of potent magic, he *shall* be king of all Britain."

The silence that greeted this pronouncement was enormous. It filled the hall.

Merlin raised a forefinger. "In one month's time, my lords. The sword from the stone."

"So say I," Arthur boomed.

"So say all of us," the men agreed.

And so it was done.

27

Doves

 MORGAUSE SENT WORD by a messenger who carried the doves across water and land. He was three weeks traveling to Cadbury.

Her assassin met the messenger from the Orkneys in a small inn on the far side of the valley. It was long after dark, and the sky was clouded over so there was neither moon nor star showing.

The best kind of night for such work, the assassin thought.

Dank and squat, the inn was scarcely more than a thatched hovel, with a surprisingly large stable for horses.

Clearly the horses slept better here than any travelers.

The two men met as prearranged, in one of the empty stalls, the messenger carrying a lantern. In the next stall but one was a roan gelding that whickered softly when they entered, expecting something to eat. It was soon disappointed, for they did not even notice it was there.

"Have you got them?" Morgause's man asked.

"The doos? Aye." Brushing slate grey hair out of his eyes and grinning, the messenger displayed a mouth full of old soldiers, teeth that were worn down from ill-usage. He settled the lantern on the door casing of the empty stall and pointed inward, farther than where the light illuminated. "They be there, master."

Morgause's man could see nothing, but he had no reason to distrust the messenger.

"All three of them?"

"Aye."

"Show me."

They walked into the stable, and against the wall was a small cage in which the doves nested.

"Are they healthy?"

"Aye." The man was closemouthed, which was good. The queen demanded such in her messengers.

"Did Queen Morgause give you ought else for me?"

It is, the assassin thought, *like pulling this man's worn teeth to get answers from him.*

The messenger licked his lips, then said, "Oh, aye."

"Well, out with it, man!"

"She said that ye maun do what maun be done." It was a large speech for him. He held out his hand, palm up. Even in the shadows it was possible to see how begrimed the hand was, how splayed the fingers. The hand remained out. Clearly he was expecting further payment than what the queen had already given.

"That I will." Before the messenger realized what was coming, Morgause's man had stuck a knife into his belly and ripped upwards, well past the heart. It was certainly easier than killing the boy, Will, had been. And less messy.

The messenger fell back, striking his head on the wall, which set the doves to gabbling.

"Hush, hush, my wee doos," whispered Morgause's man. "Dinna fesh yersel's." He spoke in the tongue of his mother. "Tha wilna be hurt. Hush. Hush." All the while he was drawing the knife from the messenger's body and wiping the blade on the dead man's coat. Then he covered the corpse with straw.

It will buy a little time, he told himself. A little time was all he needed to be gone from there back to Cadbury.

Taking the cage with the three grey doves, he slipped out of the barn, found his horse, and headed to the castle by going in a large circle and thus disguising his retreat should anyone in the inn be watching.

No one was.

In a copse not far from the castle, he took out three small cloth packets from his coat. They contained the messages he had already written to the queen. Quickly he affixed the packets to the right leg of each dove, with hammered steel wire.

Then, one by one, he took the doves from the cage, gave them each a soft kiss on the head, and tossed them into the air.

After such a long trip in a cage, they needed little urging. Circling the copse several times, the doves got their bearings, and then headed north.

North toward the Orkneys.

North toward home.

One at least, he thought, *should get through.*

He then broke the cage into pieces that he threw into the river, remounted, and rode back to Cadbury, arriving well before dawn. The guards were used to his midnight forays. They thought he had a woman in one of the farms nearby, and he had encouraged this belief. He was smiling as he went through the gates.

"Good night, sir?" asked one of the guards, a bit too familiarly.

"A very good night," he said. As indeed it had been.

THE FIRST DOVE settled to roost on a low willow branch in a small wood by a running stream. It shook itself all over, preened its breast a bit, and had just tucked its head under its wing when a poacher's net fell across its shoulders.

A thin hand caught the net up and wrung the dove's neck.

When the poacher's wife began cleaning the bird, she found the packet attached to its leg.

Since neither she nor her man could read or write, the message meant nothing to them. But they buried the packet and the wire and the message without telling a soul. After all, just catching a bird in the earl's wood could bring them their deaths.

Still, the dove was the tastiest thing they'd had to eat in a long while. The following day, their children enjoyed the thin soup made from the bird's bones.

THE SECOND DOVE was nearing the north coast of Scotland when a pigeon hawk in a perilous stoop caught it from above.

There was an explosion of feathers.

The hawk carried its prey back to its nest and its hungry nestlings deep in a tangled wood.

The packet and chain, befouled and torn, became part of the nest, which—when it was deserted—fell to pieces in an awful lightning storm. It would be centuries before that particular woodland was cleared.

THE THIRD DOVE made the crossing to Orkney without incident. If near-starvation is not counted as an incident.

It arrived bedraggled and half dead at the door of the little doocoot the queen kept in her tower window.

Eagerly, Morgause cut the packet from the bird's leg and settled it in with the others. Then she went to the table to read the message by the light of a candle.

The dove's companions quickly pecked it to death, because it did not smell or act like a healthy bird.

The queen did not notice. She was too busy reading the message the dove had brought from so far away. As she read, she twined her long fingers through her dark hair and her lips moved as if she were eating the words as she read.

"Merlinnus has conceived a sword stuck in a stone like a knife in cheese. He denies involvement, but who else could have made the thing? The legend on it reads that whosoever pulls the sword out will be king of Britain. Arthur pledges it. 'Whosoever.' The date to end the trials is the Solstice."

She smiled, serpent and beautiful woman at the same time. "Well, well, well," she said in a surprisingly sweet voice. Dropping the message onto the table, which was littered with fresh tansy and coltsfoot, she repeated what she had just said. "Well, well, well. So that was what I saw in the water—sword and stone. And the thing to be drawn out by the Solstice. When magic is doubled, and passions, also. Well, well, well."

Then she stood up and began to dance around the room, her linen skirts billowing out around her. For a moment she looked like a girl.

"Merlinnus has made a fatal misstep." She stopped dancing, caught her breath, and laughed. Suddenly the sweetness was revealed to be sour as unripe fruit. "I will remove this sword from this stone, and with it I will make my son High King." She cocked her head to one side as if hearing the sword sliding from its stone sheath. "And take the heads of Arthur and his pet mage at the same time." Then, frowning so hard her forehead became furrowed like a field, she thought, *The Solstice. It is but days away. Three weeks and more lost. So little time.*

She crushed the message in her hand, whispered a word of dismissal, then opened the hand slowly, palm toward the ceiling.

Her hand was empty except for a tiny bit of ash.

28

Hand to the Sword

THAT SAME DAY, far to the south, Gawen sat with the mage and the king around the long oak table, on which about a dozen scrolls lay half unrolled and unread. A kind of light still illumined the sky, a surly blue grey that promised fog, if not rain, in the morning.

Gawen had to work hard at listening to the conversation and not yawn. Kay had not been the only one to stay up nights guarding the king's door. Gawen had staked out a watching post down the hall the past three weeks since the thief had tried to kill the king. Those nights had taken their toll.

"When can I draw the sword, this Caliburnus?" the

king was asking. "The thing has been in the courtyard for weeks now."

Merlinnus sighed and looked over at Gawen. "Tell him, boy."

Gawen tried to reconstruct the conversation and failed, and looked blankly at the wizard.

"Tell him," Merlinnus said carefully, "why he must wait till the night of the Solstice to put his hand to the sword. And not just because it is that most potent of eves."

This, at least, Gawen knew, and leaning forward, said, "Sire, you must wait till the others have all had a go at the sword, or there will be many who will say you shortened their time, compromised the test." *Surely that is the answer Merlinnus wants!* Gawen thought.

"'*Compromised*' it? How, for the Lord's sake?" Arthur's right hand balled into a fist and he struck the table hard. Two of the scrolls rolled off. "Everyone in the kingdom has been invited to try his hand. It is the waiting on them to actually come and do it that is driving me mad."

"Some have already tried," Merlinnus said calmly.

Arthur's lips twisted wryly. "Well, a farm boy or two. And a couple of Scotti warriors. And three Picts. Jesu, they are small men! But no one else. It has been three weeks. Why have they not come forward?"

Merlinnus did not answer but merely leaned over to fetch the scrolls back.

It was left for Gawen to say. "Your Majesty, perhaps the people do not yet believe it to be true."

"Of course it is true. I said it, did I not?" Arthur's voice was a growl.

"It is not what is true that matters here," Gawen answered, glancing at Merlinnus, "but what is *seen* to be true." The mage nodded. "Truth is a matter of perception."

Arthur's face suffused with color. "Truth is true. And not just"—now he spoke in a high voice, mimicking Gawen—"a matter of perception."

Merlinnus stood and came over to Arthur's chair. He put his hand into the bosom of his robe and pulled out a wineglass brimming over with Malmseyn. "Drink this, Arthur."

"I am not thirsty."

"Drink it."

"You are evading the question, old man."

"Drink it."

Arthur took the glass and put it to his lips and drank in a huge draft. "By the bull!" he cried, spitting out what he had drunk. "What is this?"

The glass was full of nothing more than red ribands, one of which was now sticking to his lips.

"If I had had you swear a moment before that the

glass was red with wine, would you have been speaking the truth?" Merlinnus asked.

"Yes," Arthur said begrudgingly. "As I knew it then. But—" He stopped abruptly. Then he roared at the mage, "But it would *not* have been true."

Merlinnus laughed. "You are going to be a great king, Arthur. Not because you know the truth, but because you act as if you do. However, I must caution you—be careful what you drink!" With a flick of his wrist, he made both glass and ribands disappear.

Gawen had watched silently and with great concentration but could not see where the old wizard had stashed the glass. Thinking it was better not to ask, Gawen turned back to the king. "Perhaps, Majesty, you need to issue an order, not an invitation."

"The boy has done it again," Arthur said, suddenly smiling, his face a pleasing landscape after a mighty storm has passed. "Simple, direct. None of your tricksy stuff, old man. I will simply *order* everyone to try."

"Shall I get us some real wine?" Gawen asked brightly, and was sent instead to the kitchen to fetch a pitcher of plain English ale and a slab of cheese.

LATER, accompanying Merlinnus up to the tower room, Gawen said, "I am puzzled, Magister."

"About the glass and the wine?"

"Yes, and about..."

"About truth."

Gawen nodded.

"And you believe, my boy, that there is such a thing?"

"Do you not, Magister? The priests say ..."

They had reached the top of the stairs. The old man fumbled with the keys and then spoke the words of power under his breath. The door creaked open sullenly.

Merlinnus turned and said quietly, "It is not what I *believe,* Gawen. It is what I *know.* There are many truths. A priest's truth may not be a king's truth. A king's truth may not be a kingdom's truth. And an old mage may be pardoned if he plays a trick or two to secure the peace."

He went in and shut the door behind him, leaving Gawen to ponder the fact that the old man had not really offered an answer at all.

IN THE MORNING Arthur commanded the Companions to come out to the churchyard and for each to put a hand on the sword. Word of it raced through the castle, and by the time the men were assembled, dressed as if for battle, it seemed everyone in Cadbury was there to watch. There were strangers there as well.

Arthur appeared pleased. The crowd was enormous.

"Who *are* all these people?" Gawen asked Merlinnus.

"All who would be king."

"I would not," Gawen said.

"No, not thee and not me," the mage said, smiling inwardly at the boy's earnestness. "But few else can make that claim."

"Surely not Sir Kay," Gawen said, nodding at Arthur's stepbrother, who was standing at the far end of the courtyard staring fixedly at the stone, his hand playing with his luxuriant mustache.

"Do not worry," said Merlinnus, putting a hand on the boy's head. "He has not the strength to be king."

Gawen turned his face up to the old man. "You do not mean strength of arm, Magister." It was a statement, not a question.

I do like this boy, Merlinnus thought. Then he walked into the center of the courtyard and held up his hand, satisfied by the quick silence his presence brought to the place. Arthur had asked him to tell the legend again, and he had practiced how he would say it, all morning, alone in his room.

"You have heard many things about this sword and this stone," he said, his voice as strong as a young man's. "But I will tell you the truth of it."

Or the perception of the truth.

Gawen and Arthur caught each other's eyes. Clearly they had had the same thought at the same time. Almost as if he heard those thoughts, Merlinnus looked first at the boy and then at the king.

"The truth of it," he said again, "is that whosoever can draw this sword from this stone will be *in truth* High King of all Britain."

"It is a trick!" a man called out. No one saw who, but the word bubbled and ran through the crowd like a rushing stream.

"It is no trick. Look you—here is the stone and here is the sword," Merlinnus said. "It is called Caliburnus and will belong to the man who pulls it free of its stone sheath." Merlinnus opened his arms wide. "And upon so doing, that man—*whosoever* he shall be—will become High King of all Britain."

"Who can try?" This time the speaker was Agravaine, as if he still did not believe what he had been told. He took a large step toward the stone, his hands trembling.

"Why, *you* can," said Merlinnus plainly, pointing to the stone. "Will you be first today?"

But shaking his head, Agravaine moved back until he was safely with his brothers and Hwyll again.

Once against the crowd was silent.

"By the rood, I will try," cried Sir Bors, a burly and sometimes surly man, with a large black beard that so covered his mouth, it was difficult to tell when he laughed and when he frowned. He stalked over to the stone, swept off his metal-covered leather cap, and set down his own long-bladed sword on the ground by the foot of the stone. "Not that I doubt your right, Arthur, to be High King. Not at all. I am *your* man. But someone has to try first, and why not me, eh?" He put his hand around the hilt, leaned forward, then back, hauling at the sword with a powerful tug.

It did not move.

"Ah," he said, and let go as if the hilt were a panhandle hot from the fire.

A mighty sigh ran around the crowd. Then a hush.

Bors picked up his helmet and sword and stepped away from the stone.

"Anyone else?" Merlinnus asked.

When no answer was returned, Arthur said in a tight voice, "Who will be next?"

Again no one came forward.

Arthur's jaw was set and he leaned slightly forward from the waist. "I command each of my knights to put a hand to the sword. *Now.*"

Lancelot walked briskly to the stone, where he carefully set his hand on the hilt of the sword. Then he took it off. He turned to the king. "Majesty, I have done exactly as you commanded. I have no wish to be king."

The other knights lined up and each did the same as Lancelot, setting a hand to the hilt and no more.

As they filed past Arthur, his face was almost purple with frustration. He did not even give his men a nod. As soon as the last had gone by, he walked back to the stone and set his own hand upon it as if it were a house-hold pet.

Pitching his voice so that everyone in the courtyard could hear, he said, "Think on it. You have one more week till the Solstice. One more week to try your hand at pulling the sword and becoming High King. I will have all of you try before then. And *that* is an order." He turned and marched back to the castle with Merlinnus right behind him. The knights followed but several long steps behind.

Gawen stayed on, watching as a few of the towns-men came close to the stone and examined it on all sides. One fair-haired boy, not more than seven years old, put his hand on the stone carefully, as if greeting some sort of wild dog. A pocked-faced farmer touched the hilt of the blade with his forefinger. His wife brushed away his fingerprints with her skirt and tugged him home.

But no one tried to pull the sword out.

No one.

At last they all left the churchyard, and Gawen re-turned to the mage's tower to give Merlinnus a report.

V

King's Hand/ Queen's Magic

The churchyard was deserted. The sun had burst full on the square and everything was bleached out in its light: church door, square, and the stone, now the color of the tops of waves. And the strange protuberance that stuck out from the stone, like a shaft of sunlight itself.

29

May Queens All

MORGAUSE GROUND the pestle into the stone mortar with a heavy hand. She had already finished the first potion and drunk it down, but that one had been easy, made up as it was of the basic herbs she kept hanging in her herb cupboard: tansy, sweet balm, a single petal of aconite, several kinds of mallow, the whole sweetened with fresh milk, the cream skimmed off from the top. It was a potion against poison and a bane against other wizards.

But *this* one was the more difficult spell, including not only a paste of black millet, the ground liver of an unbaptized child—from a babe delivered well before its time—and the primary feathers of a male gannet.

Plus, she had added the requisite herbs gathered at midnight and kept in her darkling cabinet against such a time and such a spell.

She pressed the pestle into the grey stone cup, sweat breaking out on her brow, though it was cool enough in the tower room. Wiping the sweat away with the rough sleeve of her gown—she did not dare stop long, as the grinding had to be finished before morning or she would need to start again—she forced herself to breathe evenly. There was danger should any sweat get into the cup. It might damage the spell. And any sense of being rushed would find its way into the magic, too, and that in its turn could change the thing as well.

It was already past midnight, the forearm of morning. The only sound in the room besides her own breathing and the press of stone pestle on stone mortar was the susurration of the sea. She found herself working the pestle to the rhythm of waves coming onto the shore. It was a comforting, familiar sound. A sound of home, of childhood, the few short years of joy before Merlinnus had spoiled it all.

Still, it was dangerous to think while doing this spell or much could go wrong. So she emptied her mind of all but the rhythm of sea and stone, grinding the dark materials over and over and over again.

Finally the grinding was done. A grey silt, about a knuckle deep, sat in the bottom of the mortar. Morgause had to drink the stuff down in a single draft, and milk would not do as it was animal matter. It would corrupt the liver.

Reaching for a pitcher of Malmseyn, she poured it into the mortar, adding a touch of new ale, and a half cup of springwater that had flowed over twenty-one stones. This mixture she stirred with a small silver hammer, saying all the while, "Thrice I stir with holy crook: one for God, one for Wod, and one for Lok."

She sniffed it. Foul and fair. Fair and foul. It reeked of power. She allowed herself a satisfied smile.

Raising the cup to her lips, she drank the potion all at once. The wine and ale and water made it palatable, but she had to breathe deeply so as not to throw up the concoction.

The liquid burned all the way down her throat. She could feel it settle uneasily in her belly. Cursing her weak stomach, she thought, *It is the boys who made me thus. I was never sick on a potion before having them. They changed me utterly.* Yet she did not entirely wish them gone. Not entirely. They had their uses.

Now she just had to wait till morning.

Meanwhile there was still much to do.

Into a tiny leather flask she poured a third potion, made the day before and left out in sun and wind and rain. She had had to call the rain, but that was not difficult. Rainmaking had always been one of her most dependable spells.

She fastened the flask around her neck with a silver chain, then took off all her clothes: the three-quarter-length outer gown first, then the ankle-length tunic, finally the softer camisia. Folding them neatly, she put them into the cupboard. She slipped out of her sandals. The stone floor was cold on her bare feet.

Taking a sprig of fresh yarrow, she brushed herself with it head to foot, all the while reciting the old Celtic charm:

> *"May I be a rock on land,*
> *May I be an island at sea,*
> *Wound can I every man,*
> *Wound can no man me."*

Then she looked around. All was done here. The wax image that lay on her bed would serve as her Other until she returned. She had given it soft eyes, a hard heart, and a bitter mouth, touched with another leaf of the aconite.

No one would miss her. No one would even know she was gone.

They might, she thought smiling wryly, prefer the wax image to the real thing.

Going outside, she unfastened the lock on the doocoot, leaving the door ajar. When it was morning, the doves would follow her lead. They had no choice, of course. Magic was a hard master and a strong persuader.

She looked up at the waning moon. It was yellow and old and pockmarked. "Selene," she prayed aloud, "speed my travels."

The wind ruffled her hair and raised small bumps on her skin with the cold. But she did not mind. The mixtures she had drunk down were warm inside her.

No—they were not just warm. They were hot. She was hot.

She was burning. With passion. With desire. With hate.

Burning.

Burning.

Burning.

Like the sun.

IN THE EARLY MORNING a large white gannet flew across the roiling green-black seas, and behind it followed five plump grey doves. They flew straight to the mainland, then across the thick forests, along the spines of high-ridged mountains, and over the cultivated fields of Britain without stopping.

No one wondered that a gannet was so far from the sea.

No one wondered at the five doves behind it.

No one saw anything but a cloud across the sun, dove grey and gannet white.

It was the same all the way to a small squat and dank inn not far from King Arthur's Cadbury. There gannet and doves fell like hawks in stoop, down to the bordering field, where they alighted full feathered, then arose as six naked women, high bosomed, small headed, with rounded hips, long hair, slim fingers, and short of utterance.

May Queens all.

30

At the Gate

FIVE DAYS had gone by and no one else had been seen trying the sword. But each morning when Gawen went out to look at the thing, the hilt was covered with fingerprints. There were big splayed prints and medium-sized whorls, and small finer prints all layered one atop another, as if some strange history had been written by a series of ghostly hands.

"I do not understand," Gawen said to Merlinnus as they sorted herbs up in the tower. "Why not pull the sword during the day when they can see what they are doing? When everyone can see and declare them king?"

Merlinnus did not even bother to look up from the

clear glass bottle he was holding over an orange flame. As the liquid inside turned first green, then brown, then clear, he shook his head and made a *tch* sound with his tongue against the roof of his mouth. "And let the world watch them fail?" He shook the glass.

"But, Magister, failure is only a way stop on the road to success," Gawen said.

"Who taught you that?" The wizard's voice was sharp, but a touch of laughter hid just beneath the surface.

"My . . . mother," Gawen said in a small voice.

"Of course," Merlinnus told him, "your mother."

"What do you mean?" Now it was Gawen's voice that held the challenge.

"Only women think that way," Merlinnus said. "And mages. Men think that failure unmans them. They do it at night. And alone." He muttered something indecipherable at the glass, then said, "Get me the tongs."

Gawen found the iron tongs under the table. Days earlier when questioned about the iron—for supposedly cold iron foxed fairies and witches—the old mage had said that such was superstitious nonsense. Gawen handed the tongs to Merlinnus. "How many knights do you think have tried the sword, then, Magister?"

"How many do you think live hereabouts?" Merlinnus answered, swirling the glass once more. The liquid remained clear.

"Even Kay? Even Bedwyr? Even Lancelot and Gawaine?"

"Especially them."

Gawen grabbed up a cloth that was hanging over a stool. "I do not believe you, Magister."

"It is better to know than to believe," said Merlinnus. He glared at the liquid, then dashed it into a stone bowl, where it slowly settled into something resembling clay.

"You mean I should see for myself," Gawen said, heading out the door, cloth in hand.

When Merlinnus turned around, he found himself alone in the room. "Humph," he snorted derisively. "And where is he going with that cloth?"

The mage went over to his scrying bowl. Pouring fresh water in it, he waited until the liquid had settled. At once a picture formed on the still surface: a clear sky, and crossing it, a gannet and five grey doves.

"What can this mean?" Merlinnus whispered to himself. He glanced up, as if expecting the picture to be less than magic, only a reflection of what was actually in the sky. But the sky was cloudless, and no birds were cleaving the air. He looked back at the scrying bowl. The water was empty. And dark.

But even that small amount of scrying left him exhausted. He lay down on his bed and fell into a troubled sleep.

———

WHERE GAWEN was going was down to the court-
yard. It was a brilliant late-spring day, three days before
the Solstice Eve, the sky bursting with lark song. Doves
in their soft grey coats lined the chapel roof, cooing as if
hoping for a downpour of bread crumbs. High above, a
large buzzard circled once, twice, then flew off north.

Gawen scrambled up onto the stone and with the
cloth began polishing the sword hilt. Up close and in
daylight, the runes on the hilt were almost readable. Yet
every time Gawen bent over to try to make out one sign
or another, each rune seemed to change, crawling along
the handle like a snake, or metamorphosing into another sign altogether.

Looking straight on at it makes my head hurt, Gawen
thought. Though squinting made the runes stop crawling, they never made any more sense.

"Bother," Gawen said aloud. *I've neither the magic
nor the learning to try to decipher them further.* That sort
of thing was best left to mages.

It was while Gawen was polishing the left side of
the handle that the gates to the inner courtyard suddenly opened. Not with the usual yells from the guard,
the noise of demands and passwords and identifica-
tions. This time the doors slid open silently, as if oiled.

Six unaccompanied ladies in grey-and-white feathery cloaks came through the gate.

Five of the women had long loops of golden hair

bound up with silver pins to the sides of their heads so that the loops looked almost like wings. The women were all equally lovely to look at, with complexions the color of cream skimmed from milk. But the sixth woman had black hair in tangled elf knots, a sharp straight nose, and a broad forehead, yet she was the one who drew the eye.

The guards at the gate seemed stupefied by the beauty of the six women. They bowed to them in awed silence and spread their cloaks on the ground so the women's little silver slippers would not be soiled by mud. Then they saluted the women with closed fists over their hearts and bowed a second and a third time.

As if this were not strange enough, Gawen watched as the women raised their dove grey skirts to step on the cloaks spread before them. The dark woman had small, ordinary feet; the other women seemed to have oddly shaped shoes, almost as if each foot had three large splayed toes.

Realizing how silly that appeared, how impossible, Gawen simply slid off the stone and—leaving the cloth behind—scuttled away to the tower to tell Merlinnus what had just occurred.

"THE NORTH QUEEN!" Merlinnus said. "Of course."

"'Of course'?" Gawen did not see how the old man could jump to such a conclusion.

"I saw a gannet and five doves in the scrying bowl." Merlinnus' face darkened, and he looked over at the water basin.

"They *flew* here?" Gawen asked.

Merlinnus gave a short, barking laugh. "Of course not. Such magicks are beyond even my skills," he said. "The scrying glass was a warning, that is all. But the North Queen and her women are here nonetheless. They will be exhausted by their travels. We must tell the king."

He went to his wardrobe and drew out his second-best robe, a white garment with runes in black and red scrawled along the collar and hem and around the sleeves at the wrists.

"Should I wear something different, too?" Gawen asked.

Merlinnus turned and considered Gawen for a moment, then he came over and brushed a hand over the top of Gawen's hair.

"You will do just as you are. Yes, indeed, you will do."

31

Queen/King/Mage

THEY WENT DOWN the stairs at a slow pace, to accommodate the mage's old bones, though Gawen wanted to run. Such news needed instant delivery.

When they got to the throne room, Gawen found that they were too late. The North Queen was already there, surrounded by her five ladies-in-waiting, still in their feathery cloaks. None of the waiting women looked particularly tired. Indeed their bland lovely faces were difficult to read. The dark queen's face, though, seemed drawn and grey, and her icy eyes were red-rimmed as if she had been weeping or had spent a long time being buffeted by a cold wind.

"Merlinnus," she said when she saw the mage, in a voice that held no warmth.

"Madam," he answered, nodding. If anything, his voice was cooler.

Arthur rose from his throne slowly, as if he ached all over. "Merlinnus, see who has come for a visit," he said in an overbright voice, like a child who has been up way too late. "I have sent for her boys."

Turning back to Arthur, Morgause smiled frostily. "I am not here for my boys, my lord, for they have but recently left my side. I have come to see you, for it has been years since we have had converse."

"Had converse"? Gawen thought. *She talks as if the words were written on ancient parchment. As if speaking to real people is beyond her. Or beneath her.*

Arthur laughed. "Converse away, then."

She opened her mouth, then closed it again.

"Madam," Merlinnus said quickly, "I doubt conversation alone brought you here."

"Ah, you believe that the vaunted delights of Cadbury have pulled me from my northern rockeries," she said.

Her women seemed to shake with silent laughter.

Gawen tried to parse her sentence and failed. Tried again. It did not sound as if she were making a compliment.

"'Vaunted,' madam?" Merlinnus said. "I thought

that word meant 'an ill-made boast.' The High King does not boast of Cadbury, though others might."

"My son Gawaine does the boasting, Magister. I travel to see if these are simple flatteries or gross exaggerations."

Arthur held out a hand and drew her to the fire. "And what have you decided, my lady?"

"That my Gawaine is still a boy and prone to youthful exuberances." She smiled up at him, but it was a cold smile.

"I...am...a boy...madam, and new come to Cadbury," Gawen ventured a bit timidly at first, then with growing heat. "And there is much to boast of here. Though it is the people more than the stones that make this place what it is."

Morgause turned and stared at Gawen. "Who is this little kettle making so much noise? Hot air creates steam, I suppose."

"He is mine," said Merlinnus, "and makes much sense. It is one of his finest virtues."

"And he is mine as well," Arthur said, moving over to Gawen and setting a hand on Gawen's golden cap of hair. "An adviser of note." He winked.

"Boys and old men for advisers." Morgause laughed. "And I expect a May Queen or two for sport. My, my, this is a boy's dream of paradise. No wonder Gawaine prefers it to ruling his cold kingdom."

Just then Kay came in, shepherding Morgause's sons.

"Mother!" Gawaine said, his voice accusatory. "What are you doing here?"

"Perhaps I have come to take you home," she said, tangling a hand in her black hair.

"No!"

"Or perhaps I have come to make this *my* home."

Gawaine had no answer for this, but there was clear horror in his gaze.

The twins ran to her side to hug her, and she brushed them off as if they were overeager puppies with muddy paws. Gareth laughed and still grabbed for her fingers, but Gaheris stood to one side, looking a bit wounded.

She walked away from them, shaking out her skirts, then turned directly to Agravaine and held out her arms. "No kiss for Mother?"

He walked stiffly to her side and let himself be enfolded in her arms.

Speaking over his head, Morgause addressed Kay. "I wish to sleep now. I expect you have rooms that can be readied for my ladies and me. Do not disturb us till evening. Do not even *think* of disturbing us till evening."

Kay bowed grandly, then led the women out of the hall.

———

THE MINUTE they were gone, Arthur said, "Who was that force of nature?" Then he laughed uncomfortably.

"Mother is a whirlwind that wrecks every spit of land she touches," Gawaine said miserably.

"How can you say that?" Agravaine asked. "She is astonishing and beautiful and—"

"She has bewitched you again," Gawaine said. "Can you not see it? Can you not feel it? One embrace, and you are hers."

The twins had withdrawn to a corner of the room and were speaking together, clearly comforting each other, salving wounds only they could see.

"There will be no bewitching going on here," Merlinnus said, striking his left palm with his right middle finger as if it were a lance striking a shield. "Not while I am mage. Now go, all of you." He dismissed them with a wave of his hand. "Practice your swordsmanship. Or your bowmanship. Or something. Only go away."

As the last of the boys disappeared out the door, he turned to the king. "This is a disaster."

"This is a state visit," Arthur said. "A queen coming to visit a king."

Merlinnus shook his head.

Arthur tried again. "She is just a foolish woman hungering for a higher throne for her boys." He adjusted the cushion on his chair and sat down heavily.

"You do not believe either of those things." Merlinnus came up close. "You *cannot* believe them."

Arthur looked up, his grey eyes somewhat cloudy, like the skies after spring rains. "I can hope, though."

"We must think what to do." The mage shook his head. "Coming here three days before the eve of the Solstice—do you suppose she knows?"

"Of course she knows. We were careful to tell *every-one* in the kingdom. She could have learned about it at a dozen stops along the way here." Arthur twisted once more, as if the throne of the High King were suddenly the most uncomfortable seat in the world. "And she will want one of her boys to pull that sword."

Merlin nodded.

Arthur leaned forward. "Can they?"

"I do not believe so."

He grabbed Merlinnus by the sleeve and drew him close. "You do not *believe* so? Or you *know* so?"

Merlinnus patted Arthur's hand. "We will see."

Arthur let go of the mage's sleeves and put his head in his hands. "You are right. This *is* a disaster."

Merlinnus drew himself up so that he seemed to tower over the king, over the throne. "I will not let it be so," he said sternly. "She is only a woman, a witch, not a mage. I promise you, Arthur, her magicks will not conquer mine." Then, with his robes swirling about him—so that the runes seemed to be sending an un-readable message—the mage left the room.

Head in hands still, Arthur did not watch him go.

A WHILE LATER Kay returned to the throne room and Arthur was still there, head in hands.

"Arthur, is it my fault?" Kay said softly.

The king looked up, his face puzzled, muzzled, softened as if in pain. "Is what your fault?"

"I wrote to the queen and told her about Agravaine, when he tried to throttle Brother Josephus. When we had to put him in the dungeon." Kay's hands wrangled together. "It is my fault for telling her. She is here be-cause—"

Arthur's face creased with laughter. "Do not take this on your own shoulders, Kay. Your letter could not have gotten there in time. Think on it, man. When did you send it?"

"Soon after...after..." Kay counted the days.

"She could not have gotten your missive, much less packed up five women and traveled here so quickly." Arthur put a hand out to his stepbrother. "She has had this trip planned all along."

Relief camped on Kay's brow, smoothing out the wrinkles. "Oh, Arthur, how I dreaded telling you..."

"Never fear me, Kay. You know all my secrets."

"All?" Kay doubted that, but it was comforting to hear it from Arthur's lips anyway.

"All," Arthur said, and smiled.

MERLINNUS WENT FIRST to the grove, crossing the heaved-up path with little care. Speed was of the essence, and what was a turned ankle to the calamity before them?

When he got to his oak, he was out of breath and so his greeting was a bit broken. *"Salve, amice ... frondifer."*

The leaves were still.

"She is here, the North Witch, and with her comes a dark magic I cannot pierce. I see now she can change shape, or shape changes, more than I was aware. Have I grown too old? He held out his hands to the tree in supplication. There were liver-colored spots on the backs of his hands, more so than even the day before, and his nails were cracked and yellow. "Too old too soon?"

Now a wind puzzled through the oak leaves, and they shivered and shuddered.

"Yes, thank you, *e glande nate,* sprout of an acorn, I will go to the tower and see what I can do to soften this blow. To strengthen the stone. To put steel into Arthur's purpose."

The leaves seemed to laugh at him.

"Then will it be a woman who brings down

Cadbury in its prime? A woman who wrecks the Round Table and scatters the Companions? Oh, *amice frondifer,* what weapons do I have against a woman's wiles? Tell me it is not so."

But now the leaves were still again.

Merlinnus wept hot and bitter tears as if he were a child. Then he snuffled and dried his eyes on the hem of his robe before going back to the castle.

IN THE TOWER ROOM Gawen waited for the old man to return.

If only I had some magic, Gawen thought, holding up small and slim-fingered hands. *If only there were a miracle in these fingertips.* Only magic—not honor, not honesty, not truth or glory, Gawen was certain—could defeat the queen.

Going to the four windows, Gawen looked out to the compass points. Away to the north there, if one could see far enough across the water, was the North Queen's abode. *She has a heart as cold as her land. And as bleak.*

Turning from the north window to the south, as Merlinnus often did, Gawen saw that the corn already shone like gold in the fields. Here the turnips were just greening. Cows in their pastures moved like slow ships over a green sea. It was a pleasant land, a rich land, a land where no one would starve. *Do not let this woman ruin our king, our land,* Gawen prayed.

Going to the east window, Gawen checked on the river like a grey riband twisting past the walls of Cadbury. *If only I could bind her with a riband of steel and throw her into the dungeon.*

Gawen was about to go to the west window when the door opened and an exhausted-looking Merlinnus came in.

"Magister," Gawen whispered. "You look—"

"Never mind how I look," the mage said. "We have much work to do, and only while she sleeps may we do it." He rolled up the sleeves of his white robe. "Let us begin."

"Begin what, Magister?" Gawen asked.

"Begin work on a spell of protection," Merlinnus said, his hand shaking visibly as he passed it through the candle smoke for purification.

"Against what?" Gawen asked.

"Against theft of soul, assassination, shape change. Against everything," the old man said.

"Everything" is a very big order, Gawen thought. *I wonder if even Merlinnus can do such a thing.*

32

The Great Dinner

THAT EVENING WAS to have been a grand dinner as part of the last three days before Solstice Eve. The May Queen's next-to-last official duty included reigning at the affair.

Kay had explained all this to the boys days earlier, as they were to help the kitchen staff both with the serving and with the clearing-away.

But now, with the Orkney queen's arrival and five extra women, things had to change.

"One—the seating must be rearranged," Kay said, counting on his fingers. "Two—the menu has to be expanded. Three—a larger tun of wine has to be breached." He was about to go further, till he saw Arthur yawn.

"Just do it, Kay; do not bother me with the details."

Kay was outraged and pleased at the same time. His reaction to change was always to make more changes. But he wanted some appreciation for his hard work.

"Arthur, you do not understand," he said, moving on to the fourth finger. "We were originally to dine in the table room, though not, of course, *on* the table."

"Of course not," Arthur responded automatically.

"But that is too small now, so it will have to be the throne room. The vaulted ceiling should be impressive to the queen and—"

"She has seen the vaulted ceiling already." It was clear Arthur was trying to keep the boredom out of his voice, but Kay ignored it.

"And an awed emissary is—"

Arthur sighed. "Already half won over. Yes, I remember the old man's teachings, too, Kay. Now, I mean it—*go!*"

Kay went down to the kitchens, but if he was in a swivet, the kitchens were in an uproar. Cook was howling out orders, all the ovens were ablaze at once, whole pigs roasted merrily on spits in the giant hearths, and even the dog boy and the ostlers had been pressed into kitchen service.

"Cook!" Kay shouted above the hurly. "I need to tell you what has been changed. One—the seating must be..."

BY DINNER, the hurly had calmed and the throne room had been turned into a fine dining hall.

The Companions were shown to the long wooden tables in the center of the hall, where food was piled high. The ladies, dressed in white and green like the fey, were already seated, and the men jostled to sit by them, except for Lancelot and Gawaine, both of whom held back.

At a second and equally long table all of the outland contenders for the sword had been placed, for they had been arriving by the twos and threes all week long. Among them were seven Highlanders, each wrapped in a cloth that had dark stripes running both up-and-down and sideways. Then there were seven men who had sailed from Eire, wearing bonnets with feathers. Each of them stood taller than the tallest of the Companions, and they called themselves Fenians. A half-dozen old soldiers loyal to the Emperor Lucerius, and still in their Roman armor, were drunk already and asking for more wine. Several minor tribal kings, a half-dozen small dark Picts, and two barons who did not support Arthur had arrived only the day before. A contingent of rough-looking Saxon fighting men with their chieftain—they were known as federates—sat uneasily on one side of the table. And there were also an assortment of farm lads with bunched muscles and shocks of corn-colored hair, as well as one dark-eyed smith, with brows singed off from the smithy flames.

The pages and the knights' retinues all sat well below the salt, at the far end of both of the tables, close to the door, where they could help serve when needed.

On a dais, at a separate table, sat Arthur, with Queen Morgause at his right and Merlinnus at his left. None of them looked particularly comfortable.

Morgause was all in black, except for a heavy gold torque at her neck, gold bobs in the shape of lionesses dangling from her ears, and a simple gold fillet at her brow. She also had thirteen gold bands around her bare arms, six on her left and seven on her right. She was radiant and still.

In contrast, the king seemed unable to sit quietly. He constantly turned his head toward Merlinnus, then Morgause, as if his head were on a string, nodding left, nodding right, nodding left again. He was not laughing.

Gawen thought that Merlinnus looked like he had been washed out in a cold stream. They had worked on the protection spell right up to the moment of the dinner. But even the old mage had not predicted success with his usual certainty. All he had said was, "God is on our side." When Gawen had asked which God, Merlinnus had smiled wanly. "With luck—all of them."

"May Queens," muttered Geoffrey, speaking as though enchanted. "Do you not think so?"

"What?" Gawen had no idea what he was talking about.

"The queen's women. Beautiful May Queens."

"Are they intelligent? Do they have skills? Can they converse on matters other than embroidery?" Gawen asked in return.

"Does it matter?" Geoffrey obviously did not think so.

They hardly spoke, those soft-looking ladies, though every once in a while one would coo something to the Companions next to her. And the men sat transfixed, as if they had been bespelled.

The only woman who seemed left out of the gaiety was the actual May Queen, the pig farmer's daughter, who was to rule till the Solstice morn. Next to the bright, polished beauty of the cooing women, she appeared ordinary, stunted, even uncouth. She was ignored in these final moments of her reign, and she did not giggle a bit. Indeed, she did not even smile. She lasted through the first three courses and then abruptly left, tears making dark runnels down her cheeks.

Gawen was disgusted and would have left then, too, but Morgause suddenly laughed out loud, her head thrown back and the dark curls tumbling onto her shoulders, spilling down her back, like an enormous wave. The sound of her laugh was like a bell signaling danger.

"What do you suppose she has to laugh at?" Gawen asked Ciril, who was sitting closer to the king's table by a single chair.

Ciril turned his handsome face toward Gawen, and the wandering eye stared off into space. "Who do you mean? Dead Lot's bitch?"

Someone's hand came down hard on Ciril's shoulder.

"Be careful what you say about my mother and father." Agravaine shoved in between the two and, in a single practiced movement, took Gawen's trencher and cup for his own. Then he turned and set his face close to Ciril's, so close their noses were touching. "Or I will make your right eye go where the left eye has already flown."

"I . . . I will," Ciril began, though his eyes teared up and he looked down at his trencher.

Just then Arthur held up his hand and a hush descended on the hall. Standing, he raised his cup, a deeply engraved chalice.

"More of that awful Malmseyn, I bet," muttered

Agravaine, glaring into the cup that up to that moment had been Gawen's. "My father would not have had such piss at the table. I spit on a king who has such bad taste." He held the cup up but did not, in fact, spit.

Gawen wondered what had happened to the Agravaine who had been awed by the king. The Agravaine who was the king's own man.

His mother has happened to him, Gawen thought suddenly. *He wants to please her more than he wants to please Arthur.* Gawen wondered what this said about power and who controlled it now, and worried that there was no way to tell Merlinnus immediately.

"To the beauteous Morgause, mother of sons and dowager queen of the north," Arthur said, his cup held high.

A low murmur fluttered around the room, which was almost—though not quite—a protest, as if some of the knights did not want to praise the North Queen. Then everyone drank down a draft as a toast. They drank not so much *to* the queen—whom most hated and feared in equal measure—but because their king asked for it. And because the beautiful cooing women among them seemed to be demanding it, too.

Morgause's sons drank to her as well. Agravaine, with his stolen cup, and the twins, sharing a single vessel. Gawaine—who sat far from any of the May Queens—

drank, too, though he did not look happy at the thought of the toast.

Of all in the room—king, mage, princes, waiting women, boys, servers, and servants—only Gawen did not drink to the queen's health. Gawen no longer had a cup to drink with.

33

Curses

THAT NIGHT, everyone in the castle slept deeply and with a single dream, a dream of the North Queen sitting behind the High King's great throne.

All slept except Morgause, who got up, leaving her five waiting women abed. Draping a red cloak across her shoulders, she crept down the stairs and into the courtyard. There she stood, gazing at the stone with its sword pointing hilt upward toward the stars, saying nothing and making no sound.

All in the castle slept more deeply still, and with a single dream, now a dream of King Lot astride the High King's throne, his bones showing through his skin.

All slept except Gawen, who alone had not drunk the toast because of the goblet Agravaine had taken from him, along with his trencher. So Gawen alone of Cadbury had not been ensorcelled by the magic potion that had been poured into the Malmseyn by one of the cooing women at the behest of her queen. A potion that, as it was only a deep-sleeping draft, had not been deflected by Merlinnus' vast protection spell.

Standing rock still, hidden in a doorway across from the churchyard, Gawen watched as Morgause went around and around the stone, looking at it from every conceivable angle. She stood on tiptoe and crawled on her knees. She examined the stone top and bottom, side to side.

Twice she put her hand out toward the hilt of the sword as if preparing to pull it out herself. Twice she drew her hand back. The third time, she dared. But when her hand touched the hilt, sparks flew up, bright embers of magic, and she could not take hold.

"Well, well, well," she said, loud enough for Gawen to hear her.

Then she picked up the cloth that Gawen had dropped and wiped her right hand with it. Scrubbed away at her palm, as if to erase any of the mage's fire there. Finally, she held out that hand and something snaked from her fingers, some dark nimbus, some twisted, smoky thing. It curled up and over the stone, crawled to the sword, embraced the hilt, erased for a moment the runes along its face. Then it ran along the underside, the sharp edge of the blade, as if trying to blunt the thing. But the blade held its edge, and the smoke was halved, cut in two, lengthwise.

At the cut the North Queen shivered and let out a cry, like some small animal—a coney or a shrew. She lifted her hand higher, and the smoke reformed, left the blade's edge, crept down from the stone, and crawled up the front of her black dress till it found her hand again. There it settled and disappeared into her palm.

All this Gawen saw but was careful not to move or to make a sound. And the queen was so sure of her magicks that she did not think anyone was awake to watch, so she did not look around to see. Instead she did a strange little dance, a kind of dark exaltation, her arms waving over her head, and her feet drumming the ground. Then she turned and went back into the keep.

Watching still, Gawen saw triumph and exhaustion warring on her face and wondered which one would win.

WAITING UNTIL the queen was many minutes gone, Gawen finally ran up to the tower room, boots off so there would be no noise.

The old man was still asleep.

Plucking a candlestick from the table and lighting the beeswax candle from the embers of the hearth fire, Gawen went over to the mage's pallet and stared down at him. Merlinnus was never such a quiet sleeper. Normally the old man snorted and sighed and snored throughout the night; he kicked off his coverlet and drooled.

Either Merlinnus was ensorcelled, or he was dead. Gawen touched the old man's hand.

It was warm.

Not dead, then.

So Gawen backed carefully through the door and ran down the stone stairs to the king's chamber, expecting any minute to be challenged.

But the guards were asleep on their feet, and as deeply as the mage had been, like characters in a children's tale. Gawen passed the candle before their closed eyes. Pinched their cheeks. Tweaked their noses. Still they did not move.

"Forgive me, sire," Gawen whispered, and pushed through the chamber door. The terrible groaning of the hinges wakened neither the standing guards nor Arthur, asleep on his canopied bed.

Going over to the bed, Gawen held the candle over the king's face. Arthur's sandy hair was ashen in the light, his cheeks the color of carved stone. The shadows the candle threw made him look as if he lay on a draped catafalque, hands crossed over his broad chest, ready for a king's funeral.

Gawen passed a finger beneath Arthur's nose, reassured by the breath of life there. Yet not fully reassured. Arthur stilled was not Arthur, for his power lay in movement, his beauty in the mobility of his face. Without motion he was a stranger.

In this bed, in this light, Gawen thought, *he looks... ordinary.* It hurt to think so, for Gawen had known, from the moment of meeting the king, that Arthur was anything but ordinary. That he was larger than life. That he was life itself. And that to serve him, to be part of his story, was to be in both a whirlwind and a safe harbor, at one and the same time.

Yet here Arthur was, dreaming what everyone else was dreaming. At least that was what Gawen guessed. *And if one dreams what every man dreams, that is the very definition of ordinary.*

"What should I do?" Gawen whispered to the sleeping stranger. "If this were not magic, I would shake you and you would wake and ask me what I was doing in your chamber. I would tell you of the queen's treason, and you would leap from the bed and grab up your sword and strike her head from her shoulders." Gawen was not certain of this last. Arthur had too good a heart to strike without warning, certainly not to strike a woman. He was known to be a just king, a kind man, and honorable. There would surely be a trial, a wise judgment on the king's part; possibly Morgause would be put into a prison, in a nunnery perhaps. She would hate it there, of course, which would be the point.

"But this is magic," Gawen went on. "And I do not know if this enchantment needs a potion, a powder, a spell, or..." A small hesitation. "Or a kiss to end it."

The king slept on.

His guards slept on.

Gawen stood, candle in hand, watching over the sleeping king till the first cock crowed. At the sound, Arthur suddenly began to stretch and mutter. Gawen blew out the stub of the candle and raced from the room, leaving a tail of smoke behind.

GAWEN RAN BACK up to the tower where Merlinnus, too, was waking.

"Magister..."

Merlinnus stared at him, muzzy and unfocused. Then, when the wizard was wholly awake, the whole night's adventure tumbled from Gawen's lips.

The old man was strangely unmoved by the story. "Only a sleeping potion? That makes no sense," he stated bluntly. "And am I not awake? Is not the entire castle awake? No, boy, what you have seen is the triumph of my protection spell. As to the deep sleep, why, we just drank too much wine last night and celebrated too much, and far too long and . . ." He rubbed his hand over his white cockscomb hair and held out a hand that trembled like a leaf in the fall.

"But, Magister, celebrated what?"

"Why, we celebrated . . ." Merlinnus stopped, looking puzzled. Then he shut his eyes firmly. "I must be getting old."

"Too old to remember, Magister?" Gawen asked.

The shuttered eyes snapped open and they were an icy blue. "Too old to recognize an ensorcellment when it lies as heavy on my shoulders as a besom's shawl," the mage said. He went to his cupboard and brought out a vial of a green liquid. Holding his nose, he gulped the contents down noisily, then went over to the slops closet, where he knelt by the basin. "Boy," he whispered hoarsely, "the gods were right to send you here."

"Which gods do you mean?" Gawen asked mischievously.

Not having retched up the liquid, Merlinnus stood, then ran a hand down his robe to smooth it out. "All of them." He snapped his fingers and his hair fell back into place without need of a comb. "Come, boy, we have much work to do."

"Again," Gawen said, but was quietly delighted that the old man seemed to have recovered his wits and his humor.

34

Confessions

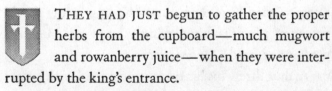 THEY HAD JUST begun to gather the proper herbs from the cupboard—much mugwort and rowanberry juice—when they were interrupted by the king's entrance.

"By the gods, Merlinnus, I slept well. And I am minded to do what we discussed last night." Arthur looked hearty enough and his eyes seemed bright, even overbright, but Gawen could not forget the vision of the dead king on the catafalque.

"And what was that, my king?" the old man asked carefully.

"Why, that I make Morgause queen."

Ignoring Gawen's gaping mouth, Merlinnus said carefully, "She is already a queen, my lord." The old man's face looked as if it had been set in stone. "She needs nothing of your making."

"Do you mean a May Queen, sire?" Gawen asked, gaping jaw closed at last. "Like the list the men gave you."

"I mean *my* queen!" Arthur said. "As she was Lot's."

"You cannot," Merlinnus told him.

Arthur's face got dark, his brows beetling. He did not look like the king Gawen knew. "I can do anything I wish, old man. Have you not made me the High King of Britain?"

"A king who does not know his ancestry." Merlinnus reminded him, then pursed his lips. "How would you know you are not marrying . . . a cousin?" His voice got low and hard. "Or a sister?"

Arthur threw his head back and roared with laughter. "You listen to too many ballads from the Continent, Merlinnus. Morgause and I are old friends, that is all."

And older enemies, Gawen thought.

"First things first, Arthur," Merlinnus cautioned. "The sword. The stone."

"Ah, yes," Arthur said, "and the lady after."

Long after.

———

WHEN AT LAST the king left, Gawen said, "You did not mention the North Queen's sorcery."

Merlinnus shook his head. "What good would it have done with him still bespelled? He would have put *me* aside, not her. No, boy, I have a much more difficult job ahead of me than I thought."

"Can I help?"

Merlinnus ruffled Gawen's fair hair. "You will have to. I have no other I can trust."

"Will it take magic?"

Nodding, Merlinnus said, "Magic and diplomacy. I have the first—and you must have the second."

Something like a chill ran down Gawen's backbone. "What makes you think I have such skills?"

"I have been watching you carefully," Merlinnus said. "So now I will send you to speak to Gawaine that we may know his mind."

"Not Gawaine, Magister. He is the queen's son." Gawen's voice was curiously flat.

"And the very reason we must seek him out." The old man had turned and was washing his hands in the basin, drying them on his wrinkled robe.

"Can we not start elsewhere? With the king perhaps? I can always speak to the king."

Merlinnus turned and stared at Gawen. "The king? Whatever for? He is clearly bespelled and will not believe. At the worst, he will take a dislike to you and send you away."

"But Gawaine—"

"Now, now, he is not like his brother, that hard-hand Agravaine," Merlinnus said. "Are you afraid of that one? If so, you have every right to be. Agravaine is a bully and a coward, a combination that is difficult to combat. He needs to be ruled by power, of which you have none. But Gawaine is different. He is a kind young man, courteous, and never willful. He is the perfect knight. It is often remarked upon at court, but I see it to be true."

Going pale, Gawen took a step back, trying to think what to say, but Merlinnus had suddenly stopped speaking. His eyes became slits and his head moved forward. He looked for all the world like an old turtle intent on a fly. "But you mentioned something about Gawaine that very first day we met. What was it?"

Gawen looked down, not able to meet the mage's eyes. "It was nothing, Magister."

"Nothing is usually something," the old man mused. "Especially with boys your age." He pulled at his beard, then looked up and snapped his fingers. "I remember! You said, *'Fearless at least with the ladies,'* and called him *'Gawaine, the Hollow Man.'* And not long ago, before he went out hunting with Gawaine, you cautioned the king about him. Said you knew him from some other time or place."

"There is certainly nothing old about your memory, Magister," Gawen said sourly.

"Ah, yes, but something is very wrong with you, my lad."

Gawen's face was suddenly shuttered.

"You have a connection with Gawaine, more than the simple conjunction of your names. I have thought so before and I will have it now. Out with it."

Gawen's face was now not only shuttered but locked and bolted as well.

"Tell me," Merlinnus said, leaning toward him and holding up a forefinger to draw Gawen's eye. "What is your connection with Prince Gawaine?"

Gawen tried to look away and could not. "He... he..."

"Go on." The mage's voice was soft, cozening.

"He..." Gawen stopped, though it was painful to do so.

"Go...on." This time there was steel in the mage's voice.

"He...compromised my sister, Mariel, Magister. He took her love and then left. Without a reason why." Gawen's voice cracked on the final word.

Merlinnus did not smile, but something like a twinkle shone in his eye. "And so that is the reason you came here to learn to be a knight? To challenge him?"

Gawen nodded.

"Did you know, before the king told you, how long any such lessons would take?"

Gawen nodded miserably. "I knew it."

"And were willing to spend that much time?" He put his finger down, as if realizing there was no need to bewitch Gawen.

"Willing to spend my whole life if need be," Gawen said.

"Or all of his," Merlinnus added.

"You did not see her face, Magister. You did not hear her cries in the night. Every night for weeks and weeks. You did not see her wasting away, her beauty eaten by grief and a splattering of boils, till she who had been lovely was loathly to look at." Gawen's own face looked pocked by the memory.

"So when you met me, you considered that magic might be faster than a sword," Merlinnus said. "Though perhaps not as satisfactory."

Gawen nodded.

"When did you know?"

"When you called me yours."

"So that is why you have become the perfect mage's apprentice."

Gawen nodded again. "Though I do it now for the king as well as my sister."

Merlinnus set his forefinger on Gawen's forehead

and whispered in a dire voice, "And what kind of magic would you learn with a heart set on such destruction?"

Gawen closed both eyes. Tears squeezed out. *How can I say the words? The words Merlinnus wants? Black magic.*

"I am sorry, Magister."

"No sorrier than I, my boy," said Merlinnus, and clearly meant it from the very depths of his heart.

For a minute neither of them spoke, then, voice breaking, Gawen said, "I will speak to Gawaine, Magister. Today." There was an agonizing pause. "But tell him what?"

"Tell him that his mother has bespelled the king." Merlinnus said it bluntly.

"Will he believe me?"

"He knows his mother," Merlinnus said. "He will believe."

GAWEN WORRIED all that day how to effect a meeting with the North Queen's son, but there never seemed a time when Gawaine was alone. Either he was surrounded by friends, by brothers, or was shadowed by Hwyll, who hovered over him like a hen with chicks.

Since it was the day before the Solstice Eve, the halls of the castle were filled with busy servants and bustling tradesmen, and out in the forecourt and down in the village it was the same. Merchants had come from miles around to set up their stalls for the Solstice fair.

A cart of traveling players was preparing an entertainment, and several musicians were already blowing and sawing away at their instruments.

Gawen followed Gawaine and his friends around for hours as they teased the girls and dropped coins in the musicians' caps and helped carters unload their wares. When at last the friends had departed, and the other sons of Lot were off squabbling at dice, and Hwyll was dancing attendance on Morgause herself, it was already night.

And Gawaine was suddenly nowhere about.

Gawen searched the keep high and low looking for him, from Merlinnus' tower down to the kitchens and back again. He asked Cook, who grunted an answer that was less than helpful.

"Try his mother's chamber."

But Gawen was not ready to go there. With the message to be delivered, it would not have been wise.

Instead Gawen asked the other boys. Ciril suggested the stables, Geoffrey the chapel, and Mark the alehouse. But though Gawen tried all three, Gawaine was not to be found.

Finally Gawen asked the king, who merely looked amused. "Was he not off on a boar hunt today? With his brothers? Possibly staying the night in some inn near the coast. Those boys do love the sound of the ocean. Why do you wish to know?"

"Merlinnus…wanted me…asking Sir Gawaine…tact," Gawen mumbled, managing to make the answer last longer than Arthur's interest. After all, Merlinnus had said clearly that Arthur was bespelled by the queen and no mention should be made.

"I do not know where he is," Arthur finally said, waving a dismissive hand at Gawen. "Ask someone else."

HAVING GOTTEN no further with his quest, Gawen went outside and, with his back to a wall, sat gazing at the stone in the churchyard. There was much to think about, and here was the one place to get away from the noise and bustle of the keep and the forecourt. He had much to worry about, too.

But Gawen had been up all the night before, when the rest of the castle was under its spell of sleep, and so without meaning to, dozed off into a dreamless sleep.

Suddenly waking, Gawen discovered it was midnight or thereabouts. A pale moon sat directly overhead.

Stiff from sitting on the ground, with a bottom that hurt as well, Gawen could hardly move. *I need to stretch…* A sound nearby caused Gawen to draw back against the wall once more, thinking, *Where is that sound? Is it the queen again?*

And then suddenly, illuminated faintly by the moon, there was Sir Kay. He began circling the stone much as Morgause had done the night before, but with much less grace. Round and about he went, as if gathering strength—of mind, of heart, of hand.

Gawen watched silently.

Finally, with a sound through his nose like that of a horse, Kay stopped, put his hand on the sword hilt, and, drawing in a deep breath, leaned back.

"Hah!" he cried out and yanked at the sword.

It did not move.

"Hah!" he cried a second time and pulled again, this time using both hands.

The sword still did not move.

Kay stepped away from the stone and, wordlessly, looked down at his hands as if they had somehow disappointed him. Then he abruptly turned and went back into the keep.

Not until the door had closed after Kay did Gawen finally stand up. Only just then another shadow moved toward the stone and once more Gawen shrank back against the wall.

The man who walked over to the stone had all the grace that Kay lacked. He walked with a light step around the stone, almost as if dancing. He reached out once, then pulled his hand back. Finally he stood still, as still as the stone itself, arms folded over his chest. He seemed perfectly at ease, but it was the ease of a warrior who could, at any moment, spring into brutal action.

Gawen left the safety of the wall. "Sir Gawaine?"

Gawaine turned. "Yes?"

He is like a coiled serpent, Gawen thought. "May I have a word with you?"

A quick smile—more like a shadow smile under that moon—graced Gawaine's face, then it was gone. "Just one?"

"I beg your pardon, sir?"

Gawaine laughed. "I hear you have been asking after me, boy."

"I have, sir."

"For what purpose?" Now he turned his entire body and focused completely on Gawen.

Gawen's knees felt wobbly. "The mage sent me."

"I do not like mages," Gawaine said plainly. "Magic has been the ruination of too many lives. And the bane of mine."

"Your mother ..."

"My mother," Gawaine said. He waved a hand as if flicking flies.

"This is *about* your mother," Gawen said again.

Gawaine moved two steps toward Gawen. He said, almost sadly, "It is *always* about my mother. Say on."

Gawen took a deep breath and said quickly, so that the words spilled over one another as water over stone,

"She set a spell last night on all who drank the toast. I did not drink and so was the only one unaffected. I saw her. She was out here checking the stone while the castle slept."

"We have *all* checked out the stone, each in our own way," Gawaine said. "Did you not just see Kay ... checking?"

"Yes." Gawen thought, *This is not going well.*

"Then why should my mother not do the same?"

"She did not just look at the thing," Gawen said.

"Do you mean to tell me she tried to pull it?" Gawaine laughed. "That would be just like her."

"No, my lord," Gawen said. "Well, yes, she *did* try. Once. But it spit sparks at her."

Gawaine laughed.

"And then she put some sort of spell upon it, a grey snaky thing."

There was a deep silence from Gawaine.

"I am not certain it worked."

Still Gawaine was silent.

"But I am not certain it did *not* work."

Gawaine seemed sunk in misery, and Gawen thought, *He has to know the rest. I hope it breaks his callous heart.* "There is more."

Gawaine looked up. "There is always more when the matter is my mother." His eyes were a misery.

"The king has told Merlinnus he will marry ..."

Gawaine's face opened, like a martyr's breast readied for the arrow.

"...your mother."

"No!" It was not a question, but a statement. Not a statement, but a cry from the heart. The sound Gawaine made was horrible, like a man who has had a sword thrust through his gut. For a moment after, he was silent, bent over. Then he straightened. "She *has* bespelled him."

Gawen nodded. "I just said that."

But Gawaine spoke as if he had not heard Gawen. "All women do that." Remarkably, his hands went to his head and he began to tear at his long fair hair.

Gawen gaped. "How can you say such a thing?"

"Because I, too, have been bespelled by a woman. And then my heart broken when my suit was rejected. Oh, Mariel!" He struck himself in the chest with a fist. "Boy, do not think to understand women. They are the great mystery of the world. What do they want? What *do* they want? How can a man hope to answer that?" He turned abruptly and walked away, through the courtyard and under the portcullis, toward the outer bailey, until Gawen could see only shadows where the man had been.

Gawen returned to the wall and sank down once more onto the ground, totally confused by the night's events.

Why had Kay come alone to try the sword? Why did Gawaine not put his hand on the hilt? Have I misunderstood my sister's plight? Who deserted whom? Whose heart was broken? Have there been other hands in this tale?

Gawen's mind was awash with questions. It was a veritable torment of misapprehension, misery, and fear.

And what of the mage's trust in me? Gawen thought. It was the hardest question of all.

35

Changes

GAWAINE WENT directly to the chambers he shared with his brothers. Only Agravaine was still awake, playing a dismal game of draughts with himself and so intent on winning, he kept switching sides.

"She is at it again," Gawaine announced.

"Mother?" Agravaine asked without looking up.

"Of course, Mother. She bespelled the court into a long sleep." He reached down and touched one of the pieces, which made Agravaine look up at him with a snarl.

"Do not touch that. I have a plan..."

"*Listen* to me. She bespelled us as well. You and me and the twins."

Agravaine's face showed that he did not understand. "Bespelled us? Why should she do that?"

"Because we mean no more to her than anyone else? Because she sees us as enemies, too? Because she can?" Gawaine shrugged dramatically before flopping into the chair on the other side of the table where the draughts were set up.

"But to what end?" Agravaine asked. He had one of the pieces in his hand, and he shook it at his brother.

"So she could do one of her magicks on the sword in that stone without being seen. So that one of *us* could then pull the sword and be High King." Gawaine said it gently, but iron was in his voice.

"I would not mind being High King," Agravaine said slowly, "or even brother to the High King...but..."

"But?"

Agravaine smiled.

He has a really nice smile, Gawaine thought, *though so rarely used.* He wondered about that.

"But it should go to the man who pulls the sword fairly."

Does he really think, Gawaine thought suddenly, *that Arthur would be pulling the stupid sword without Merlinnus' help?* And then he had a second thought: *And does it really matter? Arthur is king and should be king and that is the end of it.* He would not say further on this subject to Agravaine.

"I agree," he said. "I agree fully."

IT WAS ANOTHER hour before Gawen got up again and walked back into the keep, which held the silence of a tomb.

Has that witch bespelled the place again?

The guards standing at attention before the king's bedchamber tipped Gawen a wink.

No spell, then. Or, at least, no sleeping spell.

Gawen was halfway up to the mage's room when a sudden thought struck. *The kitchen is the place!* The idea seemed to appear from nowhere, like a magic, like a dream. But in Gawen's mind it solved every problem—the sword, the witch, the Matter of Britain. If only it would work.

It was quiet in the kitchen. Even the cats—a large calico and a wiry grey—were asleep in their willow baskets by the banked fire, for it was too late even for the mice.

Gawen looked around. No one would notice a thing missing or disturbed if . . .

COMING BACK IN from the cold, from a final visit to the stone, Gawen's hands shook with fatigue. It was still night, but soon there would be a pearling of the dark skies and then a new day would dawn, bringing—one could only hope—answers to so many questions.

As Gawen dragged up the stairs, a door opened near the apartments set aside for the North Witch's boys. The torches were unlit along this particular corridor, which in itself was unusual. Then two shadows, black on black, walked out of the room, moving silently, cautiously, almost sneaking along.

Careful to be neither seen nor heard, Gawen stopped to watch.

Was it Gawaine? Agravaine? The figures seemed too tall for the twins. But something was afoot, and after two assassination attempts on the king and a spell, Gawen was more than willing to track behind them.

The shadowy figures went up the far stairs and out to a private walkway along the northern alure, a place that Gawen knew was more private than any of the inner chambers, where folk could listen at the doors or behind a tapestry—and often did.

Gawen hurried to catch up.

Under the starry sky, the two were easier to distinguish, if not name—a man and woman. The woman had unbound her hair and was looking over one of the high crenels, shaking her long dark locks into the wind.

For a moment Gawen wondered if being there would precipitate an embarrassing situation. After all, the two could very well be the king and Morgause, out for a tryst, for the one word clearly spoken came from the woman.

"Arthur," she said.

The man bowed his head.

I have no right here, Gawen thought, starting to turn away from the two, cheeks burning with both embarrassment and anger.

Then the woman laughed. It was awful, bleak, chilling.

"Never mind about the dagger, my love. No harm done. This way is better. He will be mine and the throne will be ours without a killing." The woman was Morgause all right, but it was suddenly clear that she was not speaking *to* Arthur. She was speaking *about* him.

Gawen turned back, now guessing the man she was speaking to was Gawaine. That Gawaine should so conspire with his mother—whom just an hour past he had affected to dislike—made Gawen hate him anew. Gawaine was not to be trusted. He was a cheat and a schemer, a liar and—

"Then, my lady, how shall I give this to him?" the man said. The voice did not belong to Gawaine, but to someone older, subservient.

Something broke inside Gawen then; some bit of ice that had been like a sliver in the heart melted.

"Put the stuff in his wine or his meat or his porridge on the Solstice Eve. Whatever is easiest." The witch's voice was at once caressing and uncaring.

"Will it kill, my lady?"

"Nay, fool. That way *would* tip our hand. We dare not be so direct now. The old man has made even stronger protections against assassination since the two attempts. Discretion shall be our watchword. How politic. The mage himself would admire it." She laughed. "Poor old Merlinnus. He is not devious enough for the great magicks."

"Are you certain, my queen?" The man seemed unsure, almost cringing.

Her voice turned cold, a winter chill over a summer landscape. "Have you learned nothing from me in all these years?"

He answered smoothly, "All I know, my lady, has come from you. All that I desire."

Morgause's laugh turned soft as down, a woman flattered yet not unwilling to be flattered. "Fool indeed, my love. For loving makes us all foolish."

"But not unwise," the man answered.

"Not unwise," she agreed. "And unlike that old fool, I can learn from my mistakes. It would be unwise indeed to kill the king now. He is much beloved hereabouts. However, the potion will make him weak. As weak in the arm as he is in the soul. So weak, he will not be able to draw the sword from the stone, no matter how Merlinnus helps him." She laughed again. "Merlinnus has placed too much upon this one trick, this sword in a stone. Man's magic, to believe such foolery. And I have overlaid my hand upon his on the stone. With Arthur weak, and with a bit of help from me, my son will pull the sword unchallenged. And I will have outfoxed that old charlatan at last." She handed the man a vial.

Gawen could stand it no longer. Morgause and Hwyll were outlined against the pearling dawn and Hwyll was holding up the vial. They were both so enraptured by it and by their conspiracy, they did not notice Gawen start toward them at a run.

When Gawen had gotten close enough to see, the liquid in the vial was just turning red in the dawning light. Red like blood.

"No!" Gawen leaped for the little bottle, hoping to snatch it from Hwyll and throw it over the side of the crenellated wall so that it would shatter on the cobbles three stories below. That was all the plan Gawen's fevered mind had come up with in the moment between eavesdropping and action. "No!"

At the last minute Hwyll turned at the shout and Gawen banged into him. Frantically off-balance, Hwyll stepped backward, still holding tight to the little vial. Arms swimming in the air, he fell over a low notch in the wall.

For a moment he seemed to hang in the air, a fish without water, a bird without wings. Then wordlessly, he plunged straight down and broke—as the vial itself broke—on the stony ground where liquid and blood mixed together in one watery gush.

"Nooooooo!" This time the word was screamed by Morgause. She did not even look over to see if her man lived. Instead she stared at Gawen, lifting her hands like claws and pointing one longer finger.

"I know what you are, and not what you seem," she cried. "You gormless, shiftless besom. So, this curse I lay upon you." She threw something at Gawen's face, something large and soft.

For a moment Gawen's view was obscured. Then, lifting the cloth, Gawen saw that it was the very thing used to clean the sword the night before.

Does the cloth carry secrets? Gawen thought desperately. *Has it spoken to her of who I really am? So she implies. But she is a witch and a liar. Can she be believed?*

Before Gawen could ask, Morgause began her curse, her dark hair with its tangle of elf knots seeming to lift up off her shoulders as if having life of its own. She shook with the power of her cursing, and spittle flew from her mouth, spraying in all directions. "I curse thee that ye be shaken, flower from stem, stem from root. That yer line be blighted, yer cause be slighted, yer love unrequited, and yer person indicted."

Gawen felt every word pierce like arrows to the heart.

Morgause held her arms up. "I am bent but not broken. The old man has not heard the last of me yet. Tell him he only buys himself a small shard of time. Time is on my side, not his. And well he knows it." She shook her hands three times widdershins.

Then, as if water were running over her, washing away her sharp human features, she changed, slowly but inexorably: bones shrinking, hair whitening, silken clothes turning into feathers. Till at last she melted into the shape of a solan goose, a gannet, that leaped into the air and flapped away silently, going north—due north—through the dawn skies.

VI

Queen's Magic/ King's Sword

Now night was a surround of black. The stone was black, too, and only the hilt of the sword held any light, as if a sliver of silver pin pierced a coarse material. And day arrived, the stone, sword, and sky going bright like the philosopher's mercury that stands still and yet runs.

36

Reading the Air

GAWEN STOOD, stunned, in front of the door, unable to go inside.

Time, though, did not stop. It ground on relentlessly, and eventually the sun came up, slapping Gawen full in the face. It was a sharp shock.

Shaking all over, like a dog coming out of a bath, Gawen whispered, "Magister," knowing the old mage had to be told what had occurred.

And as if speaking the word called him up, Merlinnus suddenly appeared at the door, still in his nightshirt, his skinny legs and knobby feet showing below the coarse cloth.

"I smell death in the air." Merlinnus sniffed. "And something else."

Silently, Gawen drew him out and around to the far side of the crenellated wall. The old man peered down.

"Ah," he said. "But there is more to this than blood."

"Magic," Gawen whispered, holding out the cloth Morgause had flung at him. "Treachery."

"One an oilier smell than the other." Merlinnus took the cloth, sniffed it, looked back again over the wall at the body below. "Who is it? My old eyes cannot see so far."

"Hwyll."

"Ah, the witch's man." Merlinnus nodded again, turning back to the boy.

"You knew?" Gawen's mouth gaped open.

"He was besotted. It did not take magic to see that." Merlinnus' hands curled around one another and wrangled together, the cloth between.

"I could not."

"But you saw something else. Something troubled you."

And then it all came out, the confrontation with Gawaine at the stone and Kay's poor attempt at pulling the sword, the curse, the transformation. Everything except the trip to the kitchen and Gawen's second visit to the stone.

Merlinnus suddenly laughed. "What a night you have had, child. And no sleep. It is lucky I do not know your mother or she would have words with me." He put a hand out and tousled Gawen's fair hair.

Gawen could not stop a yawn.

"Go to bed. I will deal with the rest. Arthur shall know of Hwyll's unfortunate accident. And with the North Witch gone, her spell over him will no doubt be gone, too; otherwise I shall have to spend valuable time canceling it."

"Time!" Gawen said, hand on mouth. "She said something about time." *What was it?* Then suddenly: "She said that time was on her side, not yours."

Merlinnus shook his head. "Time is always on the side of the young," he said. "Which is why they spend it so recklessly. And recklessness will be her undoing." He put a hand under Gawen's elbow and gave a little push. "Now to bed, I say."

Gawen needed no more urging.

No sooner had Gawen fallen asleep than Merlinnus got dressed in his best robes and went down at once to visit the king.

The king was already sitting on his throne and listening to Kay. When he saw Merlinnus enter, Arthur looked up gratefully. "Here is a puzzle," he said. "Kay would have an answer and I have none. But I said that surely my mage would know. Do not fail me, Merlinnus." His voice sounded sincere, but a smile played around his lips.

Kay turned his thin face toward Merlinnus and put a hand to the flowing mustache as if stroking it lent him some wisdom.

"The women," he said. "They are gone. Stolen by magic, perhaps."

"The women?" For a moment Merlinnus seemed confused.

"The May Queens," Kay said passionately. "We must gather the Companions and—"

"Oh, *those* women," Merlinnus said, and smiled. "The birds have flown."

Kay turned back to Arthur, who was already shifting on the throne, seeking a more comfortable seat. "You see—I told you Merlinnus is too old for this, Arthur. It is not the women but his wits that have flown."

Merlinnus added, "Gone with their queen, back north."

"She is gone?" Arthur asked, with some mixed emotions.

"For the time being," Merlinnus said.

"Without a word of farewell?" Kay's voice was pouty as a boy's.

"Oh, she sent *me* a message," Merlinnus said.

"Can I read it?" Kay asked.

"Only if you can read the air," Merlinnus told him.

Kay threw his hands up in the air. "*He* is impossible!" And with that, he turned and walked out of the room.

Arthur chuckled. "Are you?"

"Am I what?"

"Impossible."

"Only to men like Kay." Merlinnus came up the steps to the throne and leaned forward. "There is much you need to know."

"About..."

Merlinnus resisted saying the word that was on the tip of his tongue: *everything*. Instead he said, "About the North Queen and what she had planned."

Arthur sighed and leaned back against the chair. "I am afraid there is much about the North Queen I do not know and may not wish to know. But still I have to know. So—tell me."

And, except for the cursing of Gawen and the threat of time, Merlinnus did.

BY MIDMORNING, when the rest of the castle had awakened and was already playing at the Solstice fair, the queen's sons were gathered in the king's chamber. They had been told of Hwyll's death and that he had planned to poison Arthur.

Of Morgause's hand in the plot Merlinnus said not a word.

Typically, Gawaine was the most disturbed by the news. Running a hand through his fair hair, he shook his head. "Are you certain, my lord?"

Merlinnus answered for Arthur. "Quite certain. He was overheard plotting and the contents of the vial, that little not soaked into the ground, have been checked."

"Plotting with whom?" Agravaine asked. His hand went to his side, where a sword would have rested were swords allowed in the king's chamber. "I will kill anyone, my lord, who would harm you." His nervous fingers played with the hem of his jerkin.

The twins glanced at him, and then each other, as if agreeing that Agravaine was their first and only suspect in the plot.

"What matters is that the king is not harmed," Gawaine said at last. "And that we take responsibility for burying Hwyll quickly."

Agravaine turned on him. "Why should we? Let him rot. Stick his head on a pike and let the crows have his eyes."

"He was a man," Gawaine began. "*Our* man."

"I never liked him, brother."

The twins said together in eerily similar voices, "But you did, Agravaine."

"Did not," Agravaine said, his face turning a burnt color.

Arthur raised his hand. "The deed is done, the doer dead. He has already been buried quietly outside of the castle, at the crossroads. We have put out that it was an unfortunate fall and have spread fresh earth where he landed. No more will be argued about it. Nor will any more be spoken of this. It will be a day's wonder in the town, no more if we say nothing. Though I thank you for your honesty, Gawaine. And you, Agravaine, for your passion. And you, my young friends"—he bowed his head to the twins—"for keeping us all on our toes."

Merlinnus thought that well said. For some things Arthur had a positive genius. He added his own weight to Arthur's. "We have other important matters now. Today is Solstice Eve and there is a fair in the castle forecourt. In case anyone has forgotten."

Arthur drew himself up till he seemed twice as tall as the others, though Gawaine and he were of a height and Agravaine was closing the gap quickly. "Then it is time."

"The sword." Again the twins spoke as one. "The stone."

"Ah." Agravaine's color dropped to a shade of white. Then he flushed again. It did not take a genius of any kind to guess what he was thinking.

Gawaine dropped to one knee before the king. "I will not put my hand on it, sire. I do not desire it."

Arthur bent over and pulled him up. "Do not be so foolish," he said. "You must try. Else your mother will trouble me over it forever."

Gawaine nodded. It was true. He would have to be seen to try.

"And you, too, Agravaine," Arthur said, glancing at the ruddy-faced boy. "I do not want men around me who will not try."

Agravaine nodded and flushed even deeper, and Merlinnus thought, *Genius indeed. There is one who will be with the king from now till the end of the kingdom, whatever his mother thinks.*

37

Out to the Stone

THE DAY was already shredded and thrown away. The fair had been a success, though Arthur and Merlinnus and Gawen had not visited it. Sales had been brisk, and no merchants would have to go home with leftover produce.

Birch and fennel, mugwort and orpine, twisted about with white lilies, hung on all the doors. Honey wine had been drunk in large quantities. There were few who walked about the forecourt sober.

Now huge bonfires of oak logs—oak for endurance and triumph—were lit in front of the church. They were used to signal the desire to drive away the dark. Inside the church, women lit candles to do the same.

Dressed in fanciful orange and red costumes, the good folk of Cadbury gathered close to the fires. Then one, then two and three began leaping the flames and crying out in ecstasy as the hot tips licked the bottoms of their bare feet.

Gawen watched the fire jumpers uneasily. Such excess, such loss of self, was frightening. *I must hold close the reason I have come to Cadbury. Not to fall under Arthur's spell. Nor to find a father in the old mage. I came to restore Mariel's honor.* And yet, had that honor been compromised by Gawaine? Or had it, rather, been someone else's fault?

"You look troubled, lad," Merlinnus said, coming over, a mug of ale in his hand.

For a moment Gawen did not answer, remembering a phrase from childhood: *To have but a mile to Midsummer.* It meant that a person was a little mad. But these jumpers seemed entirely mad, not just a little, crazed with the fire and its unleashed power. "I do not understand what all this commotion has to do with the sword and the stone."

"It is Midsummer madness," the mage told him. "Surely you celebrate the Solstice where you are from."

"The Solstice day, yes—with prayers and thanksgiving and a fast," Gawen said. "And that night, with a feast to break our fast. But this smacks of bedlam. I fail to understand what it has to do with the kingdom of Britain."

Merlinnus said seriously, "All magic—good and bad—is deemed more potent on this eve, boy. Why do you think the North Witch wanted to dose the king tonight? Why do you think I have declared this very night the time of pulling the sword?"

"And is it true?" Gawen whispered, still staring out at the people who were now driving cattle past the fires as well. The beasts were lowing their distress and several tried to turn away. But the oddly dressed herdsmen forced the cows straight ahead so that they were soon wrapped in the tatters of smoke from the flames.

"Is what true?" Merlinnus had turned all his attention to Gawen.

"That magic holds better this night." *Surely madness does,* Gawen thought.

Merlinnus smiled to himself. *The boy asks good questions.* "If the people believe that hawkweed and vervain, mullein and wormwood, plucked this midnight are more efficacious, then they are indeed. If the people own that rubbing their eyelids with fern seed gathered at the stroke of midnight lets them see the fey—then they will. If the people think that dreams dreamed tonight are more likely to come true, they do. If they hold that natural waters have special virtue this eve, then they will be strengthened by bathing in the rivers and streams before dawn."

Gawen thought a long time on this, before sighing and asking, "Are you saying that magic is merely a matter of belief?"

The old man touched his right pointer finger to the side of his nose. "Not merely. Still, belief is a large part of magic, surely. Just as history is and kingship is and—"

But what else he might have said was suddenly overpowered by men rolling burning disks past them. The roar of the flames and the heat parted the boy and the mage, and when the men had passed by to fling the disks down the embankment, the moment of truth-telling was over.

"IT IS TIME." Merlinnus had left the fire jumpers and had gone to find Arthur in the throne room.

The king was alone, placing his careful marks on the bottom of yet another piece of parchment.

"It is *always* time with you," Arthur said. "You are obsessed with time." He did not look up from his task.

"I have so little of it," the mage said quietly. "But what I mean now, Arthur, is that it is time to pull the sword from the stone." He offered his hand.

Pushing aside the hand, Arthur arose. The cushion he had been sitting on was plain, without embroidery.

"Does it help?" Merlinnus asked, nodding at the cushion, which had kept the shape of the king's backside.

"Somewhat." Arthur stretched. The kink in his back was there for a moment, then gone. "I only wish I had two of them."

Shaking his head, the old man said easily, "You are the king. Command it."

Arthur looked at him steadily. "I doubt such excess is wise."

Merlinnus only smiled.

THEY WALKED arm in arm out through the stone doorway and—with guards both leading them and following—made their way to the churchyard. Kay was in the very front of the group, his full breastplate shining. He of all the Companions still affected the Roman armor.

Seeing the king's approach, the fire dancers ceased their motions, the cattle were shepherded back to their byres, and the last fire disks were left to burn circles into the short summer grass.

In the fire-broken night, the white stone gleamed before the black hulk of the church. Darker veins in the stone meandered like streams across its surface, and grains of thin glittery minerals sparkled like fairy lanterns across the stone's broad face.

The crowd hushed, and the sword—now shadow, now light—suddenly became the focus of hundreds of eyes.

Arthur did not like ritual, but he knew how to command a crowd's attention. That command was a gift, not something he thought about consciously. Dropping the mage's arm, Arthur walked directly to the stone through two lines of guards. He nodded at Captain Cassius, who signaled the men to each take a step back.

For a moment Arthur stood still, as if waiting for some command that only he could hear. Then he knelt slowly, while at the same time reaching up to remove his circlet of office. Once it was off his brow, he shook free the sandy mane it had held so firmly in place.

A breath, a sigh, ran around the courtyard.

"The crown," someone whispered, and the word went from lip to ear, over and over, till it had circumscribed the entire yard.

Arthur stood again and this time placed the thin gold crown on top of the stone so that it lay just below the angled sword. Then he turned and, with his back to the stone, said plainly, "This crown and this land belong to the man who can pull the sword from the stone." His voice was louder than he had intended, made louder because of the silence that greeted him.

Or because it was Midsummer Eve.

"So it is written—here!" he said, gesturing broadly with his hand back toward the runes on the stone.

"Read it!" a woman cried from the crowd.

"We want to hear it again," shouted another.

A man's voice, picking up the argument, dared a further step. "Let the mage read it." Anonymity lent his words power, and the crowd muttered its agreement.

MERLINNUS' SMILE was little more than a grimace, though he was thinking that things could not have been better had he seeded the speakers in the crowd. Adjusting his robes, he squared his shoulders and walked to the stone. He glanced at the legend only briefly—for who knew better than he what was written there?—and then turned to face the people, his back to the rock.

"The message on the stone is burned here," he said, pointing to his breast. "Here in my heart. It says: 'Whoso pulleth out this sword of this stone is rightwise king born of all Britain.'"

Kay was standing nearer to the stone than all but the mage and the king. "Yes," he said loudly, "yes, that is what it says." As if his confirmation of the message made it true.

Putting his hands on his hips, Arthur said, "And so, my good people, the challenge has been flung down before us all. He who would rule, who would sit on the hard throne of the High King, must come forward and take the first step. He must put his hand upon the sword."

"And pull," Kay added.

Arthur glared at his stepbrother. "Of course," he muttered under his breath, but not so Kay could hear.

GAWEN COULD not hear, either, but unlike Kay was watching Arthur's lips and read the king's displeasure there. "Of course," Gawen echoed, liking the king especially for this small display of pique. And his unwillingness to say it aloud and shame Sir Kay.

"The sword," the king continued, "has been here for a month waiting its freedom. It has not been drawn yet from its rocky sheath. We all know that on this day, this night, what was pale becomes flushed, what was weak becomes strong."

Kay added, "What was old becomes new—" He would have gone on but Merlinnus shushed him.

Arthur did not even then turn toward Kay, but continued, "So now is the time for someone to pull the sword, even if he has tried before."

The Companions looked silently at one another, as if guessing which of them had already put a hand to the hilt.

Into the silence the king suddenly thundered: "So who will try?"

38

Trying the Sword

AT FIRST there was no sound but the dying fall of the king's voice. Then a child cried, and that started the crowd. They began talking to one another, jostling, arguing, some good-naturedly, others with a belligerent tone.

"Robin—you have the arm for it."

"Not the head, though."

"Come, Rob, or you, Trys. Here's my hand on it."

"Trys, go on. I'd like being a king's mother."

"Let go my arm; I ain't no king."

"Nor kind."

The battle rose to a roar. Some of it was in Gaelic or Erse. Some in French. Some in the Saxon tongue.

"You pushed me!"

"None but Arthur should be king."

"I would try."

"Moi aussi."

"It is the mage who will decide."

"The mage! The mage!"

And suddenly the crowd was calling for Merlinnus again. He held his arms up, waved his two pointer fingers at the milling mob, and they went unaccountably silent.

Gawen suddenly remembered Merlinnus saying that magic was mostly belief. Clearly the crowd must have thought the mage had bewitched them. *Otherwise,* Gawen thought, *they would never have quieted down so easily.*

Just then a rather sheepish farm boy was thrust from the crowd. He was taller by almost a head than Sir Kay, who was himself the tallest of the knights. Gawen recognized the boy—he had been at the dinner the night the queen had ensorcelled them all. The boy had a shock of wheat-colored hair that hung lank over one eye, and a dimple in his chin. His arms bunched with muscles. He did not look terribly bright.

"I'll try, my lord," he said. "For me mam's sake." He was plainly uncomfortable speaking up to the king, and he bobbed his head as he spoke. "I mean, it wouldna do no harm."

"No harm at all, son," said Arthur. He took the boy by the elbow and escorted him to the stone.

The boy put both his hands around the sword's hilt and then stopped. He looked over his shoulder at the crowd.

Someone shouted encouragement and then the whole push of people began to call out for him.

"Do it!"

"Pull the bastard!"

"Give it a heave, boy! A right heave!"

"Haul 'er out!" The last was a woman's voice.

Perhaps, Gawen thought, *the boy's mam.*

Buoyed by the crowd's enthusiasm, the boy put his right foot up against the stone. Then he leaned backward, and pulled. His hands slipped along the hilt and he fell on his bottom, to the delight of the crowd.

Crestfallen, the boy stood up and looked at his boots as if he did not know where else to look or how to make his feet carry him away.

Arthur put a hand on the boy's shoulder. "What is your name, boy?" he asked, and the gentleness in his voice silenced the crowd's raucous laughter.

"Percy, sir," the boy managed at last.

"Then, Percy," the king said, "because you were brave enough to try where no one else would set a hand upon the sword, you shall come to the castle and learn to be one of my knights."

"Maybe not *your* knight," someone shouted from the crowd.

A shadow passed across the king's face and he turned toward the mage. Merlinnus shook his head almost imperceptibly, but at least two people saw it—Gawen and the king.

Arthur shifted his gaze back to the crowd and smiled broadly. "No, perhaps not. We have yet to see who is to be the High King. Now, who else will try, then?"

It was a long, agonizing moment. The only sound was the snap of a branch breaking in the fire.

"I will try." It was Agravaine. He walked out quickly to the stone, put one hand on its backside a bit timidly, as if fearing some contagion. Then he put his left hand upon the sword hilt, and his right hand atop the left, and with a loud huffing sound, rather like a colt first let out to pasture, pulled. When the sword did not move a bit, he grinned broadly and, still grinning, went back to his place. "Mother," he mouthed to Gawaine, "has no power here."

Then Kay brushed his hands across his breastplate and tugged the gloves down so that the fingers fit snugly. Walking to the stone in a casual stroll that belied his nervousness, he placed his right hand on the hilt of the sword. He nodded at the king, smoothed his mustache with his left hand. Then he moved the left hand over the right, and gave the sword a small pull.

It was more for show than for real, Gawen realized. Kay already knew he did not have a chance.

Shrugging in an exaggerated manner, Kay turned to Arthur. "I am still first in your service, brother."

"And in my heart," Arthur acknowledged, fist on his breast.

Then, one by one, at Arthur's urging, the Fenians lined up and took turns pulling on the sword. Then the Highlanders. The Saxons and the old soldiers tried next. Several of the Picts gave the sword a pull, with their friends standing around the stone, cheering. Three of the four minor tribal kings placed a hand to the hilt. But neither of the barons tried, and after watching the others attempt and fail, they looked at one another, shrugged, and rode off home.

As though, Gawen thought, *they care little who is king. Or assume it will be Arthur.*

Finally Bedwyr, Gawaine, Tristan—maned like a lion—cocky Galahad, and the rest each put a hand to the sword, one after the other, and pulled. And while a few made the stone shudder, and Galahad managed to move the stone an inch, the sword never moved out of its solid scabbard.

At last, of the Companions, only Lancelot was left. He stood but a handbreadth from Gawen, watching as one after another of the men had a try at the sword. He did not speak to Gawen nor Gawen to him, but it was as if they lent one another strength, standing there together.

"And you, dearest of friends," said Arthur, coming up to Lancelot, "my right hand, the strongest of us all, will you try to pull the sword now?"

Lancelot's ruined angel face looked oddly seamed with sorrow. He ran a hand through his dark hair and the white streak disappeared, like the top of a wave disappearing in the trough, only to reappear at once when he put his hand down. "I have no wish to be king, Arthur. I only wish to serve."

Gawen shivered at his words as though having caught a chill, though the night was warm and there was no wind.

Arthur walked to Lancelot, put a hand on his shoulder, and whispered, "It is the stone's desire, not ours, that will decide this."

Gawen heard every word clearly as if they—and not the sword's legend—had been carved in the stone.

Arthur continued, "If you do not try, Lancelot, then my leadership will always be doubted. I need you as I need no other. Without your full commitment, the kingdom will not be bound."

"Then I shall put my hand to the sword, my lord," Lancelot said, "because you require it. Not because I desire it." He closed his eyes.

Gawen wondered if he wept, could not believe it, then saw tears at the corners of the man's eyes.

"Damn it, do not indulge me," Arthur whispered hoarsely. "Do not just put your hand there. You must *try,* Lancelot." His voice was fierce. "You must *really* try."

Lancelot opened his eyes and they were like deep wells wherein a spirit lives, like the Holy Well of Saint Madron's. All of Britain was spotted with such spirit wells. Gawen knew that some spirits were good and some were evil, and often it was difficult to know one from the other.

"As you wish," Lancelot said to Arthur, his voice as fierce as the king's. He bowed his head, stepped to the stone, put his hand to the sword, and seemed to address the thing, his lips moving but no sound coming out. Then slowly he let his breath out and leaned back.

The stone began to move. An inch as Galahad had done. Then an inch further.

The crowd gasped in a single voice and Gawen felt hot, cold, then hot again.

"Arthur..." Kay said, his hand over his mouth so the words were muffled. "Arthur...what if..."

Sweat appeared on Lancelot's brow, and the king had an answering band of sweat on his own.

Lancelot pulled some more, and every man in the

crowd—every woman, too—felt the weight of that pull between his shoulder blades.

The stone began to slide along the courtyard mosaic, gathering speed as it went, but even as the stone moved, the sword did not slip from its mooring. It had become a handle for the stone, nothing more.

Suddenly the gold coronet slid down the rounded prow of the stone and stopped the glide of the rock. Lancelot withdrew his hand from the hilt, bowed briefly to the king, and took two steps back.

"I cannot unsheathe the king's sword," he said. "I am not the king." His voice was remarkably composed for a man who had just moved a ton of stone.

Merlinnus stepped between the two men and slowly looked over the crowd. "Is there anyone else who would try?"

Not a person in the crowd dared meet his eyes, and there followed a long silence.

Gawen counted the seconds silently—*One ... two ... three ...*—and when the count hit fifteen, cried out, "Let King Arthur try!"

Merlinnus turned his head slightly as if trying to find the source of the cry, though Gawen was sure the mage knew all along who had spoken, and approved.

At once the crowd picked up its cue. "Arthur! Arthur! Arthur!" they shouted.

Wading into their noise like a swimmer in heavy swells breasting the waves, the king walked to the stone. Putting his right hand on the sword hilt, he turned his face to the people.

"For Britain!" he cried.

All eyes were on the king but Gawen's. Only Gawen noticed the mage crossing his fingers and sighing a spell in Latin.

Arthur's right hand clutched the sword hilt and his knuckles went white with the effort.

He first leaned into the sword, then back—and pulled.

With a slight *swoosh,* the sword slid out of its slot, and the silver blade caught the last light of the Midsummer fires.

Then the king put his left hand above his right on the hilt and lifted the sword over his head, swinging it once, twice, and then a third time, in an all-encompassing circle. Slowly the sword circumscribed the courtyard. Finally, Arthur brought the blade down slowly before him until its point touched the earth.

"Now I be king of *all* Britain," he said.

Kay nudged the gold circlet from the front of the stone, reshaped it quickly between his gloved palms, then placed it back on Arthur's head, and the chant for the king began anew.

"Arthur! Arthur! Arthur!"

The old soldiers began the chant, and the minor tribal chiefs took it up next. The Highlanders roared approval in their Scots tongue. Saxons said the words, though their eyes did not. The Picts nodded. And the Fenians threw their caps in the air.

Then the knights of the Round Table swept forward and lifted the king to their shoulders, but Arthur twisted about and sought the mage's eyes. His lips formed a command, which could only be read, not heard. "I will see you in your tower. Soon!"

Merlinnus saw and agreed with a nod.

Gawen saw, too.

And then the turmoil began anew as men, women, children shouted and danced and sang and carried the king around the church, under the archway, past a rampart, across the barbican, over the moat, and back again.

Midsummer madness, Gawen thought, *indeed.*

39

Sword of the Rightful King

MERLINNUS WAS SITTING in the tower when less than an hour later the king slipped into the room, the sword in his left hand. Gawen was at his feet, like a pup by its master.

"So, now you are king of all Britain indeed," Merlinnus said. His face was as relaxed as Gawen had ever seen it and lit by an unfamiliar grin. "None can say you no. Was I not right? A bit of legerdemain on Midsummer's—"

"What are you playing at, old man?" Arthur's face was grey in the room's candlelight. He was *not* smiling. "You know as well as I that I am not king—of Britain or elsewhere. There is another."

"Another what?" Confusion, an old enemy, camped on the mage's face.

"Another king. Another sword."

Shaking his head, Merlinnus said, "You are tired, Arthur. It has been a long day and an even longer night."

The king strode over and grabbed the old man's shoulder with his right hand. "Merlinnus—*this is not the same sword!*"

"Arthur, you are mistaken. It can be no other."

Sweeping the small crown off his head, Arthur dropped the coronet into the old man's lap. His face was a misery. "I am a simple man, Merlinnus, and I am a honest one. I read slowly and understand what I read only with help. What I know best is soldiering and people, and I am a genius at swords. You will grant me that."

And holding the kingdom's heart, Gawen thought, but knew better than to speak aloud at this moment.

Merlinnus nodded.

"The sword Caliburnus I held a month ago," Arthur said, "is not the sword I hold now. That sword had balance to it, a grace such as I had never felt before. It knew me, knew my hand. The pattern on the blade looked now like wind, now like fire."

Merlinnus stared at him, unable to speak.

The king held the sword toward the wizard. "This blade, though it has fine watering, and runes along the hilt, feels nothing like that other. This molds to my hand because I will it. It is heavier, graceless, fit for murder and not for justice."

"You are imagining—" Merlinnus began, but Arthur interrupted him.

"I am *not* an imaginative man, Merlinnus. So I am not imagining this."

"It is Midsummer..." Merlinnus tried again to interrupt the flow of Arthur's complaint. "When the weak are strong. And the unimaginative might—"

But the king would not have it. "It could be Armageddon eve and I would still say the same. Though it looks a great deal like it, this is not the sword that was in the stone." The king's face was itself a stone and his conviction graven there. "And if it is not, old man, I ask you—where is *that* sword? And what man took it? For he, not I, is the rightful-born king of all Britain. Tell me who he is and I will be the first in the land to bend my knee to him."

Merlinnus put his right hand to his head, at the throbbing vein in his temple. "I swear to you, Arthur, no man alive could move that sword lest I spoke the words."

"Unless Morgause..."

The name dropped between them like a boulder in a brook.

"She could not touch it. Her own magic precluded that. A magic hand would have set off a rebound of magic. Besides, she is gone back north, and with her all her tricks," the mage reminded him.

A slight sound near the old man's feet startled them both.

"My lords," Gawen said.

They looked down.

"If you will allow me." Gawen stood and went over to the heavy oak chest, kneeled, and opened it, then moved aside pieces of linen and silk and wool and several old sandals, and stuck a hand deep in, past dozens of rolled scrolls. Finally Gawen stood up, a sword in hand, grabbing the hilt quickly with the second hand as well, for the thing was clearly heavy.

"I am afraid I was the one who took the sword from the stone. When I found I could not put it back properly, I left a lighter substitute, an earlier version of the sword that Merlinnus had worked on. I found it when I cleaned his wardrobe." Gawen came over and knelt before Arthur, holding up the sword to him.

Arthur reached down and pulled Gawen to a standing position, the sword still between them. "It is I who should kneel to you, my young king."

A raw flush covered Gawen's cheeks and the dawning light from the window cast the slight figure in a soft glow. "I cannot be king, my lord, not now or ever. Not *rex quondam, rexque futurus.*"

"How did you pull the sword, then?" Merlinnus asked, head cocked to one side. "Speak. Speak true. Be quick about it."

Gawen placed the sword in Arthur's hand. "I brought a slab of butter from the kitchen to the stone one night, well past the midnight hour, and melted the butter over a candle flame. When it was a river of gold, I poured it into the slot, and the sword...slid right out." Gawen shrugged. "I did not fully expect it to be so easy. It was just...just...an experiment. I had to be quick about the other sword. I'll tell you!"

"A trick," Merlinnus mused. "A homey trick that any herb wife might..."

Arthur turned to the mage sadly. "No more a trick than my pulling a sword loosed by your magic, Merlinnus. And better, in a way. The boy worked it out for himself, while I relied on you for my kingdom. There is a strange justice here."

"Not justice, surely." Gawen was terrified now, more than when confronting Gawaine or pushing Hwyll over the wall.

"Cunning, then," the king told him. "A king needs such cunning, which I—alas—have little of. But a king needs a good right hand as well. I shall be yours, my lord, though I envy you this sword." He held the sword out to Gawen.

Gawen pushed the sword back at Arthur. "The sword is yours, sire, never mine. It is too heavy for my hand and much too heavy for my heart. I am not the kind of person to ever ride to war. One man slain by my hand—though all inadvertent—is enough for me. You were right to deny me the chance to be a knight. I know now I could never be one of your Companions."

Turning to Merlinnus, Arthur said, "Help me, Mage. I do not understand."

Merlinnus stood and put the crown back on Arthur's head. "I think I do, though only just now. Why I should have been so terribly slow to note it, I wonder. Age certainly dulls the mind. I have had an ague of the brain all this spring. But it makes sense, as magic must in the end."

Gawen's head drooped. *So, at last, the secret will be out. In a way, that is a blessing.*

Merlinnus continued, "I said the magic would allow no man but you, Arthur, to pull out the sword—and no *man* has." He held out his hand to Gawen. "Come, child, you shall make a lovely May Queen by next year. By then your hair should be long enough for Kay's list, though what we shall ever do about short utterances is beyond me."

Gawen nodded.

"A girl? *He* is a girl?" Arthur looked baffled. He squinted his eyes and stared at Gawen as if by looking long enough he could see what he had not seen before.

Merlinnus laughed out loud. "Magic even beyond my making, Arthur. But the North Queen guessed. Like calling to like. One strong woman to another."

"Is it true?" Arthur asked.

Gawen turned and stared into Arthur's eyes. They were like Midsummer pools, dark grey with a hint of green. "It is true, my lord. I am sorry to have fooled you. I never meant to hurt you. You are the kindest, sweetest, most honorable and just man I have ever known."

Arthur blinked, gulped, tried not to smile, and lost. "What is your name, then?" he asked. "Surely not Gawen."

"Close, my lord. It is Gwenhwyvar, called Gwen by my mother," she said. "Second daughter of Leodogran of Carohaise. I came here in disguise to learn to be a knight and thus challenge Sir Gawaine, who had dishonored my sister. But when I realized I could not best him by sword—having neither hand nor heart for it after all—I thought that by magic I might accomplish what brute strength could not."

Arthur turned abruptly to Merlinnus. "Gawaine could not possibly have—"

"I would guess his mother forbade the match and—to be certain of it—sickened the girl with a spell," Merlinnus said.

"Oh." Gwen could think of nothing more to say. But it fit with what she knew now—of Gawaine, of his mother.

"Well, I shall immediately command the match," Arthur said. "It is the least I can do. Gawaine shall marry your sister, and he shall be glad for it." This time he smiled completely. "What is her name?"

"Mariel, my lord," Gwen whispered. She suddenly felt exhausted and yet wonderfully free of the burden she had carried for so long.

"It will not be that easy, my king," Merlinnus warned him, holding up a finger. "The North Witch will not agree."

"Oh," Arthur said slyly, "I think she will. In fact, I *know* she will. For then Gawaine and I shall be brothers."

"'Brothers'?" Both Gwen and Merlinnus spoke as one.

"For I shall be married to his bride's sister."

After a moment of stunned silence, Gwen said, "It is customary, my lord, to ask what the *woman* wills."

Arthur looked chastened and his cheeks turned splotchy with embarrassment. He cleared his throat twice before speaking again. Then he said simply,

"Gawen . . . Gwen, surely you see this was meant to be. The sword has chosen not just a king—but a queen as well. The only one deserving to be on the throne by my side. After all, you are already one of my chiefest advisers, for all your youth."

"Not so young as you think, my lord," she said, blushing.

"Oh?" It was Merlinnus, not the king, who asked.

"Twenty-one this Solstice day. My father thinks me unmarriageable and is glad of it, for until I left home, I managed his household."

"'Unmarriageable'? *You?*" Arthur looked deeply puzzled, even offended.

"Short utterances," Gwen explained, keeping her tone light, "are not on my list of accomplishments, as Merlinnus has so rightly witnessed."

All three of them laughed.

"Will you, then?" Arthur asked.

"Not much of a proposal," said the mage. "Surely, Arthur, I have taught you better than that."

Never taking his eyes off Gwen, Arthur said, "You have never spoken of any such, you old fraud, and you know it. So, Gawen . . . er, Gwen—will you?"

Gwen smiled at him. "I will, Majesty, as long as I can have my sword back."

Arthur looked longingly at the sword, hefted it once, and then put it solemnly in her hand.

"Oh, not this one," Gwen said. "It is too heavy and unwieldy for me. It does not sit well in my hand. I mean the other—the one that you pulled last night."

"Oh, that!" Arthur said, the splotchiness returning to his cheeks. "With all my heart."

40

Weddings

IT WAS A YEAR and a day before the actual wedding of Arthur and Gwenhwyvar, though Gawaine and Mariel had been married six months before in a ceremony held in Carohaise, her beauty restored by Merlinnus and by love. Gawaine's mother, the North Witch, did not come, though everyone else did. Mariel's father had complained of the expense.

By the time of her own wedding, as Merlinnus had predicted, Gwen's fair hair had grown out to near shoulder length, at least long enough to be pulled up with ribands and combs and fastened with a golden circlet. At her insistence, she was carried from Carohaise to Cadbury in style, riding in a covered wagon be-decked with garlands of vervain and rose. Behind came the wagons bearing her dowry, her books, her clothing, and her mother's jewelry—or at least that which had not gone to Mariel on her wedding.

Merlinnus met Gwen at the gate and brought her through, with much more ceremony than he had done the first time. He acted more like a father than her own. In fact Leodogran of Carohaise trailed behind them, looking sour over the upcoming loss of his brilliant daughter, who had run his own castle with such effi-ciency, though he had never thought to tell her so. He ground his teeth with the knowledge that much of her mother's lands went with her as well.

The guards all nodded at Gwen, and more than a few felt themselves moved by her undisguised beauty. In a white linen dress embroidered at the hem with blue bears, a gold torque at her neck, and gold-and-blue-enameled arm bracelets, she was as fetching a woman as had been seen in the castle for months.

However, the boys Ciril and Geoffrey and Mark kept glancing at the bride under lowered lids, unable to believe it was actually Gawen come to court again.

"I knew she was a girl the whole time," Ciril whispered.

"Me, too," said Mark.

"Did not," Geoffrey retorted, then glanced again as

the bride passed him by. He could scarcely remember how his old friend had looked.

THE WEDDING PARTY came into the Great Hall, where rose petals had been strewn over the rushes and birch limbs, and fennel and orpine bedecked the torches. Fresh herbs had been thrown into the hearth fires: chamomile, pennyroyal, mugwort, and thyme. The room was redolent with their aroma.

Arthur met them midway and took Gwen's hand.

"My lady," he said stiffly.

"My lord." She was just as uncomfortable.

They walked a few steps in silence. She looked everywhere but at him, noticing that the Round Table Companions were in their full armor. Noticing that the ladies of the castle were dressed in colorful linens and wearing spring flowers in their hair. Noticing that Lancelot looked unhappy, his hands wrangling together like an old farmwife's.

This is a mistake, Gwen thought miserably. *We scarce know each other as man and woman, only as king and boy. How will I speak to him? How will he respond?* She longed to be back in her boy's clothes, her hair cropped short and out of her eyes. That boy—that hidden creature—had known how to talk to Arthur. How to cozen him and correct him. *Boys,* she thought, *have the easier time of it.* She wished at that moment that she were a boy again.

Arthur pulled them both to a stop and turned to face her. "Did you bring the sword back with you?"

"I said I would," she told him.

"We will practice every day." He smiled at her.

"And practice your writing, too," she reminded him.

His mouth twisted around. "I hate writing."

"You promised."

He grinned suddenly, and she could see the boy he once had been. When she grinned back, he remembered the mage's boy who had been his friend.

"You had doubts?" she whispered, suddenly solemn again.

He nodded. "And you?"

"Every night. Every day. But more so today than in all those nights and days together. I feared I was alone in this."

"Not alone," he told her. "Never alone again. Do you trust me?"

She tried to smile and could not, so nodded instead. "I do, my lord."

"And you will tell me when such doubts assail you again?"

This time she smiled a little. "I will tell you. I will never lie to you."

"Or I to you," he said. "Ever."

"Do you *still* have doubts?" She held her breath until he answered.

Taking her hand, he whispered, "Till this moment. But no more."

"It is all right, then," she whispered back, and he heard and sighed.

"Definitely all right."

The priest called them to kneel before the twin thrones, and said the words, both in Latin and in English.

"Man and wife," the priest ended. "King and queen." He placed a crown of laurel leaves on her head.

Gwen whispered, "Now and forever."

Only Arthur heard and he squeezed her hand. "Now and forever," he repeated so that she alone could hear.

Then they turned to the wedding guests crowded behind them, and the people set up a huge cheer with Lancelot leading them on. Wine splashed liberally into lifted cups and the king's health was drunk, and then the queen's—honey wine drunk on the Honey Moon, the one full moon in the Solstice month, to insure the queen's fertility. Like all weddings, it was meant for happy every after.

———

MERLINNUS SLIPPED AWAY, to go up to his tower. There, in his stone basin filled with fresh water gathered the night before from a nearby stream, he scryed a garden. It was a place far to the north, across the dark sea. There, with a ceaseless wind tangling elf knots into her shiny black hair, Morgause paced. He could see her face clearly. She looked discomfited, angry, soured— and suddenly old.

It made the mage smile.

The churchyard was crowded with merry-makers. Wine spilled out from the stone's open slot. Overhead larks sang and doves cooed from the rafters of the church. A sword had been pulled, a peace descended, a marriage consummated. Surely an heir would soon follow.

It was an old story but a good one.

Chatting with Jane Yolen

Question: How long have you been writing?
Jane Yolen: Since I was a child. My parents were both writers, so it seemed to me that writing was something all adults did. I wanted to get started early. But my first poems weren't published until I was in high school. I sold my first book on my twenty-second birthday.

Q: What is your writing process? Do you write every day? Do you write for a certain number of hours?
JY: I write every day, but sometimes that means ten hours of writing and zero hours of business related to my writing. Business meaning reading contracts, going over galleys, planning book tours, and the like. Sometimes that ratio is reversed. Most times it is more evenly distributed.

Q: What are some of the books that were very important for you?

JY: Anything about King Arthur, the Andrew Lang color fairy-tale collections, Stevenson's *Treasure Island,* Grahame's *The Wind in the Willows,* Burnett's *The Secret Garden,* Thurber's *White Deer,* Alcott's *Little Women,* and every horse and dog book ever written.

Q: Do personal experiences ever end up in your books? Even in your fantasy novels?

JY: Of course, but usually artfully disguised. My children, however, sometimes object to finding themselves exposed in books. Or they did when they were young. Now as adults they find it funny. And as writers themselves, they are starting to get back at me by putting me in their books and stories.

Q: You have written several books about King Arthur and Merlin. What is it about this era and these characters that draws you back again and again?

JY: I am an Arthurholic. If a story is about Camelot, I am there! Quite simply, I think it is the greatest story ever told, or more accurately, the greatest collection of stories ever told.

Q: This is the story of King Arthur and yet not the story of King Arthur. Many of the place-names are different (Cadbury instead of Camelot, for instance), and characters have names that are slanted just a degree from the familiar (such as Merlinnus). Why have you worked these small changes? What do they mean for your story?

JY: They are a signal that this telling may be different from what the reader is expecting. In some cases— very different. However, you will find Cadbury and Merlinnus as alternative names in some of the older tales. I didn't make them up, just borrowed them.

Q: You transform the well-known image of the sword in the stone into a simple bit of legerdemain, as Merlinnus puts it. Is this a cynical view of how we choose our leaders? Or something else?

JY: Sometimes people have to find a reason to believe passionately in their leaders, and Merlinnus knows this.

Q: Do you have any plans to tell the rest of Arthur's story? Why or why not?

JY: The rest of the story is about betrayal and death and I don't want to write that. I liked ending happily ever after. Besides, now that the big secret of this telling is out, what is there to do?

The Whole of
the Sword Poem

Originally I had written *Sword of the Rightful King* in eleven quite long chapters, with a poetic opening or prose poem for each chapter and a twelfth prose poem to finish the whole. These openings were each a metaphoric way of looking at the sword in the stone.

My editor wisely told me that this slowed all the action down. And though he loved all twelve poems, he thought it better to use fewer.

I made the chapters shorter (and added several new chapters with action in them, because Arthur is a man of action), and then broke everything into four sections, with one of the poems fronting each section. I wrote three new prose poems that depended on the original writing but spoke more truly to the now-changed novel. But here are all twelve of the original prose poems. I think they really do work together as a whole piece.

—J. Y.

I

Midnight by the bell. The churchyard was deserted and in darkness. By the front door, which was but a black rectangle in a blacker mass, a large square was marked off on the ground. In the square's center stood an enormous stone, which—if the moon had been shining—would have reminded any onlooker of a sleeping bear. A dead bear, obviously. For in the bear's back was thrust a great sword, its haft pointing slantwise toward the night sky.

2

The churchyard was deserted, but dawn was beginning to light the sullen square. The stone in the center blushed with the rising of the sun, and the sword in the stone's middle sprang to uncertain life. The sword's shadow was a long stain along the bulge of the stone.

3

No one was in the churchyard, but the early morning light promised that soon it would be crowded, the front door of the church opened by the priest. Before the door, but not so close as to obscure it, was a small square of stone where a forgotten anvil sat, as if waiting for a smith to take it back to his fire. In the anvil's center was an old sword, long finished, long needing refinishing. Only the morning light brightened its dull steel for a moment. Only a moment.

4

The churchyard was deserted. By the front door, a large open square of marble, the color of sunrise, seemed an invitation. An enormous stone humped up in the center of the marble square, with a large, unsightly sword thrust down in its center, put the lie to that invitation. "Do not enter," said the sword.

5

At the third hour of the day, clouds kept moving in front of the sun so that the chapel yard became a place of shadows. The shadows danced about in the center of the forecourt, and the shadow of the stone with its steel arm seemed to caper obscenely.

6

At the fourth hour of the day, a flock of blackbirds flew in to perch on the single tree in the churchyard. There were nearly a hundred birds, and they made the tree look as if it were heavily laden with black buds. Beneath them, the stone with its steel burden beckoned. Three of the blackbirds flew over the stone, widdershins. When they returned to the flock, their droppings decorated the sword hilt like opaque white gems.

7

The sun had passed its zenith and no longer stood directly above the churchyard. The sword had a new shadow now, slicing down the far side of the stone like a black wound. A single dog walked stiff legged near the stone, lifted a leg, and left another shadow on the stone.

8

Across the deserted courtyard waddled three ducks, a male and two females. They made soft cacklings as they passed the stone. The male beat his wings suddenly and rose into the air, as high as the sword. He perched on it and preened his feathers. The two females took no notice and walked on. When he realized he was alone, the male sailed down and hurried to catch up to them, calling plaintively. They did not answer.

9

Evening struck over the churchyard with a blunt fist. Everything looked squashed, smaller than before. Only the stone—with the sword stuck in it like a knife in bread— looked the same.

10

Now night was a surround of black. The stone was black, too, and only the hilt of the sword held any light, as if a sliver of silver pin pierced a coarse material. And day arrived: the stone, sword, and sky going bright like the philosopher's mercury that stands still and yet runs.

11

The churchyard was silent. The stone was a beached craft, rudderless, empty. Like waves, the shadows ebbed. Along the horizon that was the castle wall, a thin ribbon of dawn began to appear.

12

The churchyard was crowded with merrymakers. Wine spilled out from the stone's open slot. Overhead, larks sang and doves cooed from the rafters of the church. A sword had been pulled, a peace descended, a marriage consummated. Surely an heir would soon follow.

It was an old story but a good one.

Jane Yolen has written more than two hundred books for children, including the three volumes that make up the Pit Dragon Trilogy: *Dragon's Blood, Heart's Blood,* and *A Sending of Dragons*. Among her other critically acclaimed novels are *Wizard's Hall, The Devil's Arithmetic,* and *Armageddon Summer* (written with Bruce Coville). She has won the World Fantasy Award, the Nebula Award, and the Kerlan Award, as well as several of the highest awards in children's literature. She and her husband divide their time between homes in Massachusetts and Scotland. To learn more about Ms. Yolen and her books, visit her at www.janeyolen.com.